It Would Be Wrong To Steal My Sister's Boyfriend (Wouldn't It?)

It Would Be Wrong To Steal My Sister's Boyfriend (Wouldn't It?)

Sophie Ranald

It Would Be Wrong to Steal My Sister's Boyfriend (Wouldn't It?)

ISBN 13: 978-1491298015

For Hopi, who makes my dreams come true.

Chapter One

I was sitting on the sofa watching *Newsnight* with Ben when my sister brought home the man I was going to fall in love with. I'd like to say I had a sense of portent or something when I heard two sets of footsteps on the stairs outside. But instead I took another gulp of my tea and carried on half-listening to Jeremy Paxman savaging some Lib Dem MP, and said to Ben, "Sounds like Rose has a bloke in tow."

We'd been sharing the flat for four years, and generally we got along pretty well – Rose and I, that is, not me and Ben. Rose has what I suppose you'd call an active social life – she often has crowds of her rah friends over for dinner parties or 'kitchen sups' (of course I rip the piss out of her mercilessly for thinking she's the next Nigella Lawson, to which she responds that Nigella's so last decade – last century, last millennium even, and it's all about Lorraine Pascale now. And she's probably right – what would I know?). Anyway alongside the friends there's been a pretty steady stream of what Rose calls 'chaps'.

When we first moved in here Rose was going out with Danny, who she met in her final year at uni. He was an upper-class twat and I couldn't stand him. I still don't know what Rose saw in him, although he did have a fantastic body, apparently from playing polo. Polo! I ask you. Danny was actually the Honourable Daniel Someone – his father was an Earl (our Dad, who's a real old socialist, bless him, literally choked on a chickpea when Rose told him this and I thought I'd have to perform the Heimlich manoeuvre, but he recovered, which is lucky, because I've no idea how to do it). Looking back, it's possible that the Earl thing is exactly what Rose saw in Danny.

In due course Rose kicked the Hon Dan to the kerb, or the other way around, I'm not quite sure. He was followed in fairly short order by Neil, who'd been to Harvard Business School and was actually Neil Marshall III and the heir to an enormous oil-based fortune. When Neil pushed off back to America Rose started going out with Aiden, who was something in finance, then there was Mark, who was something else in finance – in fact I think he may have had a hedge fund, but I could be imagining it. You get the picture – there were lots of men in Rose's life, although to be fair never more than one at a time, that I knew of. After a while they all merged into one, and a river ran through them, so to speak. So I wasn't at all surprised that Tuesday evening to hear two sets of footsteps on the stairs: the click of Rose's high heels and the heavier tread belonging to the latest chap.

I heard the front door open and the rattle of Rose's keys as she put them in the little dish on the hall table as she always does, which is handy for me when I can't find mine, and then her voice saying, "Would you like a whisky, Ollie? Or shall I put some coffee on?" and a man's rather nice, posh-sounding voice saying he'd love a whisky.

"Ice?" Rose said.

"No thanks," said the gentleman caller, and then they both came into the living room.

Rose and I do look alike, really. If we were in a room full of other people and someone asked you to guess which of the women there were sisters, you'd get that it was us, if the light was dim enough and there weren't identical twins there too. We've got the same bone structure, the high forehead and high cheekbones and slightly beaky nose I see when I look at photos of Mum, and the same rather wispy dark blonde hair and hazel eyes, and we're both average height, not tall and not short. But that's where the similarity ends, and why when people who know one of us well are introduced to the other, they invariably say, "This is your sister?" in tones of horrified amazement, or just amazement, if they're my friends meeting Rose for the first time.

Because Rose has done what used to be called 'making the most of oneself', or what I call scrubbing up well, on the rare occasions when I do it. Rose does it all the time. She has her hair highlighted at some swanky salon in Chelsea, so instead of being mousy like mine, it's pale gold, but looks really natural, and she straightens it every day, so what's limp and shapeless on me is a smooth, shining curtain on her. She never, ever leaves the flat without having a shower, curling her eyelashes and putting makeup on – not even to go down to the corner shop for bread and Marmite on a Saturday morning with a hangover, which of course means I get sick of waiting for her to get ready and go myself. She always wears high heels, so instead of being an average five foot five, she's an elegant, slender five foot nine. And she wears really expensive, designer clothes. And did I mention the slender thing? I don't want to give you the idea that I'm some kind of lumpen heifer – I'm a perfectly ordinary, healthy size fourteen – but Rose is a size eight and puts herself through hell to stay that way.

Don't get me wrong, it's her body and her life, but it makes me sad sometimes that Rose is willing to make so many sacrifices for her looks. Part of it's principle – I genuinely believe it's wrong that women are judged so harshly on their appearance, and that there's such a very narrow definition of beauty in Western culture, and so much pressure to conform to it. Part of it's seeing my sister dragging herself off to the gym every day without fail, even if she's got a horrible cold or has only had three hours' sleep because she was out at a party the night before, and entering every single thing she eats or drinks into the calorie counting app on her iPhone, and literally stopping half-way through a plate of food when she reaches her twelve hundred calorie quota, no matter how hungry she still is. And of course I'd quite like it if I could borrow her designer clothes sometimes, on the rare occasions when I have to go somewhere smart, but none of them would ever fit me, not in a million years. But she's really nice and lets me borrow her shoes whenever I want, so it's not all bad. Except they kill my feet and I usually end up having to take them off and walk home barefoot, and once I left her silver snakeskin Jimmy Choos on the number 19 bus. She wasn't so nice about that.

Anyway, the long and the short of all this is that Rose is groomed and glossy and I'm not, and although she's eighteen months younger than me, twenty six to my twenty eight, she looks older, all sort of put-together and grown up, whereas I still look like a student, and people assume I'm the younger sister. Which I guess is why when Rose and Oliver came into the living room that night, Rose said, "This is my big sister, Elodie, and her boyfriend Benedict."

Of course, as Rose knew perfectly well, Ben is not my boyfriend. Really, not at all. He's my good mate, and he has been ever since I spilled a pint of beer down the back of his shirt in the student union bar in my final year at uni (well, since about ten minutes after, strictly speaking, once he'd finished being annoyed and I'd finished apologising). Not that he isn't the sort of bloke anyone with any sense would want to have for a boyfriend – he's super clever but never arrogant, he listens to what everyone says and treats everyone the same, and although he's so brilliant and everyone's always saying what an amazing career he has ahead of him, he never talks down to anyone, even when they're clearly wrong. And he's properly fanciable too, not in an obvious way, just really lovely, with warm smiley greyish blue eyes and a strong, open face. So understandably that first night I met him, once he had dried off a bit, I wanted to go to bed with him, and we did, and it was amazing.

For a few months we were what I suppose you'd call Friends With Benefits, and then something happened – okay, someone happened – that meant there stopped being benefits, but we carried on being friends. And we still saw each other a few times a month, sometimes alone to see a movie or go to a gig or whatever, and sometimes with a group of mates, like for the Tuesday pub quiz at The Duchess, where we'd been that night. I suppose one day we'll sign the register at each other's weddings and be godparents to each other's children, and all that stuff. Anyway, quite often I have to remind people that Ben. Is. Not. My. Boyfriend, and I felt a bit annoyed when Rose introduced him to Oliver that way.

But I didn't say that to Oliver, because I was too busy looking at him. I don't want to exaggerate but he took my breath away. Literally. I felt like I'd been punched in the stomach and I could feel a flush of heat spreading over my entire body. Which was weird, because of course I think love at first sight is a load of old pony, and anyway Oliver wasn't even my type, although his looks were, as I've said, breathtaking. He's like all the cliches: tall, dark, handsome. If he was an actor he'd have a shout at playing James Bond, he's got the right sort of steely blue eyes and beautiful, deep voice with the kind of accent you get from public school then Oxbridge, the kind of accent Rose has carefully acquired and I haven't. And, like Rose, he had that look of polish about him: his hair was beautifully cut and had just the right amount of wax or something in it, so it was in a proper style without making him look like the spiky-haired member of a boy band. His suit was beautifully cut too, even I could see that, and it emphasised his broad shoulders and long legs. His tie and his shoes and his cufflinks all looked expensive, and although it was eleven o'clock at night he looked like he'd just shaved. So, seriously, not my type. He couldn't have been more different from Ben, who was wearing a shabby grey hoodie and jeans with frayed hems and a hole on one knee, and socks but no shoes.

Anyway, once I'd caught my breath, I smiled and managed to say, "Everyone calls me Ellie," and Ben got up off the sofa and shook Oliver's hand and said everyone called him Ben.

"Have you been anywhere nice?" I asked.

Oliver said, "Nowhere special," at exactly the same moment as Rose said, "The Brompton Club," with the sort of excited smugness in her voice that made me think that it probably was somewhere very special. I caught Oliver's eye and he gave me the ghost of a wink.

For the first time in ages, I wished I'd bothered to put on a bit of make-up and do something with my hair – I was so conscious of the contrast I must present with Rose, she in her elegant little black dress and high heels and tights with seams down the back – seams! – or I suppose they might even have been proper stockings or those hold-up things that bring me out in a rash whenever I try to wear them. I was wearing a Race For Life T-shirt, old jeggings with a hole in the seam that showed a chunk of my inner thigh, and no bra, which if I'm honest is more or less what I wore most nights, so it's not like I can even say Oliver caught me at a particularly bad moment, or anything.

I tried to make conversation for a bit, letting Rose tell us who she'd seen at the Brompton place (Kate Moss and Harry Styles, since you ask), and Oliver and Ben made a few incomprehensible remarks to each other once the end bit of Newsnight came on, where they show you which markets are up and which are down, and how the pound is doing against the yen, and all that. But after Oliver's wink – if it had even been a wink – I found it really hard to know where to look, and started to feel terribly uncomfortable in my comfortable clothes with my comfortable not-boyfriend, so I finished my tea and Ben said goodnight and went home, and I went to bed, and after a while I heard Rose and Oliver do the same.

Chapter Two

A few days after that, I arrived home from work to find that the flat had been transformed. I'd left it in the morning in its normal state – not exactly a tip, but with unwashed teacups on the kitchen counter and a bit of a film of dust everywhere, and a load of washing in the washing machine that I hadn't got around to hanging up to dry. Which is probably just as well really, as Rose wouldn't have been happy if she'd brought her new man home to find a forest of my tights and knickers hanging on the airer in the living room.

Anyway, I'd had a really rubbish day and I was knackered by six o'clock, so I declined an invitation to join some of my colleagues in the pub and set off home. I work for a charity and we rely quite heavily on volunteers to meet our staffing needs, and whilst I really admire their passion and commitment and we couldn't possibly manage without them, when they are flaky or incompetent or just plain don't turn up, it makes my job harder than it would have been if they'd never been there in the first place.

My job title is Director of Communications, which sounds dead important, but actually means I spend most of my time scouring the newspapers for stories that are relevant to us and then frantically bashing out press releases to get our response to the story out there before it gets old and everyone loses interest. Occasionally a journalist will ring me up in advance of the story being printed and we get a quote in first time round – that's a good day. That Friday hadn't been a good day – there'd been some ridiculous scaremongering thing in the *Daily Mail* and one of my more hapless volunteers and I had spent the day calling and emailing all our media contacts with our response to it, except towards mid-afternoon, just as I was thinking the day was almost over, I realised that she'd emailed out my response to a story from the previous week, 'Archie, 12, is Britain's youngest Dad', rather than that day's story about the link between binge drinking and genital warts. So I'd had to call all the journalists and apologise and resend the press release, except by then most of them had decamped to the pub, and by the time I'd finished I was too tired and hacked off to do the same.

As I was saying, I knew something was up the second I walked in the door. The flat smelled of polish and lilies and something delicious cooking, and the front room had been all winter wonderlanded up with a Christmas tree loaded with gold and silver baubles and white fairy lights strung everywhere. Personally I like tinsel and multi-coloured lights but Rose says they're tacky and won't have them in the flat, and I just have to suck it up because she, as everyone knows, is the one with the taste in our household. No, really, she is, and I don't mind leaving the majority of the decorating decisions to her.

I suppose I should say at this point how extraordinarily, amazingly lucky Rose and I are to have the flat in the first place. Our dad could afford to give us a generous wedge of cash for a deposit and so, unlike so many people our age, we are happily installed on the bottom rung of the housing ladder rather than floundering around in rented accommodation, and I am really, truly grateful for our good fortune. The flat's nothing special, just a small two-bed with a decent kitchen and a lovely smart new bathroom that Dad had done for us when we moved in, and it's in a part of Battersea that used to be quite grotty but is becoming more and more chichi and gentrified – in fact one of Prince Harry's pals was mugged at the end of our road the other day, and if that's not the sign of an up-and-coming area I don't know what is.

Anyway when we moved in I gave Rose carte blanche to get on with the decorating. Actually the truth is I really can't be arsed with that sort of thing and I'd quite happily have furnished the entire place in one trip to Ikea, but Rose doesn't work that way. She went to markets and antique shops and cutesy little boutiques and found loads of lovely 'pieces' that together make the flat look lived-in and homely but at the same time really elegant. Even the things that we ended up having to buy from Ikea because Rose had blown our budget on 'pieces' look somehow chic and classic, like even if we'd had unlimited funds, we'd have chosen that particular squashy cream sofa anyway, because it's just so right. Add a few really quite good original drawings and oil paintings – Rose works for Quinn's, the auction house, so she gets to charm all the Young British Artists and snap up bits of their work that will be worth squillions of pounds one day, for next to nothing – and the flat looks like something out of *Living Etc*, it really does.

But the addition of the Christmas decorations, unnatural cleanliness and delicious smells emanating from the kitchen reminded me that Rose had told me – I'm pretty certain she had anyway – that she was going to be hosting one of her dinner parties, or possibly a kitchen supper, that night, and I'd intended to make myself scarce as I usually did on these occasions. But it was too late – I had entered the dragon's den.

"Ellie?" Rose called from the kitchen. I sidled reluctantly through and leaned in the doorway.

"Hi, Rose. The decorations look amazing, and something smells nice," I said. Rose is, in addition to all her other talents, a fantastic cook. In my gap year I went backpacking around South-East Asia; Rose worked as a chalet girl before embarking on an art-themed grand tour of Europe, and during the course of it she learned how to make mayonnaise and decant claret and all that gubbins. Personally I'm quite happy with a jacket potato in front of the telly, and anyway I'm a vegetarian so most of Rose's cordon bleu masterpieces are wasted on me, but her friends always bang on about how wonderful her food is, and whenever she has one of her dinner parties she spends a fortune at Waitrose and Borough Market on ingredients and hours in the kitchen.

"I hope you don't mind me putting the tree up, although it's only the tenth," Rose said. She looked flushed and pleased – she really loves doing this kind of thing. "We're having rib of veal with chanterelles, and smoked, herb-crusted goat's cheese with chanterelles for you and Simon."

"What?" I said. My hopes of sending an SOS text message to Ben and if he wasn't free ringing my best friend Claire, and legging it down to the Latchmere, were fading fast. "Rose, I'm really sorry, but I'd completely forgotten about this and I... er... I have plans."

"No you don't," she said. "I reminded you the other night, don't you remember, and you said you were free."

A hazy memory surfaced of her mentioning something, and me muttering a response before going back to gawping at Oliver. Rose is a chatterer – even if she can see I'm watching something on telly or reading my Kindle, she chats. About her day at work, about the new shoes she's bought, about her plans for the evening – chat, chat, chat. Bless her, it's quite sweet really, but the ability to tune her out has been a vital life skill I acquired in childhood and have honed to a fine art since we've shared the flat.

Clearly I was trapped – she'd gone and made a special veggie main course for me and this Simon, and I wasn't going to be able to get out of it without hurting her feelings and making myself feel like a total evil shit.

"Do you need a hand with anything?" I asked.

"No, it's all under control," said Rose. Then she gave me one of her Looks. "Why don't you just have a shower and get ready? Use some of my Molton Brown revitalising stuff if you've had a tiring day."

Which I interpreted as, "Go and wash your hair and change into something decent, or you'll show me up in front of my friends."

"So who's coming?" I asked, opening the fridge and nicking one of Rose's home-made chocolate and sloe gin truffles.

"Just a few people," Rose said, checking them off on her fingers. "There's Simon, who works with me, and his partner Khalid." So at least she wasn't trying to set me up with Simon, which was a relief. "And Vanessa and Tom." Vanessa was one of Rose's more annoying friends from school, whose wedding the previous year to Tom Willoughby-Archer had graced the pages of *Tatler* and *Hello*, according to Rose. "And Pip, she was going to bring Sebastian but they've had an epic row apparently so she's coming on her own, and I invited Oliver at the last minute so we'll be an even number."

I felt a little fizz of pleasure. "Right, I'll go and make myself look presentable then," I said, and went upstairs to shower.

To be fair to Rose, I'm never going to win any best-dressed-woman awards in my work attire. I have to wear suits in the office and I absolutely hate it, and resent paying a single penny more than I have to for them, so I tend to descend on Matalan and Next and M&S at sale time and buy a job lot in various colours and throw them in the washing machine once a week, which is why they don't last nearly as long as they should. That day I was wearing a particularly uninspiring mushroom-coloured ensemble that had seen better days, and quite frankly even its best days hadn't been that good.

Steaming gently, a towel wrapped around my hair, I gloomily surveyed the contents of my wardrobe. I don't much care about fashion – it strikes me as a bit shallow and pointless to spend as much money as Rose does on what you wear – but that night I felt really depressed by my lack of clothes and if I'm being honest by my appearance generally. I was going to be sitting around a table with former model Vanessa, who has the long limbs and perfect bone structure achieved by generations of rich, thick men marrying generations of thick, beautiful women; Pip, who if I remembered correctly was an up-and-coming fashion designer and the daughter of some 1970s rock god and a famous actress; Simon and Khalid who being gay men were bound to be toe-curlingly stylish; and my sister, who always looks gorgeous. And Oliver. Of course. It was Oliver, Rose's Oliver, who I was really thinking about as I raked through my wardrobe, inspecting and discarding garment after garment. The turquoise silk tunic I bought in China would have been perfect, but had a grease stain in the middle of the front and I kept forgetting to take it to the dry cleaner's. My black velvet batwing top, which I found in a load of Mum's old things that Dad was going to take to the Oxfam shop, and rescued for nothing more than sentimental reasons really, except now it's suddenly madly fashionable, was in a crumpled ball at the bottom of the laundry basket. My only dress, a red beaded sheath from Monsoon, had suffered cruelly when I ignored the 'dry clean only' instruction on its label.

In the end I settled for jeans, of course. That's what I always do: spend half an hour frantically digging through my wardrobe trying stuff on and dropping it on the floor and end up with my bedroom looking like a branch of JD Sports after the rioters have been round, and wearing jeans. Still, I managed to find a rather nice sparkly scarf in Rose's accessories drawer (she has an accessories drawer, and a makeup drawer, and a shelf in her wardrobe where all her handbags live in linen drawstring bags. And I'm sure you don't need me to tell you that her shoes are all in plastic boxes with a photo of the shoe stuck to the front), and used her GHDs to straighten my hair and put on some of her Tom Ford scent, and by the time I was ready I looked okay, I thought.

Now you might be wondering whether in addition to nicking Rose's scent and her hair straighteners and her scarf (oh, and some lovely shimmery Shu Uemara eyeliner – let me not hold back), I had set my sights on her boyfriend. Honestly, I hadn't. I was... intrigued, I guess, by Oliver. There was something about him that made me want him to think well of me. I didn't want him to see me as Rose's fat, slobby older sister, but I didn't want *him,* if you see what I mean. Not then. Rose and I had never, ever gone for the same sort of men – I fancy blokes who see the world in the same way I do, who care about important things like ideas and politics and the environment, and don't care about things like looks and money. I didn't know Oliver, but just the fact that he'd appealed to Rose pretty much automatically made him not my type. Still, when I went downstairs to set the table under Rose's strict guidance, I found myself developing a severe case of Mentionitis.

"Oooh, you look amazing!" Rose said, when I came into the kitchen. "That scarf is fab on you. You should wear it more often." That's another thing about Rose, she's incredibly generous. She doesn't mind at all when I borrow her stuff without asking – although the flip side of that is she has no reservations at all about borrowing mine. Not that it matters, because I've got nothing she'd want. She does help herself to my fat-free natural yoghurt though, when she's run out, which is a bit annoying. After all, you can't just put it back like you can a scarf.

"Thanks," I said. "I thought I'd make a bit of an effort so as not to look like the fugly sister. So, tell me more about this Oliver then." When I said his name, I could feel myself blushing – stupid or what?

"Isn't he lovely?" said Rose, with a little sort of happy sigh, arranging a small battalion of gold candles of different heights on the dining room table. "I met him at work. He came in a couple of weeks ago for the contemporary art sale preview, and then I bid on a couple of Marcus Brands for him, and won them, and he took me out for a drink to say thanks."

"Wow, Marcus Brand," I said, putting wine glasses on the table and watching Rose move them to the other side of the plates. Marcus Brand is one of the hottest of Rose's YBAs. He was long-listed for the Turner Prize a couple of years back and his paintings (to use the term loosely – they're mostly mixed-media monstrosities made from 'objets trouvées that epitomise the urban environment', according to the brochure Rose showed me once, which means empty paper coffee cups, Big Mac boxes, chicken bones and in one instance – and I'm not making this up – a used tampon) are madly sought after and sell for ridiculous amounts. So this told me that Oliver had a) lots of money, and b) not much taste. "He must be loaded."

"He certainly likes investing in art," said Rose rather primly. "And I suppose he can afford it; he's a partner at Longfellow Reeves."

Business as usual for my sister, I thought. My boyfriends have tended to have interesting but not lucrative careers – Wallace worked in admin for Amnesty International, Sean was a journalist, Chris was training to be a GP, although he changed his mind and decided to go into cosmetic surgery at around the same time as he cheated on me with some blonde nurse. Go figure. And although of course he isn't my boyfriend, Ben works as a parliamentary adviser for an MP – Lucille Field, who used to be a shadow cabinet minister before she – yeah, that one. But Rose won't consider going out with anyone who doesn't have a load of noughts on the end of his net worth. Not that she's shallow or superficial, she just... Well, I suppose she is, a bit. In some ways.

"So never mind about his bank balance," I said, "When he stayed over on Tuesday, was that, you know, your chance to put him through his paces for the first time?"

"God, Ellie, you're so nosey!" Rose was leaning over the table lighting the candles, but I suspected the glow on her cheeks wasn't just from the naked flames. "Since you ask, I stayed over at his place a couple of days before. On our fourth date."

"And?" I said. It's great fun interrogating Rose when she doesn't want to be interrogated – she gets all flustered.

She didn't this time though, she stood back and inspected the table from all angles, then she said quite seriously, "It's not a buyer's market out there, Ellie."

I was about to ask her what on earth art auctions had to do with what Oliver was like in bed, when she looked at her watch and said, "Christ! I'd better get changed," and legged it upstairs, and I poured myself a hefty G&T and sat down to wait for Rose's friends to arrive.

"And what do you do, Ellie?" asked Simon, or it may have been Khalid, as we all tucked in to our main course – to be honest I can't remember which of the glossy pair of them it was, as things were a little hazy by this point. I'd had a G&T and then another, and then a couple of glasses of the champagne Rose had splashed about while people ate their canapés (seriously, canapés. God love her), and then obviously loads of wine with dinner.

I caught Rose's eye across the table and I could see her thinking, "Don't mention the minge bus!" That's the thing about my job – it does tend to take over the conversation rather. It's not called the minge bus, obviously. The name of the charity is YEESH, which stands for Youth Empowerment and Education for Sexual Health, and in addition to all the media and campaigns stuff that I look after, we've got a crack team of doctors, nurses and educators who travel around the place ('up and down the country', our press releases say) visiting schools and youth groups and giving talks and then offering counselling and contraceptive advice and smear tests and the morning-after pill and referral for treatment of STIs and counselling for terminations and stuff in their mobile consulting room – hence my name for it, the minge bus. Anyway, if I say so myself, it's a fantastic organisation and it does brilliant work, but sometimes people – or rather, narrow-minded idiots – view what we do as controversial, mainly because we're up-front about the fact that teenagers are biologically programmed to have sex, and that's what they're going to do whether you like it or not, and the best way to deal with the issue is to provide them with the knowledge and equipment they need to have it safely. As you can imagine, we get a lot of flak from the right-wing press, and Rose knows from bitter experience that once I start talking about it, it can be difficult to shut me up.

So I said all this in answer to Khalid – or Simon – and they made approving noises, because like most gay men they took a sensible view of these things.

Then Vanessa said, "But aren't you just encouraging girls to be promiscuous? Isn't it better to teach them to say no?"

I splashed more wine into my glass. "Here's the thing," I said. "You're a fourteen-year-old girl and your boyfriend says he's going to finish with you if you won't have sex with him, and all your friends say they're sleeping with their boyfriends, and no one is giving any sensible advice about contraception because they still believe the rubbish about not getting pregnant the first time, or if you do it standing up," I could see Rose wincing, "or if you use an empty crisp packet as a condom, and your boyfriend won't take no for an answer, and then you don't have access to emergency contraception or proper advice, and you wonder why we have a teenage pregnancy rate higher than anywhere else in Europe." By this stage I suppose I was getting a bit loud, but I'm passionate about what I do.

Before Rose could tactfully steer the conversation on to more innocuous subjects, Vanessa chimed in again, "But how can a fourteen-year-old girl make the decision to terminate a pregnancy?" And then I'm afraid I went off on one a bit, launching into my standard rant about how abortion is safer than childbirth and if you don't allow women absolute control over decisions about their reproductive health then we become little more than brood mares for society, and by the time I'd finished, the polite hum of conversation around the table had fallen silent, and Vanessa was looking shocked and embarrassed.

"Well, of course you're entitled to your opinion, Ellie," she said, and I said it wasn't an opinion, it was a fact, and she was entitled to have opinions too but only if she was willing to accept that they were just plain wrong. Which I suppose is why Rose doesn't like it when I talk about the minge bus at her dinner parties – but then I can't help it if some of her friends have ridiculous, antediluvian views, can I?

"Would anyone like some pudding?" asked Rose in a rather tight sort of voice, and stood up and started clearing plates. Vanessa got up to help her and I knew that when they were in the kitchen Rose would be apologising to her for my behaviour and Vanessa would be lying and telling her it was fine, she wasn't offended, at all. Then they came back with a bowl of what Rose announced was chestnut panacotta with mincemeat sauce, and the conversation around the table more or less resumed. I decided I'd better keep quiet for a bit and try not to cause any more ructions, so I concentrated on eating my pudding – which was gorgeous – and listened to Oliver talking to Tom about his art collection and some guy called Jamie Cunningham who was apparently the next big thing. Rose chimed in and said that he'd asked her to sit for him, and everyone made suitably impressed noises.

When everyone had finished, I started to clear the table – Rose has me well trained – and Oliver got up to help me. We carried the plates and bowls through to the kitchen and while I was stacking the dishwasher Oliver said, "That was impressive work back there, Ellie. You're absolutely right, those sort of views need to be challenged." I looked up at him and he smiled and I felt my stomach turn over in a way that had nothing to do with my having eaten way too much panacotta.

Chapter Three

I woke up the next morning feeling as rough as a badger's arse. My tongue had cleaved itself to the roof of my mouth and tasted as if I'd been licking dried cat sick. My eyelashes were stuck together with lumps of sleep and mascara. I had a pounding headache and a horrible sense of impending doom. I tried to roll over and get back to sleep for a while – always the sensible thing to do in these situations – but it was no good; I needed to wee and The Fear had me well and truly in its grasp, and besides there was a lovely smell of coffee and bacon wafting up the stairs.

I know I said I'm a vegetarian, and I am, it's something I really believe is important. It's not just about the morality of killing animals to eat, there are so many other issues: food miles, the environmental impact of animal husbandry, the economics of it all. Do you know how many acres of pasture it takes to produce a pound of beef, and how much grain could be produced from the same area of land? Well, I can't exactly remember, but trust me, it's a lot. Of course vegetarianism isn't without its ethical compromises. Ben pointed out to me a few years ago that if you're a vegetarian who eats dairy products you're inadvertently contributing to the murder of thousands of male dairy calves, which are born but have no use in milk production. I have no idea what I thought happened to them – either they lived out their days happily scampering around green pastures, or the bad meat eaters ate them, I suppose. But it's neither of the above: they basically get slaughtered at birth and used for pet food. And that really shocked me, so much so that I gave up dairy (and eggs, on the basis that if a thing's worth doing…) and became a vegan for more than a year. But I just couldn't hack it. My hair started falling out, I was tired and run down and constantly getting colds, I piled on about a stone because I craved sugar all the time and there's this lovely little vegan cafe down the road that does amazing peanut butter cupcakes, and I was getting through about five of them a week, in addition to mountains of nuts and avocado pears. Then Ben told me about the terrible deforestation that's going on in the Amazon and how fragile natural habitat is being destroyed to clear land for soya production, and pointed out that by following a vegan diet I was basically complicit in that. So I made myself a cheese omelette and felt much, much better.

Anyway my point is that if you try to live in a decent and ethical way, you find yourself constantly coming up against dilemmas that seem fundamentally insoluble. Is it worse to eat free range chicken than battery eggs? Is the destruction of the rain forest for soya production a price worth paying to feed people in the developing world who might otherwise starve? Is the carbon footprint of a South African avocado pear more or less than that of a Welsh lamb chop? And so on and on. You can't get by without making some compromises, and as far as I'm concerned it's never going to be possible to be morally pure when it comes to food – or indeed anything else – and what's important is that one is mindful of the choices one makes. Which is why I try not to feel guilty about the fact that I love the smell of bacon and still long for a bacon sandwich, just sometimes, if I have a really stinking hangover.

I showered and cleaned my teeth and swallowed two paracetamol with water from the bathroom tap, and got dressed in skinny jeans and ballet pumps and a rather pretty camisole top and waterfall cardigan (from Primark – don't get me started on the ethics of *that*) and poured loads of eyedrops into my eyes before I went downstairs. Not that I was expecting Oliver to be there, or anything. But he was. He was alone in the kitchen, standing at the stove poking with a spatula at a pan full of bacon.

"Morning," I said, feeling desperately shy all of a sudden.

"Morning," Oliver said. He was wearing the smart white shirt he'd had on the previous night, with the cufflinks and everything, and I presume boxer shorts, although I couldn't see because the shirt tail hung down to the tops of his thighs, which I couldn't help staring at. His legs and his feet were bare and he'd obviously just had a shower (Rose has her own en-suite shower room; in the course of negotiations about that, I got sole use of the main bathroom and the bigger bedroom that faces the garden, so I'm not complaining), because his hair was damp, although it had been carefully combed. His top half looked like a banker and his bottom half like a teenage boy – it was odd and quite touching. I noticed that he had lovely legs, lean and muscular with a dusting of dark hair, which was worn away at the tops of his legs where his jeans would rub. I realised he'd noticed me staring, and also that a rather awkward sort of silence had fallen.

"Did you sleep..." I said, at the same moment as Oliver said, "I hope you don't mind..."

"After you," he said.

"No, no," I said. "Guests speak first in this house. Anyway I was only going to ask you if you'd slept okay, which is pretty dull as conversation-starters go."

Oliver laughed. "And I was going to apologise for taking over your kitchen. I promised Madam breakfast in bed – it seems she's feeling a little fragile this morning. So am I, in fact. I think bringing out the Calvados was probably a strategic error. You'd very sensibly called it a night by then."

I don't know if you've noticed this, but finding out that someone else has a hangover worse than your own has almost supernatural restorative powers. Perhaps it's realising that they will be too occupied dealing with their own crawling sense of shame to worry about anything stupid you might have said or done the night before, or it's a simple question of realising there are others worse off than yourself, but trust me, it works every time. I certainly felt heaps better knowing Rose and Oliver were suffering too, anyway.

"Coffee?" Oliver asked, pushing the cafetière across the table.

"Lovely." I located my favourite Marmite mug in the cupboard, sloshed in coffee and milk, and sat down at the kitchen table, sipping gratefully. "Do you have anything exciting planned for the day?" I asked, realising as soon as I said it that it sounded like a none-too-subtle way of asking when I could expect him to clear off out of our kitchen.

Oliver lifted the slices of bacon out of the pan and arranged them on a plate lined with kitchen paper to drain. Impressive – I'm more of a slap straight on to bread and eat leaning over the sink girl myself. "Work, unfortunately," he said. "We have our year-end in December and it means that the run-up to Christmas is ridiculously busy and January doubly depressing because there are no looming deadlines to distract one."

I suppose that may have been my cue to ask Oliver what he did for a living, but I had a hazy recollection of it having been discussed at some length the night before, so I just made sympathetic noises. Oliver opened the breadbin and took out a loaf of wholemeal sourdough – Rose refuses to have white bread in the house, she says she can't resist eating it and it plays havoc with her weight and her IBS – and started to slice it.

"I always feel plastic white is the best medium for a bacon sarnie," Oliver said, "but I'm sure there are benefits to this, too."

I said I totally agreed with him, and placed the blame for the organic stone-ground stuff on Rose. I didn't mention her IBS though – that would just have been low.

"But where do you stand on the red sauce versus brown sauce debate?" I asked.

"Sauce? What kind of philistine would adulterate a bacon sandwich with sauce?" Oliver said. "Lots of butter," he spread a thick layer on the bread, "Bacon, a generous dusting of white pepper, and there you have it – perfection. Would you like one the same? Oh, no, sorry, of course – you don't…"

I looked at Oliver and I looked the slices of bacon, the fat golden and crisp at the edges, and thought about my principles and the poor pigs, and how shallow and wrong it would be to do something I disapproved of in order to please him, and I said, "Oh, go on then."

And he was right – it was delicious. We ate and he asked me about my plans for the weekend and I said I was going to visit my best mate Claire, who lives a couple of miles away in Brixton, in a very tiny, very dodgy studio flat with her gorgeous baby girl Persephone, who's my god-daughter. I told him all about how Claire's boyfriend Ty had succumbed to a fit of commitment-phobia towards the end of Claire's pregnancy and ditched her, leaving her and Persephone to make do on almost no money whilst Claire's on maternity leave from her job as a drama teacher in a youth outreach programme, which pays next to nothing at the best of times. I told him how Claire had asked me to be her birth partner after Ty buggered off – although I suspect he would have been about as much use as a chocolate teapot anyway; I saw him almost faint once watching Claire trimming chicken livers for a paté.

"It was the most amazing experience," I said to Oliver. "So, like, elemental. And Claire was... Just, wow. Even though she was screaming and mooing like a cow, bless her, she was just so strong. She did a hypnobirthing course and I think the techniques helped her deal with the pain, because she just zoned out – it was like she'd entered another plane. And seeing how proud she was when she held Pers for the first time was incredible. It's really going to be tough for her being a single mum but I know she'll make a go of it."

And Oliver talked a bit about a friend of his who's a barrister specialising in family law, and how hard it can sometimes be to get absent fathers to do their duty by their kids, and what a disgrace it is that so many men seem to want to abdicate responsibility rather than embracing fatherhood, and how things really have improved over the past few decades in terms of the way the courts can appropriate income for child support. I was really surprised by how sound his views were actually – I suspect most of Rose's friends would come over all chuntery about how women shouldn't go having babies they can't afford, which is nonsense of course because as we all know, it takes two to tango. Anyway we had more coffee and I found a carton of grapefruit juice in the fridge, and by the time Rose came downstairs showered, dressed, fully made up and looking rather crossly for her breakfast, Oliver and I were chatting away like old friends and we'd finished all the bacon.

"So Rose has a new boyfriend?" asked Claire, once we'd got the formalities out of the way. The formalities consisted of me presenting Claire with a bottle of wine and a box of brownies I'd bought at Waitrose on the way, and Pers with a fluffy pink pig, and then spending about half an hour kissing her adorable squashy tummy and telling Claire how much she'd grown since I last saw her two weeks before.

Poor Claire, since Ty dumped her and she had Pers her social life has been a bit limited, so she's developed a slightly obsessive interest in other people's, and of course Rose's is a pretty good one to pick if you're in the market for living vicariously. Although Pers was totally gorgeous and brilliant company, and was terribly advanced for eight months, she didn't have an awful lot to say for herself yet, and Claire missed human interaction, even though she and Pers try to go out at least once every day.

Their flat is truly, truly horrible. I die a little bit inside every time I go there and am struck afresh by how awful it is, and by the fact that it's home for my best friend and her baby daughter. Claire's done her best to make it nice, but ultimately with a kitchen that hasn't been updated since the 1970s, a wonky floor covered in manky, ancient carpet tiles that lets the downstairs neighbour's skunk smoke seep through, and a huge patch of mould on the bathroom wall that comes creeping back within days of Claire spending an afternoon scrubbing it off, the amount of difference flourishing plants and cheerful framed posters on the walls can make is limited. And yet Claire and Pers emerge from this hovel every day to go to their baby massage class or their mums and tots yoga or storytime at the library or whatever, Claire in her charity-shop clothes and Pers in the little outfits Claire puts together from hand-me-downs and eBay purchases, and they look like they've stepped out of the Boden catalogue.

Claire, you see, is seriously beautiful. Not like me and Rose. Claire's a ten without doing anything. She's got clear, glowing olive skin that doesn't need makeup and smooth, shiny hair the colour of bitter chocolate that doesn't need straighteners, and a slim, lithe figure that doesn't appear to need diet or exercise to stay that way, and a perfect oval face with high cheekbones and full lips that always seem to be smiling. I suppose it's partly her looks that got her into the mess she's in now. In the same way as people with vast amounts of money tend to go out with and marry other people with vast amounts of money, I've noticed that utterly gorgeous people end up sleeping with other utterly gorgeous people. You'd think there'd be some disadvantage to it in terms of the diversity of the gene pool or whatever, but apparently there isn't, and that's how it was with Claire and Ty. He's as beautiful as she is, all long limbs and honey-coloured skin, and the most amazing green eyes I've ever seen. For almost a year the two of them were inseparable, constantly intertwining their lissome bodies and exchanging dazzling smiles and gazing into each other's exquisite faces. You could see that, however much they pretended they were glad to see you, they really couldn't wait for you to go so they could be alone again. It was at once deeply annoying and really, really lovely and sweet, because they were both so happy, but anyone with more than about five minutes' experience of life could tell it was going to end badly, and so it did.

When Claire found out she was pregnant, it was like nature cranked up the dial a bit and allowed her special dispensation to go from being a ten out of ten to being an unprecedented eleven. Joy shone out of her. She was never sick, she barely put on weight, she didn't seem to get swollen ankles or stretch marks or varicose veins or any of the other disfiguring horrors that plague pregnant women. She just glowed with a kind of serene excitement, thrilled by what was happening in her body. And therein lay the problem. For the first time in their relationship, Claire's attention was focussed inwards, at the tiny new life inside her, rather than outwards at Ty. Initially he made an effort and shared Claire's excitement about the baby – I really believe he did. But as month followed month and he carried on being not-quite-as-important, he started to withdraw. When Claire wanted to stay in and drink tea and have a warm bath and go to bed with another Georgette Heyer novel (she became obsessed with them whilst up the duff), Ty wanted to go out. At first Claire reluctantly went with him; then Ty reluctantly stayed in; later still he took to going out alone, and one night he didn't come back.

Claire rang me, frantic with worry, and I went round and stayed overnight in the slightly less grotty one-bedroom flat she and Ty shared, while she paced and fretted, sure he had been stabbed to death on the mean streets of Brixton. I pointed out to her that the streets of Brixton are hardly mean any more, property prices there have rocketed in recent years and there's even a farmers' market, for heaven's sake, but she was too anxious to listen. I was right, of course, and the next morning Ty sloped in, sullen and belligerent and clearly feeling guilty as hell. I made myself scarce, but Claire told me later that after spending the day crying (her) and shouting and punching the walls (him), Ty had admitted that he'd spent the night with a girl called Olya who worked on the Chanel counter at Harrods, and he couldn't help it but he was in love with her and was taking himself off to Bayswater to twine his limbs with hers and gaze into her eyes, and Claire could forget it if she thought she'd be getting child support because Ty, being an out-of-work musician, hadn't got two quid to rub together.

So in spite of having a genetic inheritance that will probably make her a supermodel, poor darling Pers has had a hard start in life from the point of view of material things. But Claire adores her and I adore her and Ty and Olya adore her (Claire's been incredibly grown up and allows them to see her every other weekend, although they can't take her out on their own for very long because Claire's still breastfeeding on demand and Pers does demand rather a lot). This also curtails Claire's social life, and although I know she wouldn't swap places with anyone, she does get a rather wistful look about her when she remembers the days – just a couple of years ago – when she was out every night at various gigs drinking and smoking and dancing and being admired and pulling. It will get easier for her, of course, once Pers is a bit older and she has a bit more freedom and a bit more money, but for now I think she does feel a bit trapped sometimes, and so she loves hearing about Rose's active social life and my less active one.

"He's called Oliver," I said. "He's some sort of City trader, and he collects art."

"Really?" Claire shrieked with laughter and rolled her eyes. "That is just, like, so Rose. Is he as vile as he sounds? Does he wear peach-coloured cashmere jumpers and have floppy Tory-boy hair? Does he pop his collar and have a box at Twickenham? Would I find his picture on lookatmyfuck-ingredtrousers.com? Does he belong to a swanky golf club that won't let women be members? Or is he the wide boy type, whose idea of a fun night out is snorting coke off strip-pers' bums?"

I said, feeling a bit defensive for some reason, I hadn't seen Oliver in a cashmere jumper or red trousers and he hadn't mentioned golf or strippers, and his hair was actu-ally quite sensible and ordinary. Claire looked a bit disap-pointed and switched Pers over to her other side to finish her lunch.

"Actually, Claire," I said, "he's really nice. Like, as in nice. I like him." I felt myself blushing furiously but she didn't see because she was gazing down at Pers's fluffy little head.

"You like him? Great," she said. Claire's heard all the horror stories over the years about Danny, Neil, Aiden and all the rest of them, and has had to listen to me wailing about the prospect of Rose one day marrying one of them, and my poor future nieces and nephews being saddled with Danny, Neil or Aiden for a father.

"Mmmm," I said, helping myself to another brownie. "The thing is, I think maybe I like him a bit too much."

This got Claire's attention. She looked up at me. "You fancy Rose's new boyfriend? Really? You're not just making it up because my life is bereft of excitement and romance and I have to live vicariously?"

I laughed. "I wish I was. He's sweet, he really is. He seems really interested in what I have to say. And, Claire, he's so fucking drop-dead gorgeous I could just sit and stare at him for ever. He's as lovely looking as you and you know what a compliment that is."

"Shut up!" Claire said. "But... you won't do anything about it, will you? You wouldn't try and steal Rose's boyfriend off her? Because that would be so totally evil I don't think I could be your friend anymore." But she was smiling and I could tell part of her was thinking that it would be really, really interesting if I tried to steal Rose's boyfriend, and would provide her with enough gossip to keep her going until Pers was practically old enough to leave home. You see, Claire, while a kind person and a true friend, loves nothing more than a juicy bit of scandal.

"Of course not. That would be wrong. I suppose I should find someone new really. I need to get out more," I said gloomily.

"I still wish you and Ben..." Claire began, but I silenced her with a hard stare.

"Ben. Is. Not. My. Boyfriend," I said. "And he won't be, not ever." I didn't need to tell Claire why – she knew all about Nina. "So I need someone new. I need to check my phone every five minutes to make sure it's working, and feel my head spin when I'm kissed, and experience the horrible disappointment of realising he doesn't really understand *American Psycho*, and all that stuff."

"Yes, I vaguely remember all that," Claire smiled ruefully. "Anyway, even if you had set your sights on Rose's chap, it wouldn't work, because if Rose is his type, you aren't, right? Not that you aren't wonderful and beautiful and everything," she added hastily, "but Rose is just... different. High maintenance. Knows important people. Goes to flash parties. You know."

I did know, and after the little smart of hurt I felt whenever I suspected anyone of drawing comparisons between me and Rose had faded, I realised she had a point. Why on earth would Oliver want me, or even think about wanting me, when he had Rose? But why not, if all or at least some of the things he liked about Rose were there to like about me too, mightn't he – totally of his own volition, without me needing to do any stealing at all – just sort of... notice me? Look at me and think about me in a bit the same way as I couldn't help looking at and thinking about him? Because when I talked to Claire about all the knee-trembling intensity of the beginning of a new relationship – the breathless anticipation, the round-the-clock sex, the tenderness everything about Him (even unto dirty socks) can inspire, I wasn't imagining experiencing those feelings for just any random new man. I was imagining experiencing them for Oliver. With Oliver.

Then Claire said, "Obviously trying to steal your sister's boyfriend would be bad and wrong, but..."

"But what?" I said.

"If you were to decide to just sort of gently entice him away a bit, which would obviously make you a really horrible person..."

"Then what?" I said.

"Then it might help if you had a friend who was a really bad person too, and had a brilliant, evil master plan that could help you do it."

I said, "I know you're breastfeeding, but shall we open another bottle of wine?"

"My midwife reckons that unless you get so pissed you forget you even have a baby, it's all good," Claire said. "There's some Viognier in the fridge."

Chapter Four

"Night out tonight at mystery venue?" I texted to Ben. "Meet at mine at 8 for warm-up drinks. Dress like you're auditioning for *Made in Chelsea.* E xx."

It was the last working day of the year and Rose and I were getting the train to Buckinghamshire the next day to spent Christmas with Dad and Serena. But, as you generally do at this time of year, I felt the need for one last big night out before we left London. Usually I would have met a group of mates and headed to Brixton or Camden for a gig, or to the South Bank if we felt the need to imbibe some culture with our drinks, or out for dinner if we were feeling flush. Tonight, though, I had a different plan.

I'd picked Rose's brains earlier in the day.

"Where do your flash friends hang out these days?" I'd asked as we walked to the station together, Rose to head north to St James's, where Quinn's has its palatial headquarters; I to get the train to Waterloo and then the tube to London Bridge and the considerably shabbier offices of YEESH.

"Which ones?" Rose asked. "The media ones, or the art ones, or the bankers, or the young and trendy?"

"The young and trendy, I guess," I said. "I want to show Ben how the other half lives."

"Then Mahiki, probably," she said. "It's not new but it's still on trend. Prince Harry goes there sometimes, and loads of models and football players."

"That sounds perfect," I said. "I suppose I need to book?"

"Book?" Rose laughed. "Too late for that, I think. You'll have to turn up and queue with the commoners and get turned away by the door bitch. Their entrance policy is brutal. Borrow my Louis Vuitton bag if you like – it's no guarantee but it won't hurt."

"Really?" I said. The Louis Vuitton bag was new – an early Christmas present from one of her art-loving admirers, and it was very close to Rose's heart. "Thanks. You're an angel. I promise I'll look after it." By this stage we'd reached the station and we said goodbye, and I went up to platform three and Rose walked into the tunnel in the direction of the coffee shop and platform twelve.

Normally nothing – but nothing – would persuade me to try and get into a place that had a door policy based on anything other than making a reservation or first come first served. The idea that someone can get to queue-jump on the basis of who they are or what they look like is absolute anathema to me – and of course as a committed republican the idea of hanging out in Prince Harry's favourite haunts doesn't exactly float my boat either. But I had decided to dip my toe into Rose's world – the world I would have to inhabit if I were to appear as more than the faintest blip on Oliver's radar – and besides, I had a secret weapon.

My friend Ashira works on the arts and ents pages of the *Evening Standard*, and she's always saying that they can get in absolutely anywhere, places are competing so desperately for favourable publicity. Ashira's job involves reviewing films, plays and world music by unknown directors and artists, but the clubs and restaurants don't know that, and as soon as she mentions the paper's name, she's in, she says. So when I got to the office, while I was in that drinking coffee, checking emails, chatting to colleagues about last night's X Factor stage of the morning during which nothing important ever gets done, I sent her an email asking her to get me and Ben into Mahiki.

"Mahiki??!!" she emailed back. "Are you having a giraffe? You don't want to go to Mahiki, it's full of pretentious wankers in blazers."

So I hastily made up some story about a callow ex-university friend of Ben's who was up in London from the provinces and whose life ambition it was to see Rosie Huntington-Whiteley in the flesh, and we'd said we would try and sort it. I considered saying that the friend had some terrible disease and Ben and I were acting as a two-person Reach for a Dream foundation, but I thought that might be a bit much, so I left it there, and a few minutes later Ash mailed me back to say it was all sorted and there would be a table for three booked in my name at eleven that evening, and I finished my coffee and punched the air and went "Yessss!" and Ruth and Duncan stopped their conversation on the other side of the office and looked at me as if I was barking mad. Then I texted Ben and told him to prepare for my magical mystery evening.

By the time eight o'clock rolled round I was feeling a bit less chipper. My wardrobe had revealed its shortcomings yet again, especially as I'd realised that jeans for women in smart nightclubs simply are not done. I'd checked the *Heat* magazine website and every single Z-list celebrity photographed arriving at or falling out of Mahiki had been wearing a dress, presumably to allow the long lenses of the paparazzi easier access to their knickers. So I'd had to do an emergency dash to Debenhams at lunchtime, and all I had managed to find was a rather dull black dress that made me look like I was going to a funeral, but was at least slimming. But it kept gaping open at the front, revealing my cleavage-boosting yet in itself terribly unattractive flesh-coloured bra, and the copious amounts of Rose's tit tape I'd used kept sticking to strands of my hair, and I'd got a bit sweaty wrestling into control-top pants in my overheated bedroom and my nose had gone all shiny and in short I was feeling about as far from a young and trendy nightclub-goer as it's possible to get.

But when Ben turned up at the door he did a huge double-take and said, "Wow, Ellie, you look gorgeous!" Bless Ben, he always can make me feel better about myself. And actually he was looking not un-hot himself, in a long tweed overcoat that almost brushed his Converse high-tops, a black jumper and jeans that – I had to lean over and peer at his bottom to check, which is never a hardship – had a designer label.

"True Religion?" I said, "Get you!" And he explained that they were actually the result of a lunchtime panic-buying trip to TK Maxx, and I explained about my lunchtime panic-buying trip to Debenhams, and we ripped the piss out of each other about our fashion failure while Ben opened a bottle of fizz and poured us both a glass.

"So," he said, "Am I allowed to ask where we're going?"

"Mahiki," I said.

"Mahiki?" Ben used exactly the same incredulous tone that had come across in Ash's email. "Isn't that full of cunts?"

I looked at him, my mate Ben, with his champagne glass frozen half way to his lips. I thought how nice it would be to tell him everything: my stupid crush on Oliver, how I'd told Claire about it and the advice she'd given me, trusting that I wasn't going to follow it, how I'd got Ash to blag us on to the guest list because I thought it was the kind of place where people like Oliver might go, and since I'd become friends with Oliver on Facebook I wanted to post status updates that made me sound as if I lived his and Rose's kind of life. But it was all too complicated, and it made me sound like the kind of person Ben wouldn't much like, and nor would I for that matter, so I just said, "I need to broaden my horizons." I did tell him about his mythical friend with the crush on Rosie Huntington-Whiteley, though, and we had a good laugh about that while we finished the bottle of cava and a tub of cheese footballs. Then we put on our coats and I picked up Rose's bag – a really beautiful, floppy envelope made of soft gold leather – and checked I had keys, phone and lipstick, and we headed out into the frosty night.

When I saw the queue outside the door I almost grabbed Ben and legged it. I don't know when I've felt more intimidated than I did walking past that crowd of designer-clad, swishy-haired lovelies – and that was just the men. All of them gazed covetously at Ben as we passed, or perhaps they were looking at Rose's handbag, or resenting our ability to stride to the front of the queue while they waited in the cold. I was expecting a hard hand to land on my shoulder at any moment and a sinister voice to say something like, "You don't belong here, missus. Your hair is all wrong and your frock is from Debenhams and we know that bag isn't yours and we've heard reports that you read the *Guardian.* Now come quietly, we don't want any trouble." But we reached the door unmolested, gave our names to the beautiful, reed-thin blonde girl who wielded the Clipboard of Power, and we were admitted and shown to our table, which was behind a gigantic fern-like plant next to the loos, so clearly there were limits to Ash's miracle-working.

Ben peered at the cocktail menu in the gloom. "Is your name Vicky?" he said.

"What?" I leaned forward. The chairs were the kind that sort of trap you in a semi-recumbent position so you're closer to the people at the next-door table than you are to the person at your own, and the music was so loud I'd be willing to bet people carried on conversations all night without hearing a word. Or perhaps I'm just getting old, deaf and carmudgeonly.

"I said, what the hell's tiki?" Ben shouted.

I explained, mostly by the medium of sign language, that it involved tropical islands and lots of rum, and we ordered some absurd cocktails that came in hollowed-out pineapples, and sat sipping and observing the crowd.

Whenever Rose told me about nights out with her friends, she made them sound like the best fun ever. Whether or not you care about Tara getting off with Tristram and Pippa Middleton being seen fixing a ladder in her tights in the ladies', Rose and her mates always seemed to spend nights out dancing until their feet were killing them and laughing until their stomachs ached and generally having a fantastic time. But all I could see around us were groups of people trying to look achingly cool and hence looking like they weren't having much fun at all, ordering bottles of vodka and champagne and bellowing conversations at one another. All the girls were impossibly thin and beautiful and had glossy, artfully tousled hair and the sort of make-up that's meant to be shiny, as opposed to getting that way towards the end of the night, as mine does. They might not have looked like they were enjoying themselves, but my god, they looked good. Even if I spent the next month being starved, plucked, scrubbed and styled, I didn't think I could look like that. The men seemed to fall into two categories: those wearing suits with no ties, lounging against pillars holding glasses of vodka, and the loud, lairy, sweaty rugby-player types, dragging girls on to the dance floor. I looked at Ben and wondered if he was feeling as out of place as I was, but he was drinking his pina colada with apparent relish and looking around grinning like he was having the time of his life.

I noticed that in between looking cool and indifferent, lots of people were frantically tapping away at high-end iPhones and Blackberries, presumably reassuring themselves that this was, in fact, the very coolest place to be at that particular moment and there wasn't a much better party taking place a few hundred yards down the road. I wondered what would happen if Kate Moss or Peaches Geldof or someone were spotted elsewhere – presumably the news would spread like wildfire on Twitter and there would be a run on the place, possibly with fatalities as everyone tried to get to the door at once. I considered testing the theory but I didn't actually know the names of anywhere nearby where I could pretend to have spotted them, and anyway only about twenty of my friends follow me on Twitter.

I got my phone out of Rose's bag anyway, and tweeted, "At Mahiki with @BenedictTheRed. Have complicated cocktail and designer bag. No selebs spotted yet – boo hiss." I'm sure I am not alone in observing that mobile phone use is contagious. It's like when you're with someone and they yawn, and seconds later you can't help yawning too. Anyway, as I typed I looked over at Ben and saw him fight for self-control and lose, then, compelled by an irresistible force, take out his own phone and start tapping away.

To be fair to Ben, he does have a very good reason to be surgically attached to his phone. I think I mentioned that he works as an adviser to Lucille Field, the MP. Anyone who takes an interest in politics will have followed the story of her fall from grace with horrified relish – it was widely reported in the press as one of the first casualties of social media use. Lucille was a shadow cabinet minister with responsibility for children and the family or some such – basically a role covering soft issues that most politicians don't actually think are all that important but which they have to be seen to care about because the electorate does. But she's considered to be very brilliant and was tipped to have a bright future ahead of her. Then she launched herself on to the Twitterverse. Lucille thought this would be a great way to communicate with her constituents whilst appearing to be down with the kids, and before you knew it she had loads of random voters and the more technically savvy MPs following her. All went well for a while until Lucille had a disagreement with the Leader of the Opposition over something or other, and posted a tweet saying, "I don't so much mind our dear leader's lack of policy – it's his eyewatering halitosis (never to be mentioned) that brings shame upon us all" – exactly one hundred and forty characters, which I thought showed commendable accuracy. Unfortunately Lucille didn't send the tweet in reply to one of her trusted allies, but to all her fourteen thousand followers, all of whom instantly went off to Google images of people recoiling from close contact with said dear leader, and attach them to retweets of Lucille's trenchant words, and the story even made the front pages of the tabloids for a couple of days. The net result was she was shuffled off the shadow cabinet sharpish, and poor Ben spends an awful lot of time on Twitter pretending to be Lucille, because he won't allow her to send her own tweets any more. I'm just waiting for the day when he too slips up and tweets something like "Off to meet @EllieMottram to get off our tits on Stella and have a curry" from Lucille's account instead of his own, but I think he is probably too technically proficient to make such a rookie error, and anyway he's really discreet about his personal life.

I checked Rose's Twitter feed and saw that she was at her work end-of-year party, and checked Oliver's but it was full of incomprehensible stuff about the futures market. Then I put my phone away and we ordered another cocktail – one that came in a coconut shell this time, with two straws so that we could share it. We drank it and looked around at the beautiful people some more, and tried to have a conversation about them over the music, and I realised that I was terribly bored. There – I said it. I was with one of my favourite people in a fabulous place, and all I could think was how much more fun we'd be having if we were drinking pints of lager or rough red wine in a low-key bar, chatting about a film or exhibition we'd just seen. This is what it must be like to be a proper socialite, I thought – not only do you have to put a huge amount of effort into the way you look, but you have to turn up to places where you don't necessarily want to be and talk to people who you don't want to talk to. Thankfully I was spared that fate, because I didn't know anyone there except Ben, but I thought about all the parties Rose has been to over the years with the sole purpose of 'networking', and I wondered how on earth she found the stamina for it. That's Rose for you though

– when she sets out to achieve something, she doesn't give up. The room was warm and I was actually feeling quite sleepy from the two cocktails – it was after one in the morning, too, the night starts late when you are a socialite, I suppose, and have nothing more important to get up for in the morning than an eleven o'clock with your pedicurist. I felt my jaw creak and the next thing my face split in a huge yawn, and when I looked sideways at Ben I saw him yawn too. I stretched my leg out and poked his thigh with the pointy toe of my shoe.

"Shall we go?" I mouthed.

Ben nodded with undisguised enthusiasm and stood up, and we ploughed a path through the beautiful people towards the door, and there, at the heart of a cluster of the most beautiful people of all, was Oliver. He was in the suit-with-no-tie camp, his hair was flopping over his forehead, and his long, elegant fingers were wrapped around the stem of a cocktail glass. No coconuts or pineapples for Oliver, I noticed – he was drinking a martini with olives in it. I instantly resolved to shun sweet, pink drinks forthwith and learn to like dry martinis if it killed me, which it probably would because, let's face it, they are bloody horrible things. I'd like to say that the music faded to silence and the crowds melted away, leaving us alone as our eyes locked together and our lips met in a kiss that seemed to last forever, but that would obviously be ridiculous. I stopped in my tracks when I saw him, and said lamely, "Hello! Fancy bumping into you here," and we kissed each other's cheeks, or rather sort of clashed jaws, like you do, and Oliver said, "What a coincidence," and then he winked at me, so I knew he'd seen my tweet and wasn't surprised to see me at all. I wondered whether, just maybe, it was knowing that I'd be there that had made Oliver decide to come, but that was way too far-fetched. He probably dropped in all the time.

"What would you like to drink?" Oliver asked.

I opened my mouth to say I'd love a dry martini, but Ben said, "Nothing, thanks, we were just leaving actually." He didn't look particularly pleased to see Oliver. I'd have thought the two of them would get on quite well, both being bright and more or less the same age and having so much else in common, but they didn't appear to be hitting it off much.

"Are you sure?" Oliver said. "Ellie?"

"No, really, we ought to be going," I said. "I've an early start tomorrow. Rose and I are off to spend Christmas with our dad and stepmum." Which of course made me sound dull, prim and about twelve years old.

"Shame," Oliver said, and Ben said, yes, it was a shame, but we must all get together soon, with a whopping great note of insincerity in his voice. Then we exchanged the usual pleasantries about Christmas, and established that Rose had invited Oliver to our place for New Year's Eve, which meant that Ben and he would be bonding over drinks rather sooner than Ben had bargained for.

We waited outside for what felt like hours while one taxi after another sailed past with its light off, and eventually when we did get one to stop, the driver refused to go south of the river, the bastard, even though the cabbie's code says they have to.

"You go on," I said to Ben. "I'll get a bus."

He paused, his hand on the cab's open door. "Are you getting in or not, mate?" said the driver.

Then Ben said, "Why not come back to mine?"

I said, "Okay."

I didn't exactly stay over at Ben's often, but I sometimes did, if we'd been out and I'd missed the last train or something. We'd get a kebab from the place at the bottom of Ben's road – falafel in pita with extra chilli sauce, no onion on Ben's, and a giant bag of greasy chips – and give fingerfuls of hummus to Winston Purrchill, Ben's black and white rescue cat, who has cosmopolitan taste in food. Then I'd clean my teeth with a dollop of toothpaste on my finger and wash my face with Ben's soap, which always left my skin feeling dry and tight the next day, and he'd offer to sleep on the sofa and let me have his bed, and I'd say I'd be fine on the sofa, and it would all be totally normal.

But that night things felt a bit different. We sat in silence in the back of the taxi, the space between us feeling like it was somehow either too large or two small. After a bit I said, "So what did you think?"

"Full of cunts," Ben said. "Why did you make us go? Just, why, Ellie?"

"Didn't you like looking at the hot women?" I asked.

Ben shrugged. "They were okay. I don't really get girls who just want to parade around in designer clothes and swish their hair, you know that. I don't do arm candy – apart from you of course," he added gallantly.

I slid over and elbowed him in the ribs to show I treated that comment with the contempt it deserved, and then stayed there, our arms touching. I couldn't really think of anything else to say. I wondered about Ben's perception of all those glossy, swishy-haired girls. Did he really not fancy them? Maybe he was right and they were just waiting for some rich bloke to come along and snap them up and marry them. But maybe they were also, I don't know, hedge fund managers or heads of marketing for multinationals or whatever, who just cared a lot about their appearance and liked going to clubs with their friends, like Rose does. Like Rose, they'd have homes, and sisters who borrowed their shoes, and they'd leave hair in the bath, and sometimes eat a whole packet of Jaffa cakes even though they'd pay for it the next day with their IBS and have to spend an extra two hours in the gym. There was more to Rose than her glossy beauty – there was her sweetness and her cleverness and her fantastic sense of humour and her great taste. So surely Ben – or Oliver, or any man – would choose someone who was all of those things and looked like Rose, rather than someone like me who was some of them and didn't.

How many calories had I eaten that day, I wondered. Two thousand? Three thousand? Rose only allowed herself (or as she puts it, "I am only allowed…" as if there was some external agency that dictated what she could and couldn't eat) twelve hundred a day. I'd had a bowl of cornflakes for breakfast and a tuna sandwich for lunch, and a Mars bar mid-afternoon because I was feeling a bit peckish and needed something to pass the time until five o'clock, and two pieces of toast and peanut butter before going out for the evening to line my stomach. And the tub of cheese footballs Ben and I had polished off (those things are like crack, and their arrival in the shops signals to me that Christmas has come). That was normal, surely? Okay, I hadn't got my five a day, but I generally did. I ate a normal amount of food, didn't I? But it wouldn't be normal for the lithe army of size-eight girls I'd jealously admired earlier in the evening.

So I was relieved as well as disappointed that Ben didn't ask the cab driver to stop at the kebab shop. We drove straight to his flat and went upstairs. Ben didn't turn on the light, and when he went over to the window the street lamp outside shone briefly and brightly on his face before he pulled down the blind.

"Shall I take the sofa?" I asked. But Ben shook his head.

"Come here a second," he said. I walked towards him slowly, still in my high heels and my black dress.

"Turn around," he said. I did, and he unzipped my dress. But instead of sliding seductively to the floor, the dress stayed obstinately up, attached to the yards of industrial-strength tit tape that was holding it on to my unsexy flesh-coloured bra. And I was still wearing my horrible suck-it-all-in knickers (the sort that have a special flap thing for you to wee through, and leave deep red furrows on your skin, every stitch on every seam indelibly impressed).

"That'll be all, Jeeves," I said. "I can take care of the rest of the scaffolding."

I heard Ben take a deep breath, as if he was going to say something important. But he just said, "Take the bed, then. I'll sleep in here."

I found an old T-shirt of his and put it on and got under the dark blue duvet, surrounded by the warm smell of him. Even with Winston's comforting, purring weight on my hip, it took me a long time to fall asleep.

The next morning Rose and I caught our train with seconds to spare, and collapsed laughing in our seats, surrounded by carrier bags bulging with presents (Rose's tastefully wrapped in shiny silver with grey chiffon ribbons, mine roughly swaddled in brown paper and string).

"So how was Mahiki?" Rose asked.

"Brilliant," I said. "We had a fabulous time."

Chapter Five

"I bags the bed by the window!" Rose ran through the door and threw herself and her suitcase down on one of the twin beds.

I laughed. "You can have whichever one you like, it's your room after all." Strictly speaking it wasn't any more, of course, it was Dad and Serena's guest room, and tastefully decorated with pristine white duvets and an abstract painting with splashes of bright jewel colours hanging above the fireplace. But it used to be Rose's – she'd fallen in love with it as a ten-year-old because if you leaned out of the window and craned your neck you could see a little slice of river, and sometimes swans gliding past.

The room that used to be mine is at the very top of the house, converted from an attic, and I didn't care that all you could see out of its tiny windows was sky. I loved the idea of my own little kingdom right at the top of the house, where I could shut myself away for hours with a book, impervious to Rose's entreaties to come down and play with her. That room has been turned into a study for Serena, with a squashy sofa that pulls out into a double bed where Granny and Grandpa sleep. Every Christmas Dad tactfully asks them if they wouldn't prefer to stay in Rose's room, and every Christmas they tell him not to be ridiculous, and insist they can manage the stairs perfectly well.

Granny and Grandpa are Mum's parents, and they've spent every Christmas with us since we moved here. It's strange to remember the first year, with Mum and Dad so full of excitement and plans to keep chickens and geese in the garden and perhaps even a pig. Mum had all sorts of ideas about sustainability and getting back to the land – she was always a bit of an early adopter, as the market research types call it. Sometimes I look at photos of her and Dad when they first met, and she was all dyed black hair and trailing lace shawls and elbow-length gloves, and it's clear that she was right in there when the whole Goth thing was taking off, too. In fact she and Dad met at a Joy Division concert – Dad says he took one look at her figure in her purple brocade corset and leather skirt and realised then and there that she was the one for him. God knows what Granny and Grandpa must have made of their eccentric only daughter, who went off to university to study computer science and came back after her first term dressed like a vampire, and after her second, pregnant with me.

In those days lots of people still felt they 'had to get married', but Mum and Dad were unconventional enough that they wouldn't have bothered, except they were so madly in love they thought it seemed like a brilliant idea. So off to Chelsea Register Office they went, Mum's corset laced more tightly than ever, and then off to France to spend a weekend camping by way of a honeymoon. This, as I remember asking Mum to tell me over and over again as a bedtime story, was an unmitigated disaster. It rained and rained and their tent leaked and their meagre supply of food got waterlogged, and they ended up hitchhiking to the nearest village and taking shelter in a tiny little café where they could at least use a clean loo and have something to eat. Mum said it was such a relief to be warm and dry and the cassoulet was the most delicious thing she'd ever tasted, and the waitress was so kind and pretty that Mum said to Dad, "Luke, if this baby is a girl, we are going to name her after that woman." She hadn't even asked the waitress her name at that stage – it could have been Clothilde or something vile, but it was Elodie. By the time Rose was born Mum had got over herself a bit and ditched the black clothes and she and Dad were living in a little flat in Earl's Court while Dad and his business partner Stu worked silly hours to get their software developing business off the ground. She always said that she and Dad loved me so much they simply couldn't wait to have another baby to love as well, even though they were grindingly poor, and that when Rose came along they were so overwhelmed by her beauty (utter nonsense, I've seen pictures and she was a wrinkly little troll of a child) that they called her Rosamund – rose of the world. But grandiose names for children don't tend to stick and by the time we reached school age I was Ellie and Rose was Rose.

I suppose there would have been more children, Mum being the sort of woman who is never happier than when she's pretending the cupboard under the stairs is a castle or cutting out clothes for paper dolls or baking gingerbread men. But they tried for a few years after Rose was born and eventually when no third baby was forthcoming Mum went to the doctor and had some tests and she was diagnosed with cervical cancer and had to have a radical hysterectomy. She was only twenty-eight. By that stage Dad and Stu's business was starting to make waves. They developed an application called WebSurfer, one of the earliest internet browsers, and in the early nineties Dad accepted an offer from an American computing giant to buy the business and we moved to this little stone house with its two acres of garden and small slices of view of the Thames, with the plan of Dad taking early retirement and he and Mum living out their Good Life fantasies of chickens and pigs and a biodynamic orchard and all the rest. Except then Mum started feeling ill and tired all the time and when she went to the doctor she was told the cancer had come back and metastised and before the next Christmas she was dead.

I can't imagine what it must have been like for Dad, even though he is a great one for sharing and has always encouraged us to talk about our feelings, and talked to us about his. But he kept buggering on, staying at home and looking after us as a full-time father with occasional long visits from Granny and Grandpa to help him out. I kept myself to myself, drowning my loneliness in books and schoolwork – and lonely I was, because Rose abruptly announced, when she was due to start secondary school, that she wanted to go away to boarding school.

I have no idea what Mallory Towers-inspired fantasies led to this decision, but in spite of all Dad's gentle discouragement and my shameful emotional blackmail, Rose set her face in a stubborn mask and insisted she wanted to go, and in due course she did. I suppose that was the beginning of Rose and me becoming so different. It was during her time at Cheltenham Ladies' College – because Rose didn't want just any boarding school, she wanted that one – that my sister first acquired her poise, her graceful straight-backed walk, her ability to 'get on' with strangers, her careful neatness and love of art and fashion. All the things that set her apart from me.

Of course at the time I was just another teenager, happy enough if isolated at the local grammar school, studying hard and getting the results that would eventually win me a place at UCL to read English Lit. It didn't occur to me that my sister was working towards a different goal. I'm not even sure if she knew it herself at the time, but Rose was aiming high, above where she perceived Dad and me to be, and if she left us behind she would be sad, but not regret it.

Anyway as I said, Dad was really noble and dedicated himself full-time to us. I don't know if he had any girlfriends – if he did he certainly kept them away from his daughters. I suppose he felt that we were bound to resent any woman who aspired to take Mum's place. It was only after we'd both gone to university and Dad had plunged back into the world of work (he started writing software for web-based interactive war games as a hobby and predictably he's been hugely successful at it; for a man who genuinely couldn't care less about money, Dad has an unfair share of the Midas touch) that Serena came on the scene.

She's a graphics animator and she and Dad met when she pitched for the design of his latest game – apparently when the fire-breathing dragon she'd created burst on to the screen Dad literally screamed with fright. Anyway, Serena's great. She's quite a bit younger than Dad, when they got married she was thirty-four, the same age Mum was when she died (make of that what you will, Freudians), and Dad turned fifty last year so there's twelve or thirteen years between them, but Dad is so young in every important way it really doesn't matter. Serena is tiny and dark with close-cropped hair that she styles into artful disarray with wax or pomade or something, and designer steel-framed glasses. She's never attempted to mother Rose and me, instead approaching us with calm friendliness, presumably hoping we'll see how happy she makes Dad and accept her for that if not on her own merits.

This has never been a problem for me – I think she's fab and really, although we miss Mum, it would have been mad to expect Dad to have stayed single for ever. It's been a bit more of an adjustment for Rose, though, and sometimes she makes things very difficult for poor Serena.

I was musing on all this whilst I unpacked my little wheelie case of four days' worth of clothes and folded everything carefully away in the cupboard – Rose goes a bit mental if I'm messy when we're sharing a room – but mostly I was just excited. All the traditions started by Mum, faithfully continued by Dad and sensibly left unchanged by Serena were set to unfold over the next few days. There would be the spag bol supper on Christmas Eve followed by a walk to the pub. The midnight service in the village church for those who wanted to go, which means Granny and Grandpa and occasionally Rose or me, but never Dad. The Christmas stockings that Dad still makes for me and Rose although we really, truly are too old for them now (and the bits of lovely Benefit make-up, cashmere mittens and the like that have started appearing in them in recent years lead me to suspect that the responsibility for assembling them has been passed to Serena). The turkey and bread sauce and the special nut roast Granny makes for Dad and me, and the Christmas punch that Grandpa mixes up. Every year it's the same and every year from about the first of December I can feel a warm, fizzy excitement building in me as I think about it. I know it's a bit tragic and I ought to have grown out of it by now, but I love Christmas, and although she'd never admit to something so uncool I know Rose does too. When I was putting my stuff away in the drawer Serena had carefully lined with white tissue paper, I saw she'd brought her special knickers that have little reindeer and sprigs of holly on them.

I was woken the next morning by bright light flooding into the room through the filmy white curtains, and realised the snow, which had been beginning to fall as we walked home from the Rose and Crown after last orders, had settled. I turned over and lay quietly for a while, enjoying the peculiar silence a blanket of snow brings with it, looking at the enticing lumpiness of my Christmas stocking, and wondering whether it would be safe to wake Rose. It wasn't long before the anticipation got too much for me and I got up, showered and dressed, by which time she was awake.

"Happy Christmas," I said, and she said happy Christmas, grinning cheesily and doing a little bounce on her bed.

"Shall we open them?" she asked.

"Let's," I said, "And then let's do the noble thing and take some coffee up to the olds."

We ripped the wrapping paper off a wonderful haul of Burt's Bees lip salve, Urban Decay eyeshadow, stripy wooly tights, chocolate seashells, a bottle of truffle oil for Rose and a giant jar of Marmite for me, paperback books and iPod socks, taking as much pleasure in the opening as we did when we were kids unveiling new clothes for our Sindy dolls and boxes of crayons. Finally everything was unwrapped, and the chocolate oranges unearthed from the stockings' toes, and our beds were littered with shiny paper.

"Good loot," I said.

"Good loot," agreed Rose. "You go on down, I'll get myself ready and be there in a sec."

When I went into the kitchen Serena was already there, wearing rather racy red satin pyjamas and manhandling a massive turkey into the oven.

"Christ, what was I thinking when I bought this monster?" she said. "It only needs to feed seven and it's the size of a hippo. I'll be eating leftovers for months. Happy Christmas, Ellie."

"Happy Christmas," I said, and once she'd parked the turkey I kissed her smooth, honey-coloured cheek. "We've just opened our stockings. Gorgeous stuff. I never knew Dad had discovered Burt's Bees."

Serena laughed. "I'd tell you I'm trying to turn him into a metrosexual but you'd never buy it," she said. "Although of course it's not Luke who's the metrosexual, it's Father Christmas. Maybe it's one of Rudolph's jobs to get him *Grazia* every week."

I started singing to the tune of Rudolph the Red-nosed Reindeer, "You know *Grazia* and *Cosmo* and *Tatler* and *Stylist, Harpers* and... No, it's no good. I can't think of any more."

"*Vogue* wouldn't fit the meter," mused Serena, "And *Marie-Claire's* no good either, nor *Elle. InStyle* doesn't quite scan." She tried singing it, and it sounded so daft the two of us were leaning against the kitchen counter giggling like loons when Rose walked in, looking absolutely radiant and appropriate in that way Rose has, in a cream-coloured silk wrap dress with her hair piled up on top of her head with a couple of lovely sparkly combs, and caramel-coloured slouchy boots and the chunky outsize pearl beads that she'd had in her stocking, which I took as a sign that she wanted to make Serena happy, and made me feel a bit relieved.

Once all the food had been prepared to Rose's standards, Dad, Rose and I bundled up in layers and layers of scarves and coats and mittens and went outside and built a snowman, finishing it off with a carrot for a nose and the battered tweed cap Grandpa wears when he's out walking in the Lake District, where they live. I made a mental note to retrieve it before the end of the day because Grandpa really is quite bizarrely fond of it. We were all glowing and warm with laughter despite the freezing day, and I looked at the snowman and thought how excited it would make Pers, and I wondered if Claire had taken her down to the park to build a snowman of their own, and just fleetingly I thought that there was something a bit sad and empty about a Christmas with no children. I haven't been hit with the broody stick or anything – I adore Pers and I expect I'll have kids of my own one day, but for the moment I simply can't imagine the responsibility.

Perhaps Rose would marry Oliver, I thought, and in a couple of years' time there would be a tiny child trotting around Dad's garden in the snow and sitting down suddenly on its bottom and looking startled in that cute way they have. Then I wondered what it would be like living on my own in the flat in Battersea with Rose and Oliver living somewhere else – I think he'd mentioned that he had an apartment in the Barbican – and I suddenly felt cold again. By that stage Stu, Dad's old business partner, and Serena's parents Gill and Michael had arrived so we all trooped back inside and shed our layers and opened some champagne.

Eventually – late as it always is on Christmas day – lunch was ready and we all filed through to the dining room and watched Dad carve the turkey, and then embarked on a very civilised feeding frenzy. After the main course but before the pudding, once everyone had said no, they couldn't possibly manage another chipolata sausage or Brussels sprout and then had three, and Rose and I had carried the plates through to the kitchen and stacked them next to, but not in, the dishwasher, because a job postponed is a job halved, and Dad had filled everyone's glasses, Grandpa stood up and tinged his glass with the mustard spoon.

He made the little speech he'd made every year for the past thirteen Christmases. I suppose he used to do it before then too, but I'd dismissed it as one of those random things grown-ups did that had no real meaning for me, but since then, obviously, it had become a bit of a big deal. He talked quickly and sweetly about how Christmas is a time for family and friends – sending a warm smile in the direction of Stu, who was looking borderline comatose from punch – and that, at this time of year, we think most fondly and most sadly about those who we would love to be here, but who aren't.

Then he said, "So I will propose my usual Christmas toast, to absent friends," and everyone murmured, "Absent friends," and took a grateful glug of their drink, and Dad reached over to Serena and gave her hand a squeeze to let her know that although he and everyone else was thinking of Mum, she was the one who was there and the one he loved the most right then. And Serena squeezed his hand back and then Dad gave a little cough, and half stood up too, but thought better of it and stayed sat down.

"I've got something to say too," he said, "and today, with all of us here together, seems like the right time and place to say it."

I looked at his face, all sort of pleased and shy, and at Serena's expression of glowy excitement, and the glass of fizzy water she was holding in her hand that wore the titanium wedding band matching Dad's, and of course I knew exactly what he was going to say. But Rose didn't. She was half-turned towards Granny, impatient to continue their conversation, and she just looked perplexed and a bit annoyed. I wanted to stop Dad and tell him this was a really bad idea, and to save it for another day, but there was no way I could. Dad is crap at speaking in public at the best of times, but in this setting, facing his daughters and his in-laws (two sets of them, how harsh is that?) and his best mate, he became positively loquacious.

"Family is enormously important to me and Serena," he said. "She's become a wonderful and close friend to Ellie" – true, she has – "and Rose" – steady on, Dad – "and Gill and Michael have welcomed me as a son, albeit an ageing, crusty one." He was really getting into his stride. I dug my fingernails into my palms and willed him to wrap it up. Or better still shut up, but it was too late for that.

"And we're so excited that we are going to be adding a new generation to the family," Dad blurted out in a rush. "Serena's going to have a baby in June. Actually she's going to have twins, and we're both so delighted and proud."

The crowd, as they say, went wild. Granny and Grandpa pushed back their chairs and went over to Dad and were careful to tell him how happy they were for him and Serena, and Granny wiped away a tear and said it felt as if Elizabeth were in the room giving them her blessing. I got up, wanting to give Serena a proper squeezy hug so she'd know I was genuinely pleased and didn't mind and wasn't in the least bit upset or jealous. Gill and Michael were holding hands, looking terribly chuffed with each other and their daughter who, at the ripe old age of thirty nine, was going to present them with not one grandchild but two. Stu stood to go and congratulate God knows who, and caught his foot in the legs of his chair and went flying, taking the jug of punch with him. I rapidly changed direction and went to see if he was okay, because nothing would fuck Christmas up like a guest with concussion.

Only Rose stayed in her place. She sat there, immobile, for a few long moments while the drink Stu had spilled cascaded over the crimson tablecloth and soaked into her cream dress. Then she stood up very, very slowly, holding on to the edge of the table as if she needed it to balance by, which perhaps she did, she'd had an awful lot of champagne.

"How fucking dare you?" she said quietly, yet amidst the mayhem we all heard every word. "How fucking dare you do that to Mum?" And she turned around and left the room, dripping punch off her lap all over the beautiful wool rug that Serena had bought on her travels in Tibet, of which she was immensely proud, and walked slowly and gracefully up the stairs, her piled-up golden hair and her long neck and her straight slim back gradually disappearing as she reached the landing. Then the glasses and dishes on the table and the baubles on the Christmas tree shuddered with the force of our bedroom door slamming against its frame.

There was a moment of total silence. Then Stu scrambled to his feet and started apologising for the mess and Serena and I rallied round and fetched cloths and sponges and Serena told him it didn't matter, and Granny suggested to Gill and Michael that they all go through to the sitting room and she would take the Christmas pudding and mince pies out there on a tray with some coffee and port, and really it would be best to leave the two of us to get on with clearing up.

Dad sighed heavily and said, "I suppose I'd better go up and have a word with Rose."

I didn't say anything. I carried on sponging the carpet with stain remover, and feeling a bubble of resentment gradually building inside me. I was furious with Rose – not just for hurting Dad and being a bitch to Serena, but for taking the role of the sister who was special, who was different and sensitive and needed to be treated as such, otherwise she would withdraw herself and her affection from the family. Where did that leave me, I fumed? Being the one who cleaned up the mess and didn't get the rich handsome men and smoothed over the hurt feelings, all my life for ever and ever, like some kind of latter-day Cinderella?

I got up and tipped the bucketful of water down the kitchen sink, dried my hands and went into the front room, where everyone was sitting around rather awkwardly with cups of coffee and plates of pudding and glasses of port. I poured myself a brandy and sat down and tried to chat to Gill, who asked me about my plans for New Year's Eve, presumably thinking it was a safe subject.

"Rose and I are having a party at our flat," I said, and I saw Gill's lips tighten at the mention of her name.

"I'm really sorry about what she said back there," I said. "She's had a lot to drink and I suppose with it being Christmas it brings back memories of Mum and the feelings are a bit raw. I'm sure she'll be down soon and feeling absolutely mortified."

Gill sort of sniffed, and I realised that Serena would have confided in her over the years about all the little examples of Rose being 'difficult' – the loads of clothes put in the washing machine with all Serena's left behind in the laundry basket; the lovingly cooked meals loaded with chilli, which Serena can't eat; the china figurine of a cat that had been a wedding present to Dad and Serena, which Rose accidentally smashed. Admittedly it was a bit hideous, but still.

Then Dad came downstairs looking no happier, and took me aside and said, "I'm afraid Rose has decided to go back to London, Ellie."

"But how can she?" I asked stupidly. "There aren't any trains until tomorrow."

"She's rung a boyfriend. Some bloke called Oliver. He's on his way to fetch her now."

I couldn't help feeling a lurch of excitement at the prospect of seeing him.

Chapter Six

When I arrived home three days later, Rose was out. The flat had that slightly stuffy, dusty smell places get when they've been empty for a few days, and the beautifully-decorated Christmas tree was shedding its needles on to the parquet floor. I dumped the huge carrier bag of Christmas presents for Rose, which she hadn't bothered to take with her, in the hall and headed up to my room, put my bag on the floor and then sat down on the bed, looking down at my hands and feeling sad, anticlimactic and generally at a loose end.

We'd tried to maintain the pretence of a normal Christmas after Rose left with Oliver, who had introduced himself politely to all the family but refused anything to eat or drink, clearly finding the situation as cringily awkward as the rest of us. He barely spoke to me, simply perched on the edge of a chair and made desultory conversation while we all waited for Rose to reappear, and when she did she said, "Shall we go, Ollie? Goodbye everyone, enjoy the rest of the day. Ellie, I'll text you." Then she and Oliver had walked out to his car (a low-slung sporty thing I think may have been a Jaguar) and they drove away, leaving silence and a feeling of emptiness behind them. Frankly it was all just shit and although I tried not to show it I felt so angry with Rose and embarrassed for her and myself, as if I were somehow to blame. And Oliver, of course, remained as remote and untouchable as ever.

Part of me had really wanted to leave myself, head back home and go out with my friends or to work or somewhere – anywhere – to escape the bad atmosphere. But the office was closed until the second of January, I didn't want to go back to the flat in case Rose was there with Oliver, there was no room for me in Claire and Pers's little matchbox and besides I didn't want Dad and Serena to feel like they'd been deserted by another daughter. So I stuck it out for three more nights, chatting to them about the babies and making pots of tea and being dutiful, and instead of enjoying having them to myself, by the end of it I was really relieved to go. But now that I was home, I couldn't seem to decide what to do with myself. If we were going to go ahead with Rose's ambitious New Year's Eve party plans, we'd have to have a conversation at some stage, but she hadn't been in touch with me and I was buggered if I was going to be the one to give in and call her first.

After a while I got up, unpacked, found homes for all my Christmas presents, swept up the pine needles and whisked a duster around in a half-hearted way, then went out to the corner shop and stocked up on bread, milk and – randomly – a cabbage, because I vaguely felt we should have something healthy in the fridge to make up for all the chocolate I'd eaten over the past couple of days. When I got back I flipped through the channels on the telly, called Ben and left a message for him, called Claire and left a message for her, and then of course I caved in and called Rose. I should have known I would – I have no willpower in these things and absolutely no ability to sustain any kind of cold war. Whenever I've had rows with boyfriends and stormed out into the night in a huff, I'm always back knocking on their door apologising within a few minutes. If I have a disagreement with someone at work, I literally have to sit on my hands to stop myself sending conciliatory emails and end up sending them anyway. I'm a complete sucker that way. Peace-loving, I suppose you could say if you were being kind.

Anyway Rose answered her phone before I even heard it ring, so I suspected she'd been waiting for my call as anxiously as I'd been waiting for the moment when I'd give in and call her.

"Hey," she said.

"Hey," I said.

"Are you home?" she asked, and I said yes, I'd got back a couple of hours before.

Then I said, "Rose, listen…"

"No, Ellie," she said. "I'm not going to listen and I'm not going to talk about it. I'm just not, okay?"

I think I've mentioned that Rose is ridiculously stubborn. I didn't say anything, and thought for a bit. I could try and talk sense into her and convince her that she was being childish, bratty and cruel, but then we'd end up rowing about it and there'd be a fug of tension in the flat that could last for weeks. Or she might decide to stay where she was and not come home and that would be just as bad.

So I said, "Where are you?"

"I'm at Vanessa's," she said surprisingly. "I've been staying here for the last few days – Ollie had stuff on. We're planning our outfits for New Year's. Did you see the update on the Facebook page?"

"No," I said, rather sullenly if I'm being honest.

"We've decided to make it an eighties theme," she said. "You'll need to find a costume – I'm going as Madonna, with a pointy bra and everything, and Ness is going as Tina Turner."

"What?" I said, well and truly distracted from my original point. "But I hate fancy dress. You know I do."

"Oh come on, Ellie, don't be a spoil-sport," Rose said. "It's going to be brilliant. We're going to have disco music and lights and retro food and everything. Ness wanted a prawn ring but I said no because we have our standards, but I'm thinking miniature chicken kievs and devilled eggs and stuff."

"Cheese and pineapple hedgehog?" In spite of myself, I was entering into the spirit of the thing.

"Exactly!" said Rose. "See, there's no need to be so prickly."

"As long as you promise the prawn ring idea's going to be spiked," I said, starting to giggle. Rose and I love playing this game.

"Don't worry, I talked Ness out if it," Rose said. "She's quite spineless really." I could hear the smile in her voice too.

"Did you have sharp words?" I asked.

"Nah," Rose said, "Ness lacks the quillpower." I could hear Vanessa groan loudly in the background. She just doesn't get it.

"Know what I don't understand about them?" I asked.

"What?" said Rose.

"Why they can't just share the hedge." I heard Rose dissolve into laughter, and ended the call, feeling much better. I didn't know what was going to happen with Oliver, or with Dad and Serena, but for now I had my sister back. I sat down at my laptop and started Googling 1980s fashion, and when Rose walked in a couple of hours later I was feeling quite enthusiastic about the idea and had decided to go as Siouxie Sioux.

"Now if we hang the mirror ball here, in the middle of the room from the light fitting," Rose said, "And the coloured fairy lights round the edges, it will look totally tremaze." It was five o'clock on New Year's Eve and she had been in full-on preparation mode all day, the two of us working like slaves piping filling into scooped-out boiled eggs, sticking spikes on not one but three cheese hedgehogs, one with pineapple, one with green and red glacé cherries, and one with blue cocktail onions – god knows where Rose managed to track those down, I thought they would have been banned years ago owing to their frightening E-number content. After all, even Smarties have been made all healthy and naturally coloured now, and look like they've been presucked, which is wrong if you ask me. Anyway Rose had managed to locate her lurid pickled onions from somewhere, and made a huge black forest gateau and loads of vol-au-vents and sausage rolls and sticks of celery stuffed with blue cheese and walnuts, and it may all have been kitscher than a kitsch thing, but it looked delicious.

Finally, Rose climbed the step ladder and carefully hung up the mirror ball.

"There." She stood back and surveyed our handiwork. "Now we'd better go and get ready, Ellie – it's going to take me ages to get my hair right with those stupid heated rollers."

We went into Rose's bedroom together and it was just like getting ready for parties used to be when we were teenagers. Rose teased my hair and sprayed it purple and I helped her arrange the rollers in hers. She lent me a black vinyl mini-skirt she'd found in one of her drawers and which I just managed to squeeze my arse into and we put careful rips and ladders in a pair of my M&S opaque tights and I finished off the ensemble with Mum's velvet batwing top that I'd remembered to iron, and put loads of black eyeliner on my eyes and some on my lips too. Rose hadn't managed to find a pointy bra but she put on a white basque thing and a full, short skirt and white lace gloves and white fishnet stockings that she said had cost a fortune at a bridal boutique, and masses of red lipstick and once she'd spayed half a can of Elnett on her curled hair she looked beyond hot.

Then the doorbell rang and it was Rose's friend Simon wearing a suit and tie, and apart from the fact that the suit was a bit padded-shouldery and the knot of the tie a bit on the huge side, he looked pretty normal, and we all went, "Booo, party pooper!" but then he handed over a carrier bag that contained a magnum of Krug, pulled a mask out from behind his back and put it on, and he was Nigel Lawson. We all fell about laughing and Rose opened a bottle and found an Abba album on her iPod and put it on and we turned out the lights and started dancing even though it was only seven thirty and none of our other friends had arrived yet.

Soon Ben arrived, dressed as Robert Smith with madly back-combed hair, a baggy white shirt, red lipstick and masses of black eyeliner. He looked the very spit of the Cure frontman circa 1984, only less podgy and rather sexy, and we laughed about our totally accidental outfit co-ordination, and we seemed to have returned to normal after the so-brief-I-might-have-imagined-it weirdness before Christmas. But there was still a bit of a shadow between us after our last evening together, and for the first time ever, I actually felt shy around him. Claire turned up, looking absolutely stunning in fluorescent yellow legwarmers and an outsize black and white stripy jumper, with Pers strapped in her sling. Pers is such a chillaxed baby, she's been with Claire to Occupy London demos and any number of parties and even a couple of pro-choice marches, and she's really good at meeting people and in no time at all Ben and Simon and even Rose were cooing over her and making her do jazz hands with her pudgy little arms, and she was giggling like a loon and loving it.

To be honest I envied little Pers her effortlessly sociable nature. As more people began to arrive – Vanessa and Tom, Pip and Sebastian, a gaggle of Rose's old friends from uni who I didn't know; my mate Ash and her boyfriend Dave, Ruth from work and her girlfriend Diana, Ben's brother Alex and various other mutual friends of ours – I got the urge to retreat to a quiet corner and spectate for a bit, and I noticed a strange thing. Even though almost everyone was in fancy dress (except Alex, who'd forgotten, and turned up in jeans and a jumper, the noodle), if you had to play a game of spotting who was my friend and who was Rose's, I reckon you'd be able to do it with about ninety-five percent accuracy. My lot all looked just a little bit scruffy. Their fancy-dress outfits had obviously been thrown together at the last minute, based around stuff they'd found lying around in their wardrobes, as mine was. I think the only one who'd spent any money was Diana, who'd decided to come as Princess Diana and invested in a sparkly plastic tiara from Claire's Accessories. They mostly had beers in their hands, or glasses of wine, and they were standing around in small groups, engaged in quite interesting and serious-seeming conversations. Ben and Claire, for instance, were sitting on the sofa with Pers on Ben's lap. They'd only met once or twice before, I realised, which was weird given that I'd known Ben for years, and Claire – well, her Mum was best friends with my Mum, so I suppose you could say I've known her for ever. But she and Ben were obviously getting on, and when I walked past them on my way to the kitchen I could hear them earnestly discussing the future of education in inner London and how much more important a stable home life is to a child than private schooling, which is just as well because Claire wouldn't be able to educate Pers privately in a million years, unless she won the lottery or something.

Rose's friends, on the other hand, were standing around in big groups all talking very loudly at once, with occasional outbursts of loud laughter, braying from the men and shrieky from the women. Rose was flitting from group to group, and I wondered if she was stressing because Oliver still hadn't turned up – every now and then, in between her flitting, she stopped and checked her mobile phone, then bit her lip and looked cross, except as the evening wore on and there was still no sign of him, she began to look more anxious than cross.

It was when Rose went off to boarding school that this great divide between our friends opened up, I suppose. When I look at other sisters I know, their social circles are pretty homogeneous. There might be this one's friends from her book group or that one's friends from her running club, but by and large they're much the same kind of people and they all sort of fit together. But when Rose first brought Vanessa to stay with us for a week over the summer holidays almost fifteen years ago, it was like an alien had landed in our house. Although she was only twelve, Vanessa had her hair highlighted, her toenails painted lime green and her legs waxed. She wore matching bras and pants from Sloggi. She had a mobile phone of her own, which was virtually unheard of for anyone under the age of eighteen in those days. She had not one but two ponies, and every night of that week she rang her mother, who she called Mummy, and had a long conversation about how Dapples and Buzz's schooling was progressing ahead of the pony club championships later in the summer. She really did. The following holiday Rose went off to stay with Vanessa's family in Gloucestershire, and came home with highlights, painted toenails and waxed legs of her own. Granny went completely mental and told her that painted toenails are vulgar at any age and totally unacceptable for a child of thirteen, and made her clean it off. I paint mine now, of course, every couple of weeks in the summer, although it has to be the most boring activity in the world, ever, but every time I do I can still hear the note of horror in Granny's voice as she told Rose off.

"As they used to say to us at school, care to share the joke?" I'd been so lost in thought I hadn't even noticed that Oliver had turned up at last, was standing next to me, and I must have been grinning away to myself. I told him about Granny and Rose's toenails, and he laughed. Then he said, "Rose certainly knows how to throw a party. I'm afraid I'm letting her down rather, I'm not much of a mixer really."

"Nor am I," I said. "Give me a couple of friends down the pub and I'm perfectly happy, but Rose loves doing things like this."

Oliver said his worst nightmare was having to entertain clients at work, when you've got nothing whatsoever in common with them and you can't think of a single thing to say and nor can they.

I laughed. "Sounds like hell. Why do you do it?"

"They expect it," he shrugged. "Schmoozing's part of the job, even though I don't think many of us enjoy it much. The guys who have children, especially, hate it when they've been in the office since seven and they're stuck there until eleven and not even doing anything productive."

I murmured something sympathetic.

"Your friend's daughter is gorgeous," Oliver said. "Kids are great at that age – still babies but starting to get really interesting."

This came as a surprise to me, although I suppose it shouldn't really – among the people I know it's generally the men who like babies and the women who don't. Before she found out she was having Pers, Claire was pretty relaxed about whether she'd ever have a family, and even now she's told me she finds other people's kids terribly boring. Rose is positively anti the idea of motherhood too. But Ben and Alex are brilliant with kids, love nothing better than chatting to them and playing peek-a-boo and god knows what else. I wouldn't have thought Oliver was the paternal type though, and I looked at him with renewed interest, and said so.

"I'd have liked to have settled down in my twenties," he said, "only I hadn't met the right person. I thought I had for a while, but I was wrong." We both looked at Rose in her white basque and stockings, her golden curls beginning to soften and drop down her neck. As always, she was at the centre of a shrieking, braying crowd of her friends.

"D'you think you have now?" I asked.

"Well, it's early days," said Oliver, "but I think…"

But before he could finish whatever he was going to say, Rose started rounding everyone up to go on to the roof terrace, from which if it's a clear night and you're quite tall and you crane your neck a lot, you get a reasonable view of the fireworks in the South Bank. She came bustling over to Oliver and me with a tray laden with glasses and said, "Would you mind carrying those upstairs, Ollie?" and thrust a couple of bottles at me, and I took them and we all left the flat and filed upstairs.

It was bloody cold up there but the view is amazing, I have to say. You can see the chimneys of Battersea power station sort of looming over everything, and in the distance the glimmering lights of Westminster. There was a thin drizzle falling, not enough to actually count as rain, and I could see little beads of moisture sparkling in the amber light on my madly teased hair.

Ben and Oliver opened the bottles of champagne and Rose filled up the forest of glasses on the trays, and someone got out their iPhone and found the BBC broadcast, and we all started to count down to midnight. It was pretty cool really – we could hear the tinny sound of the chimes over the phone's speaker, then a few seconds later the real thing, ringing out faintly but clearly in the still, damp air. And we could just see the first glimmer of fireworks in the distance. Everyone hugged and kissed everyone else – I embraced Claire, warm in her fuzzy jumper, and Pers who was fast asleep on her chest, not in the least fazed by the bangs. I hugged Rose and we grinned at each other for a moment, happy that we were sisters, and for the moment at least, friends. I kissed Ben, who I realised I'd hardly spoken to all night, I even did a 'mwah, mwah' air-kissy thing with Vanessa. Then Oliver approached me and I felt all shy and awkward for a second, and we moved together for a polite kiss, the kind you give your sister's bloke, only somehow it went wrong and our noses bumped together and then I felt his lips against mine, warm and dry and tasting slightly of champagne – or maybe that was the champagne on my own mouth, I don't know. It only lasted a second but I literally reeled with his closeness. His shoulders felt lean and strong under my hands, and the bit of his hair brushing against my skin felt so silky I longed to twine it around my fingers. Then we pulled away from each other and smiled, and everyone joined hands and bellowed out a tuneless rendition of Auld Lang Syne, and Oliver, who still had my hand in his, asked softly, "So what are your resolutions for this year, Ellie?"

I hadn't really thought about it in any detail, but I heard my voice say very confidently, "Oh, this is going to be a big year for me. Lots of things are going to change." And I looked at the last golden glimmer of fireworks beyond the bend in the river, and suddenly I was very sure it would be true.

Chapter Seven

"I'm hungry," I said to Ben. "It's the fifth of January and I've been Hank fucking Marvin for five fucking days."

It was true. Well, not strictly, strictly true – there'd been moments when the hunger had faded, like two spoons into a particularly dreary bowl of tomato soup – but true enough. Of course I'd experienced hunger before in my life, but only in a 'great, what's for dinner?' sort of way. This was an annoying, background hunger that seemed to wipe out the possibility of all rational thought, and I hated it. I'd woken up on New Year's Day with a bit of a hangover but a deep sense of purpose, told myself that today was the first day of the rest of my life and all that stuff, and made myself a cup of tea and two pieces of Rose's organic wholemeal toast, with Marmite but no butter, and when I'd finished it I'd still felt hungry, and that had pretty much set the tone for the year so far.

I sipped my Perrier water morosely and looked at Ben's pint with an expression that I imagine must appear on the faces of those poor mentally ill women who abduct babies from supermarkets, the moment before they snatch the buggy and leg it.

"I'm doing Weight Watchers," I said. "Well, kind of. I'm basically eating dry toast and soup and boiled vegetables."

"That's not Weight Watchers," Ben said. "Lucille did that last year and she ate normal food."

"Yeah, but I can't have normal food in the house," I said. "If there's nice stuff in the fridge, even tofu kind of nice, not family pack of Mars bars nice, I'll lose the plot and eat it. I've no control, I'm scaring myself."

"What about Rose's food?" Ben asked.

"Well, she never buys anything interesting apart from smoked salmon, and she gets given boxes of chocolates from grateful clients," I said. "But I made her do a ritual cleansing of it all before she went off skiing. It's the scorched earth policy. It worked for Napoleon and hopefully it will work for me."

"You threw away chocolate?" There was a look of genuine horror on his face. "Ellie, these are bad times."

"I know," I said gloomily. "And it was the good stuff too – those salted caramel ball things, and the beautiful swirly-topped ones that look like something from Fabergé, and three giant-sized Toblerones. Although those were mine, obviously, not Rose's. And we didn't actually bin them, I took them round to Claire's – she can be trusted not to eat them all at once."

"Hmmm," said Ben. "It sounds like it's time for me to stage an intervention."

"What do you mean?" I said, pushing aside a vision of him turning up with all our friends and them making me trough bars of Galaxy like some sort of feeder orgy.

"If you want to lose weight – not that you need to – you need to do it sensibly," he said. "I'm not having you giving yourself rickets or something because you're living off boiled potatoes and frozen peas, which if I know you is what you're doing."

"I had tomato soup last night," I protested. "And Ryvitas with cottage cheese."

"Whoop de do," Ben went sarcastically. "Apart from anything else, you need to eat in a way you can sustain, right? And can you see yourself eating tomato soup and fucking Ryvitas every night for the rest of your life?"

"Well, no," I said. I thought about it for a bit. I suppose you could say I'm lucky, because I've never really needed to diet. I've always been just kind of normal sized, and apart from my brief and ill-starred foray into veganism a couple of years ago, my weight hasn't really varied since I went off to university and piled on a stone, the way everyone does. So this was new territory for me, and I imagined that I'd need to go through a few weeks of pain, then I'd be a size ten (even a size eight, in my fonder fantasies) and I could go back to normal, only I'd be magically, permanently thinner and the first step of Project Transform Ellie, as I'd codenamed it not very catchily in my head, would be complete.

"You need protein," Ben lectured. "Protein's what stops you feeling hungry. And you need food you enjoy, otherwise you'll turn into a total misery guts. In fact I can see it happening already, and that's why I'm going to buy you a vodka and slimline tonic before I lecture you some more."

"Okay," I said obediently. He went off to the bar and came back with another pint for himself and a voddie for me, and let me tell you, it was the best thing I'd tasted for a long time. Five days, to be exact. We were in The Duchess, my local pub, which used to be rough as, with gang members knifing one another in the beer garden by way of an evening's entertainment, but now, like the rest of Battersea, it's really civilised and has poetry nights and knitting evenings and everything. They've done that thing of replacing the flock wallpaper and ancient, sticky carpets with pale-coloured walls and polished floorboards and loads of mismatched furniture and lamps and shelves of dusty old books, which always makes me think there must be a company somewhere making a killing clearing out old people's houses after they've died and flogging the contents to trendy pubs, but anyway it looks really authentic and quite nice. I do miss the old days of overhearing dodgy geezers planning their illegal betting scams and dog fights when you passed them en route to the bar, though. Ben had also got a bowl of olives – you wouldn't have been able to get olives here in the old days, a wrap of crack would have been about the limit of their bar snacks – and I ate one, then took another.

"Fat," Ben said.

"What?" I demanded, looking at the olive in horror. It was green, how could it be made of fat?

"Fat is vital in your diet," Ben said. "It sends satiety signals to the brain, and is important for all sorts of metabolic processes. God, did you not learn anything about nutrition at school?"

I said I supposed I hadn't, or perhaps I'd been reading *Jane Eyre* under my desk when we had that lesson.

"Anyway," Ben said, "here's another thing. Exercise. Look at me."

Ben sort of waved a hand at himself, and I looked, and as ever it was no hardship. I don't think I've mentioned it but Ben's an exercise nut – he's run marathons and is training for an Iron Man triathlon and consequently he has one of those lean, muscular bodies. Not in a bulgy sort of way, just streamlined, with lovely ridges on his torso and stomach. A lot of the time I don't really notice Ben's looks, because... well, I've sort of trained myself not to. But sometimes I'm stopped in my tracks by how hot he is – on a totally objective level, of course – and I think how lucky the girl will be who finally falls in love with him, assuming he falls in love back, of course. He was wearing a dark grey suit and a silvery tie and a purple shirt that made his eyes look very blue, and his hair, which is sort of darkish brown, was partly sticking up and partly flopping down.

"Do I deprive myself of food?" he asked.

"No," I admitted. "In fact you're constantly bloody hoovering. You're like a one-man plague of locusts."

"Exactly," Ben said, a bit smugly. "That, Ellie, is the magic of exercise. Do enough of it and you can eat absolutely what the hell you like."

This sounded tempting. I'd sort of assumed there was a different rule for boys, and they could eat like Ben does and not get fat, whereas women have to control every calorie, like Rose does.

"Now," he said, "we're going back to yours and stopping at Tesco on the way, and I'm going to cook you a proper meal, and in the morning you're going to get up and go for a run. Deal?"

I thought about it for a bit. I hate getting up in the mornings almost as much as I hate running. I mean, what are buses for? I did the Race for Life a couple of years ago, but it took me nearly an hour and to be honest I walked almost all of it. I was just there for the good cause and the whole sisterhood thing, really. But I was hungry, and it sounded like a run was the price I was going to have to pay for Ben's cooking, which is actually really good.

"Deal," I said, and finished my drink, and we got up and left the pub.

Ten minutes later the kitchen counter was scattered with vegetables, and Ben was continuing his lecture.

"Butternut squash," he said. "Hardly any calories, versatile, filling. Cauliflower, ditto. Low-fat coconut milk. Curry paste. Brown rice. In about twenty minutes we will have a dinner as delicious as it's nutritious."

"Bloody hell," I said. "Want to move in? Or you could be like one of those delivery companies Hollywood stars use that drop off your day's food every morning and I wouldn't have anything else in the fridge except Evian water and nail varnish, and I'd stay so thin I'd have to bath with a coathanger between my teeth in case I slid down the plughole."

Ben laughed. "So anyway, Ellie, what's the aim of this diet mission? I've never known you to bother before and like I said, you certainly don't need to."

I sat down at the kitchen table and poured a glass of wine, and presented Ben with a sort of edited highlights of the Oliver situation.

"I really, really like him," I said. "I know he's going out with Rose at the moment but she'll find someone else, she always does. She has an unfair advantage, being so beautiful.. And that makes her Oliver's type, and I'm not. Not yet. So I'm just making a few changes, to place myself a bit more in his sphere of fanciability, if things go wrong with them. You know what I mean."

Ben went quiet, and the knife he was using to cut up some ginger thumped on the chopping board with a force I thought excessive.

"So you're on a diet because you want to nick your sister's boyfriend?" he said.

"No, no," I protested. "Not nick him. That would be wrong. Just kind of present myself in a light that will make me more attractive to him, so he might realise he's chosen the wrong one of us."

Ben threw all the chopped vegetables into a pan and added stuff from various tins and jars and boiled water to cook the rice. Then he said, "Put some plates on the table, will you? And do you mind if we have the news on while we eat?"

I set the table and we had our dinner, which was delicious, but we didn't talk because Ben was tapping away on his phone, pretending to be Lucille on Twitter again, I suppose. Afterwards I stacked everything in the dishwasher and put the kettle on.

We drank our tea in silence, and after a bit Ben said he'd better head off, because he had to get up at six to cycle a hundred miles before work, or something. Then he said, "You do know, don't you, Ellie, that if Oliver dumps Rose for you, especially if he does it on the basis of you losing a stone and getting some highlights done, that would make him a bit of a cunt?" He picked up his coat and laptop bag and plugged himself into his iPod and gave me a quick kiss on the cheek before striding out of the front door, slamming it thunderously behind him as he always did.

The next morning, as I lay in that pleasant state of semi-consciousness in between pressing the snooze button and actually getting out of bed, I remembered waking up next to Ben after our first night together. I'd swum foggily out of sleep – not that there had been much of it, because whenever I'd felt myself drifting into that borderline reality that precedes a dream, Ben's presence next to me had brought me to nerve-tingling wakefulness, and I'd reach out and touch him. The sheets were damp and twisted and I was feeling hungover and a bit sore from all the sex, and the night of sweat and gasped, surprising words and sudden glimpses of Ben's face – so very, very close – was over. I opened my eyes cautiously to the bright morning. My clothes were scattered on the not-very-clean carpet and the room had that smell single blokes' rooms have, sort of essence of man.

I turned over slowly, not wanting to disturb my companion from the night before, should he prove to be an embarrassingly hideous product of beer goggles. But he wasn't. He was Ben, and he was wide awake, his bright blue eyes watching me quite solemnly, but his white, even teeth showing in a grin. I grinned back and reached across the bed for him.

Later, as we slurped our way through copious amounts of builder's tea and crunched slice after slice of and toast and Marmite, Ben said, "So, what's the plan? The delights of London lie at our feet. We can visit any one of the capital's myriad galleries and museums, admire the glorious autumn foliage in its many parks, take in world-class theatre or opera..." He dropped the travel documentary schtick. "Okay, we can't do that, because I'm skint. But we can do any of the others. Or we can stay here and gaze mindlessly at daytime telly."

"Admiring the ads for loan sharks and ambulance-chasers?" I said.

"Not today," Ben said. "Today will be brought to you by *Saturday Kitchen*, *Come Dine With Me* and the footie."

I remembered it was the weekend. "We can't have that," I said. "No point wasting the day indoors watching daytime telly unless it's properly shit."

"Good point," Ben said. "More toast?"

I looked at his strong forearms and bony, almost elegant hands as he scooped the knife into the Marmite jar, coming out with a proper huge dollop and spreading it thickly on a piece of toast. My throat felt tight with something in between longing and apprehension. "No, thanks," I said.

In the end we just sort of drifted out into the bright October day, and we walked, and we chatted. And in between finding out that we liked the same books, and hated reality TV but loved the shopping channels, and liked Razorlight but thought McFly were over-rated, I felt myself beginning to panic. This wasn't meant to be happening. I was off men, officially. I'd decided. I was going to be single and not get my fingers burned and not get hurt.

So when we stopped on the South Bank, leaning over the parapet and watching the water, shimmering like crumpled blue foil under the clear sky, I blurted out, "You know what would be cool?"

"What?" Ben said.

"If you could have all the good parts of going out with someone, but none of the shit," I said. I'd been reading Jean-Paul Sartre, and I burbled on for a bit about how monogamy was a bourgeois construct, limiting personal freedom and stifling growth. I'm not making this up. I thought how desirable I must sound – how interesting and independent and grown-up. I suppose part of me even believed the twaddle I was spouting.

"To exist is to be free," I said. "Consciousness is what makes us different from cauliflowers."

"Different from cauli… Right," Ben said. "How about a pint?"

I felt smugly confident that my little speech would have the desired effect. Ben would think I was the ultimate cool girl, offering great sex but not asking for commitment or fidelity. I wasn't going to be clingy and demanding, and I wasn't going to fall in love. That way no one would get hurt.

Well, that worked out well for you, didn't it, I said to myself as my alarm jerked me awake for the final time and I reluctantly swung my feet out of bed and into my waiting running shoes.

Chapter Eight

My new regimen might have been austere, but after five days of morning runs, porridge for breakfast and increasingly inventive vegetable-based dinners, I was forced to admit that Ben was on to something. My clothes were feeling looser, my skin had lost that pasty winter pallor and Duncan at work asked me if I was in love.

"Because you're glowing, sweetie," he said. "This is January, it isn't natural."

We were in a meeting to discuss our new outdoor advertising campaign, which wasn't actually outdoors at all. It was a series of digital escalator panels, paid for by a generous donation from a deceased estate and a huge deal for us because we didn't usually have any budget at all for advertising. The meeting got off to a bad start, though, because Ruth was a bit late and by the time she walked in Duncan and I were already deep in discussion about the DEPs, and Ruth misheard and sort of blanched and said, "I know we're all for being up-front about sexual education but surely we shouldn't be running a London-wide campaign about double penetration?" And by the time we'd finished laughing and set her straight and I'd gone across the road to squander some of our funds on takeaway cappuccinos from the Fairtrade coffee place, and we'd had a bit of general chit-chat, it was nearly lunchtime and we had yet to make any decisions.

"Don't you think Ellie looks well, Ruth?" Duncan said.

"Ellie always looks lovely," said Ruth. When I first started working there I wondered if Ruth was hitting on me, but in fact she's just a naturally kind person who makes a point of saying nice things that make other people feel good about themselves.

"I've started getting up early in the mornings and going running," I explained, "and I'm putting on a bit of slap before work too, and ironing my shirts. Just trying to clean up my act, that's all."

"She is in love!" Duncan crowed. "She so is! Tell all, Ellie, who is he?"

I wasn't going to explain the whole Oliver situation to Duncan, who is a terrible gossip, so it was a relief when my phone rang and Ruth said, "Shall we reconvene at the same time tomorrow, and then we really must make some decisions," and they sort of drifted away and I checked my phone and saw Claire's name flashing up on the screen.

"Hey Ellie!" her voice sounded a bit squeaky, the way it does when she's excited about something. Being a drama teacher, Claire knows all about breath control and resonance and all those good things, but she's never seemed to stop this tell-tale change of pitch in her own voice, and I think it's really sweet so I've never mentioned it to her. "I need a huge favour. Are you free this evening?"

"Rose is due back from her holiday," I said, "but we haven't made any plans. Why?"

"Can you possibly look after Pers? Just for three hours?"

I said of course, it would be a pleasure, and we made arrangements for Claire to drop her off at the flat, which she said would be easy for her as she was going into town to meet someone. Of course I was avid to know who he was and whether this meant romance was blooming again for Claire, but before I could ask her I heard a piercing shriek from Pers and Claire said, "Oh for God's sake, not the curtains. No – Persephone!" and then there was a crash and Claire, half-laughing, said, "Shit, my child is set on destroying the flat. Must go – I'll see you at seven."

I was really excited about an evening in with Pers, and stopped on my way home and bought copies of *Owl Babies* and *The Very Hungry Caterpillar* (Pers had chewed her old copy to the point where it was unreadable) and laid in a stash of pita bread, hummus, mango, carrot sticks and cucumber, because Claire's a great believer in what she says is called baby-led weaning, which as far as I can tell means Claire not having to mess about with jars and purées and stuff, and Pers getting to suck and chew on bits of grown-up food and make an incredible mess, which of course she loves.

It was almost quarter past seven when Claire arrived, looking amazing in a long, belted velvet coat and high-heeled brown boots.

"Late!" she said. "Stupid fucking buses. I am late, late, late! Here's some milk for her – if she won't drink it out of the bottle put it in a cup and don't use it in your tea whatever you do, it's expressed breastmilk. And here's wipes and nappies and her Camelduck" – this was a shapeless toy knitted by me, which looked like no creature on earth, of which Pers was inordinately fond – "and I'll see you at ten. Be good for auntie Ellie, sweetheart," and she thrust Pers and all her stuff at me, kissed us both and ran off back down the road, her dark hair flying, before I could interrogate her about her date.

I knew from experience that Pers would only go to sleep when she was ready, so we had a bath with bubbles and watched some telly – Pers was absolutely transfixed by *University Challenge* – and I had a glass of wine and Pers had some of her milk, which she seemed quite happy to drink out of her bottle after all, and I'd just finished changing her nappy and was about to make us some dinner when the doorbell rang.

"Who's that, Pers?" I said, in the daft way you do when you're talking to babies, even though you know it makes you sound like a total loon. "Who's come to visit us? Has Auntie Rose come back from her holiday and forgotten her keys?"

I scooped her up and went and opened the front door, and there stood Oliver.

I couldn't quite believe it at first, because as far as I knew he was on his way back from Switzerland with Rose. "Er... hi," I said. Pers recognised him and gave one of her massive gummy grins and babbled away incomprehensibly, holding out her arms for a cuddle, and Oliver kissed her and then kissed me too.

"I'm awfully sorry to disturb you," Oliver said. "I take it Rose isn't back yet?"

I said she wasn't. "Come in though, and have a drink. You're welcome to have some supper too, if you like carrot sticks and hummus."

He followed me into the flat and I gave him a glass of wine, and then it occurred to me that in all the excitement of having Pers, I hadn't checked my phone since I left the office. There was a missed call and a text message from Rose.

"She says she's stuck at Geneva airport," I said. "Grounded by heavy snow, apparently."

Of course I was dying to ask Oliver why he wasn't with her, also grounded by heavy snow in Geneva, and why Rose had told me but not him. But I couldn't think of any way to do it that was even slightly tactful, so I watched him sip his wine and thought for the millionth time how beautiful he was. I'd never seen him in casual clothes before, and he looked just as desirable in jeans and a shabby cream jumper as he did in a suit.

"I came back a couple of days early," Oliver volunteered after a bit. "There was a crisis at work and I couldn't sort it out over email. I'd arranged with Rose to meet her here tonight and more or less assumed it would still be on, even though when I left..." his voice sort of tailed off, and I guessed that they'd had a row – presumably Rose hadn't been too pleased about her new boyfriend rating a crisis at work as more important than his holiday with her and her friends. Which is not entirely unreasonable – it's the sort of thing that would piss anyone off, but most people would simmer down after a day or two. Not Rose though – she can sustain a sulk like no one else I know.

While I was pondering all this I was arranging salad and bread and cheese and stuff on a platter – a lot more decoratively than I would have done if it had just been me and Pers, I must admit – and Pers was sitting on the floor contentedly chewing her new copy of *The Very Hungry Caterpillar.* "Perhaps she texted you but it didn't get through," I said. "They take ages sometimes. Stay and have some food anyway."

Oliver looked unconvinced, but said he'd love to stay, and I put some plates and the bottle of wine on the table, and put some bits of food on a tray and gave it to Pers on the floor, because obviously we don't have a high chair to sit her in. I asked Oliver how the skiing was and he said various incomprehensible things about what the snow was like. I've only been skiing once, when Rose persuaded me to join a bunch of her mates in St Moritz for a week, and quite honestly I have never hated anything so much in my life. It's a mystery to me how an activity manages to be both boring and terrifying, but skiing, in my opinion, has cracked it. Consequently I spent most of the holiday in the bar getting slowly sozzled on gluhwein, eating cake and reading *A Suitable Boy*. I didn't tell Oliver this, saying instead how gutted I was that I hadn't been able to have joined them this year, but we were terribly busy at work, and I told him about Ruth and Duncan and the DEP campaign, and he laughed.

I was so engrossed in talking to Oliver that I'd almost forgotten Pers was there. He was telling me about some near miss he'd had on a black run when there was a sort of strangled squeak from the floor behind me, and I looked around to see if she was okay. I could tell straight away that she wasn't. Her face was brick red, except around her mouth which was bluey-pale, and her eyes were bulging. I said stupidly, "Shit. I think she's choking and I don't know how to perform the Heimlich manoeuvre." And I froze, and everything started moving in slow motion. I could feel a huge lump in my throat and my hands were shaking so hard I couldn't hold my phone to call 999.

Before I could even start dialling, Oliver had picked Pers up. "You don't perform the Heimlich manoeuvre on babies," he said, completely calmly. Then he sort of laid her along his leg and gave her a series of gentle thumps between her little shoulder blades. I stood watching, numb with panic, and after about the sixth thump a soggy lump of pita bread shot out of Pers's mouth on to the floor, and I heard her take a huge gasping breath and start to wail. I'm afraid to say I wailed too, and Oliver ended up with both of us in his arms, absolutely howling, until his strong, soothing presence and "there, there, it's okay" noises calmed us down.

The way I felt about Oliver changed completely after that night. Of course before that I'd fancied him, I'd been fascinated by the world he represented: the world of money and designer clothes and friends with titles, of which Rose was a part and I categorically was not. I'd been faltering at the entrance to a dangerous arena, playing a game against my sister at which she was far more skilled than I was. I knew it was wrong, and my conscience had held me back. But that night, in spite of myself, I fell in love. My head disengaged and my heart took over – and my body was still very, very much involved.

Oliver was amazing that evening, he really was. He comforted me and Pers, heated up some milk for her, changed her nappy without so much as flinching, and read her a story until she fell asleep, all sort of sprawled out on his lap. He said he'd wait with me until Claire came to pick her up, because I'd had a horrible fright and must be feeling really shaken up – which I was – and we sat together on the sofa and finished the bottle of wine and watched *Masterchef*, except I wasn't watching the telly so much as Oliver, transfixed by the beauty of his profile, the way his long eyelashes swooped down over his cheekbones when he blinked, the soft lick of dark hair that flopped down over his forehead, his perfect skin, tanned golden from skiing. Occasionally he made some innocuous comment about the contestants or the food, and we both laughed, but I didn't really listen to what he was saying just basked in the warmth of his smooth, resonant voice that sounded as if it could turn into a laugh at any moment.

I know I sound like a fifteen-year-old with a crush on the captain of the hockey team, but honestly, that's how I felt. I hadn't had that shy, almost reverent feeling for someone, that sense of desire so strong it hurts to swallow, since I was travelling in Asia on my gap year, and fell headlong for a shaggy-haired, guitar-playing waste of space called Kyle. Of course I hadn't known at the time that Kyle was a loser, and I squandered nine months of my life that I'll never get back finding out: nine months putting up with his infidelities, his unreliability, his pointless and persistent drug use, all because I was in luuurve. I more or less swore off that sort of emotional incontinence post-Kyle. A couple of weeks after he finally dumped me because one of the other girls he was shagging was proving to be even more of an all-forgiving, bankrolling sucker than I was, I met Sean and we went out for almost a year, but I was never particularly serious about him if I'm honest, just swept away by his glorious looks and the fact that he wrote poetry that was actually rather good. Then along came Chris, but he cheated on me and my tolerance for that sort of thing was pretty low after Kyle, so I dumped him as soon as I found out (he literally came home with another girl's knickers in the pocket of his jeans), and swore off emotional involvement forthwith. Then I met Ben, and after a few months of not being each other's boyfriend or girlfriend, he met Nina, so I was properly single again. I stayed that way for ages and was pretty sex-starved to be honest, until I got together with Wallace. That really was his name. And (I am cringing slightly remembering this) he used to like me saying it while we had sex. As in, "Fuck me, Wally! Fuck me harder! Give me your hard cock, Wally!" Call me shallow, but after a month or so of this I realised I simply couldn't live with myself and I certainly couldn't live with Wally, so I told him to sling his hook. That had been a couple of years ago and, barring the occasional drunken post-pub shag, I'd been more or less celibate. I was about due for an emotional shake-up, and it had well and truly come.

At ten o'clock we heard Claire knock at the door, and I let her in and between me and Oliver the whole story came spilling out, and Claire said Pers quite often gagged on her food and generally managed to sort it out herself, but it sounded like Oliver had done exactly the right thing if we were worried. And she gave Pers a massive cuddle and said she'd better get her home to bed, so yet again I failed to glean any meaningful information about where she'd been and who she'd been seeing. A few minutes after Claire and Pers left, Oliver said he'd better be going too.

"Are you okay now, Ellie?" he asked.

"Yes, I'm fine. Sorry I went all wobbly on you, and thanks so much for taking care of Pers."

"No, thank you." He gave a lovely, soppy smile. "She's an absolute sweetheart, I've really enjoyed spending the evening with both of you. I used to... I miss... Anyway, it's been a pleasure."

He reached out and tucked a strand of hair that had escaped from my ponytail away behind my ear, and when his finger brushed my cheek it felt like an electric shock. He pulled me into his arms and gave me what I really, really hoped was a bit more than a brotherly hug, and said he'd see me soon. And I went to bed, cherishing the memory of his lean, strong arms around me and his scratchy jumper against my lips, with the heat of his body beneath it.

I'd arranged to work from home the next day, and normally I get an amazing amount of work done in bed with my laptop, endless cups of tea and Radio 4 in the background, but that day I simply couldn't focus. Every time I tried to think of catchy lines for our ad campaign or draft a lucid and compelling press release, my thoughts scurried off in the direction of Oliver. Every time I heard the sound of a woman's heels on the pavement outside, I worried it would be Rose, and felt a horrible sinking sense of guilt and shame, as if she was going to walk in on me trying to squeeze my lardy thighs into her jeans, or something. After a couple of hours I lost patience with myself and went to have a shower, and the rush of the water must have muffled the sound of the front door because when I came downstairs in search of toast and Marmite, there she was in the kitchen filling the fridge with the various noxious-smelling cheeses she'd brought back with her.

"Hey," I said.

"Hey, Ellie." Like Oliver, Rose had a gorgeous, golden tan, but she looked tired and her hair was all over the place – I suppose she'd spent the night stranded in some airport lounge.

"How was it?"

"Apart from the stupid delay at the end we had an amazing time," she said. "Pip's finally dumped Sebastian, she shamed him by getting off with a ski instructor called Hans in front of everyone, and Sebastian's furious. We spent most of the holiday making jokes about Hans off to wind him up, I wish you'd been there."

"All Hans on dick?" I suggested with a grin, and Rose laughed.

"Exactly. And Vanessa said she'd picked up a stomach bug so she wasn't drinking, or eating much, but actually she was panic-dieting. She told me she put on a stone over Christmas."

"Marriage will do that to you," I said.

"And I brought you chocolate. Loads of chocolate, and a bottle of this lethal aquavit stuff."

I felt another wave of guilt. Great, thanks, Rose, come back from your holiday with presents for me and I'll just try and steal your boyfriend, it's all good.

"Thanks. I'll try and resist it though, I'm sort-of dieting, too."

"Really? You're looking amazing, actually, I noticed as soon as I saw you. Not that you aren't always gorgeous of course. My lucky sister, who was at the front of the queue when the cleavages were handed out." That was Rose's kind way of saying I was fatter than her.

"Oh, and," I tried to make my voice sound casual, "Oliver came round last night. I was babysitting Pers and he stayed for a bit. I think he was expecting you to be here."

Rose's smile disappeared and her face smoothed into a sort of blank mask, the way it does when she's upset. "Did he, now?" she said.

"Yes," I blundered on. "Honestly, Rose, I do think it's a bit unfair of you not to have told him you weren't going to be here. Even if you'd had a row."

"What makes you think we'd had a row?" she snapped. "What did Ollie say?"

I hastily assured her that he hadn't said anything at all, beyond general ski-related chitchat. Then I told her about Pers choking, so she'd understand that Oliver and I had had more important things to talk about than any row they may or may not have had.

"But it was obvious," I said. "You texted me to tell me your plane had been delayed, why didn't you text him? It's not his fault he had to come back early. Especially as you'd made arrangements to meet him."

"Well, Ellie, it's very good of you to be so concerned about Oliver not experiencing any inconvenience," she said, "but frankly if he chooses to treat our relationship like it's some meaningless, casual fling then he should be expected to be treated the same way."

Then of course it all came spilling out. Unlike me, Rose can never resist confiding all the gory details about her boyfriends: what they get up to in bed, what they row about, when they do and don't call. I suppose it's an outlet for the insecurity and turmoil that everyone feels when they're in love, even if they're as poised and beautiful as Rose.

It was on the sixth night of their holiday, she told me, a gorgeous, radiant evening, with the moon and the stars pouring light down on to the glittering expanse of snow and the mountains looming over it all like white ghosts. She and Oliver had gone for a walk, taking a bottle of champagne with them.

"It was like something out of a fairytale," she said. "You know, the little gingerbread-style houses and the narrow, cobbled streets, and Ollie and me walking along hand in hand. It was so romantic, it was just perfect. I know we haven't even been together that long but I was sure he'd brought me out there for a reason."

So Rose, swept away by these surroundings and, if I know her and her mates on holiday, emboldened by copious amounts of wine, had decided to seize the moment. Like a total numpty, instead of shutting up and letting Oliver do the talking, she'd mentioned Commitment.

"And he just went all remote, Ellie," she said, sniffing. "He said I'm a lovely girl – cold fucking comfort – but it was early days and we should get to know each other better and have fun and," her voice wobbled a bit, "maybe see other people. The complete fucking fucker! See other people! Just because some silly cow he lived with upped and left him, he thinks he can play the broken heart card for ever."

"What silly cow?" I said. I knew nothing about Oliver's relationship history and of course I was intrigued, as I was by anything to do with him.

"I don't know," Rose said. "He won't talk about it. Just kind of burbles wistfully about the one that got away. But we've all got one. Look at me. I've got loads and I don't let it stop me. Anyway, then the next day he said he'd had a call from work and had to fly back to London, and there I was left there looking like a total loser."

"I'm sure you didn't look like a loser," I said soothingly.

"Oh, I so did," said Rose. "And I had to play gooseberry to Pip and bloody Hans while they practically shagged each other in the bar every night."

"Ugh, grim," I said.

"Oh, Ellie," Rose said, and there was a wobble in her voice that made me worry she was about to cry. "What am I going to do?"

"You need to think about this rationally," I said. "What's gone wrong with previous boyfriends, where can you spot parallels with the Oliver situation, and how can you prevent yourself falling into the same traps again?" I pulled my shorthand notebook out of my handbag and picked up a pen. "Come on, you were talking about your one that got away – or several that got away – let's do a Venn diagram."

Rose sniffed, blew her nose and managed a watery giggle. "Okay, Venn diagram it is then."

"So, Danny. What happened with him?"

"It was all going really well," Rose said. "We'd got to the stage where we were seeing each other almost every night and I mentioned moving in together – because after all we were practically living together anyway – and after that he just sort of switched off, and then I found out he was seeing someone else, so I finished with him."

"Right," I said. "Infidelity following premature suggestion about commitment." I wrote it down. "Next?"

"Neil," Rose said. "I was, like, so in love with Neil. Even though he was a lot older than me. I thought that was a good thing, I thought it would mean he'd be more mature and stable, more likely to want to settle down."

"But?" I said.

"But he's American, obviously, and he was only out here for six months, buying art. So I thought perhaps I might go back with him. I even looked into getting a Green Card and talked to Quinn's Manhattan office about getting a job there. I was really excited about it, and then when I told Neil my idea he told me not to be ridiculous."

"What was ridiculous about it?"

"I was just a fling, he said. 'A summer full of fun' was his phrase. Dickhead."

"Okay, so dumped by dickhead after taking casual fling too seriously." I wrote. "Aiden was next, right?"

Rose nodded. "We'd been going out for about a year. Then this new woman started working with him and he talked about her, like, a lot. And you know how you sometimes just know something's going on?"

"Mmmm," I said non-committally.

"So I checked the messages on his phone, and I didn't find anything, but he went completely mental at me for snooping, and after that things weren't right any more, and we drifted apart."

"Okay, I'll put 'drifted apart after snooping caused by fear of affair and worry about commitment'," I said. "I don't know about you, but I'm beginning to discern a pattern here. Now, Mark."

"Okay, okay," Rose said. "That only lasted five weeks. He dumped me after I said I thought we were seeing each other exclusively, and he thought we were dating other people too."

"Commitment-phobe frightened off by demands for exclusivity," I said. "I think we have the answer, Rose. You need to forget commitment, and work on being less clingy. Think cool, elusive, remote. Think Scarlett O'Hara meets Buffy."

"Ellie, you're a genius. You and your Venn diagrams! From now on Oliver bloody Farquahar can do the running. I'm not calling him, I'm not texting him, and if he comes round here I shall be out. And we'll see if a couple of weeks of that treatment doesn't change his mind."

And she hefted her bag of skiing stuff on to her shoulder and stalked off upstairs.

My advice had been good, I knew that, but I wondered whether I'd also invoked the law of unintended consequences. After all, if Rose was going to be giving Oliver the cold shoulder, then Oliver might find himself at a loose end, and in need of company occasionally. I logged on to Facebook.

Chapter Nine

Rose was true to her word. A couple of weeks passed and Oliver's number remained untexted, his Facebook wall unwritten on. Every now and then I heard Rose talking to him on the phone, sounding breezy and cheerful, saying things like, "Oh, I'm so sorry, Ollie, but I've got a... something on on Thursday," and, "I'm working late that evening otherwise I'd love to have seen you," and so on. She has nerves of steel, she really does. Unfortunately this meant that I didn't get to see Oliver either, and what with the launch of YEESH's digital poster campaign on the Tube and my continuing regimen of early morning runs, vegetable soup and no booze, I felt that my social life was going from below average to non-existent.

After a week of heinously late nights – I think I'd left work after eleven o'clock on Tuesday, Wednesday and Thursday – the artwork was finally signed off on Friday afternoon. It had really gone to the wire – the boards were due to go up on Monday morning so London commuters would be faced after a weekend of debauchery with hard-hitting messages about STIs that were sure to get their week off to a truly horrible start. The initial creative from the design agency had been all wrong – totally off-brand, Duncan complained – and it had had to go back again and again, while Ruth and I sweated blood over the copy. Eventually we'd settled on two images: one of a girl's face and chest on a pillow, dimly lit but clearly in the throes of sexual ecstasy, and one of a bloke's face, similarly contorted but seen from below. The copy read, "She [or he]'s not the only thing you picked up tonight," and then there were a few scary bullet points about the increasing rates of various infections, and our freephone number and web address. I'd questioned whether showing sex taking place in the missionary position in both images was reinforcing gender stereotypes, but as Duncan pointed out, you can never overestimate the ability of the general public to fail to get the message, so we'd kept it simple.

Anyway, at last Ruth clicked 'send' on the final email to the production guy, and we all sat back in our chairs and looked shell-shocked with relief.

"Drink?" Duncan suggested, but to be honest by this stage we were sick of the sight of one another, and Ruth said she'd arranged to take Diana out for dinner and Duncan said he was desperate to get to the gym and I suggested we have a night out the following week, and we switched everything off and locked the office and drifted away, zombie-like with post-deadline fatigue.

I'd ring Claire, I decided, and see if she could leave Pers with Portia, her neighbour, and pop out for a beer or two, or otherwise I could just go round to hers and we could order a curry and watch a cheesy film, or something.

She took ages to answer her phone but eventually I heard her say, "Hey Ellie, how's it going?" She sounded flustered and out of breath.

I told her about the work stuff, and asked how she and Pers were doing.

"We're fine, just great! Just a bit mad at the moment, I'm getting ready to drop Pers off at Portia's while I'm out."

"Fab!" I said. "Where are you going? Mind if I come along?"

There was a sort of awkward, pregnant pause, then Claire said, "Oh, it's not really that kind of out, Ellie. You see, I'm meeting..." then there was a crash and a wail, and as so often happens during conversations with Claire, she said, "Shit! Got to go. I'll call tomorrow, petal, okay?"

Feeling a bit deflated, I texted Ben to see what he was up to, then got off the train a stop early and walked along the river and through the park. It was a gorgeous, sunny February day – one of those days when you start to feel like you have broken the back of winter and spring genuinely can't be far away. The river sparkled in the setting sun and there were drifts of snowdrops and crocuses scattered through the grass. It all perked me up a great deal, and by the time I got home I was thinking that actually a night out to celebrate was just what I needed, so I got in the shower and shaved my legs and scrubbed my tired, greasy hair and used some of Rose's Dermalogica exfoliating stuff on my face. By the time I'd finished straightening my hair – which was really looking horrible, I noticed, straggly-ended and split to fuck – Ben had replied.

"Sorry, Ellie, busy tonight. Maybe catch up next week? Bx."

Oh, I thought. That was a bit shit.

By this time my feeling of wellbeing had totally evaporated, and when Rose came home she found me sitting at the kitchen table, still in my towelling dressing gown, morosely drinking vodka and slimline tonic.

"Hey, Ellie," she said, sort of skipping into the room and dumping a load of Selfridges and House of Fraser carrier bags on a chair. "What's up? I've barely seen you all week."

I told her we'd cracked the deadline and I'd really been looking forward to a night out to celebrate, but Ben and Claire were both busy.

"But you must come out with us!" Rose said. "Come on! It'll be brilliant."

"Who's 'us'?" I asked suspiciously, imagining myself playing gooseberry to Rose and Oliver.

"Pip, Ness, Chloë, me," she said. "Just a low-key girls' night out, I promise. We're going to a new bar that's opened down the road. It's meant to be really nice."

I hesitated. I knew Rose's idea of a low-key night out – the last one I'd been to had ended after four o'clock in a club in Chelsea, with us having to scrape Chloë off some rugby player she'd picked up. Music too loud to talk over, nowhere to sit, skinny girls shrieking at each other – not my idea of fun. But, I realised, it must be Oliver's, if it were Rose's.

"It won't be like last time, I promise," Rose said, seeming to read my thoughts as she so often does. "This place is really new, no one's discovered it yet, and Pip knows the owner so we'll get a table."

"Okay," I said. "But if it's horrible, I'll..." I cast around for a dire threat, "I'll tell Vanessa about the time you shagged Mick."

"Waaah!" Rose said, "No! Anything but that!"

I hadn't mentioned Mick in a while, but clearly the memory had lost none of its power. Rose had been in sixth form and I was in my first year at uni, and we were both back at Dad's for the summer holidays. We'd been out to the local nightclub – a total dive called Mask-u-raids – with some of my old schoolfriends, and Rose, presumably feeling there was no need to act cool as none of her crowd were there, had really let her hair down and got totally plastered on alcopops.

By around midnight she was superglued to a brawny, tattooed, shaven-headed twenty-something man. I considered trying to break it up, but figured he was probably harmless and Rose was quite capable of looking after herself, and sure enough she staggered home the next day, brutally hungover but in one piece.

"Oooh, my head," she moaned. "And oooh, my knees and elbows. I feel like I did ten rounds with Mike Tyson." I laughed, and Rose went on, "The weird thing is, he looked sort of familiar. Do you think he's on telly or something?" I gazed at her in horror and pissed myself laughing. "You mean you didn't realise?" I said. "That was Mick, who's been our bin-man for, like, eight years." And ever since then, when I've wanted to coerce Rose into loading the dishwasher when it's my turn, or doing the Ocado order or whatever, I've wheeled out the prospect of revealing all to Vanessa, who, being an appalling snob, would mock Rose mercilessly and quite possibly defriend her.

Rose and I had a giggle about Mick the binman, and as usual I realised that she had made me feel much more cheerful, so I headed upstairs to get dressed. Sadly my good mood didn't last long, as I realised that my recent weight loss had left me with absolutely no clothes that fitted – even my bras were too big. I ended up wearing a denim mini skirt that sat so low on my hips that it was barely a mini any more, a slouchy black jumper that wasn't really meant to be slouchy, leopard-print tights and black boots. Rose said I looked amazing and she couldn't believe how thin I'd got, but I suspect she was just being kind – half a stone isn't much really and there was no way I could compete with her in her designer skinny jeans, flat over-the-knee boots and backless gold top.

Her friends were being kind too, though, because when we walked into the bar – it was called Eve's and it was decorated in a style that I suppose was meant to echo the garden of Eden, with loads of lush plants, murals of tropical jungle scenes on the walls, snakeskin print fabric sofas and bowls of fake apples everywhere – they all broke into a chorus of, "Wow, Ellie, you look amazing! How fabulous to see you!" It was quite sweet really.

We sat down at our table and all ordered fancy cocktails and started chatting away. Pip told us about the filthy text messages she'd been getting from Hans the ski instructor, and had us all in stitches with his 'damn you, autocorrect' moments. Apparently the latest message had said he wanted to kick her aunt. Chloë was checking out a group of men in suits at the next-door table, but when they came over and said hello and she found out that they were estate agents, she lost interest. Rose produced some juicy gossip about her friend Gervase, who was apparently having a passionate affair with a married man he'd met at work. After the second round I found myself telling Vanessa all about Ben's running-and-porridge boot camp, and how none of my clothes fitted any more.

"But you must come and see me at work," she said. "I'd love to sort you out with a new wardrobe, I adore doing that sort of thing, and I'll get you a discount too. Go on, you can't deprive me of a chance to play personal shopper," and the next thing she'd whipped out her Blackberry and we were comparing diaries and discovering that we were both free the next afternoon at two (actually I hadn't needed to consult my diary to know that, but it's just as well to play along in these situations).

Vanessa's a fashion buyer for Black & White, the uber-smart department store on Bond Street. I'd only been in there once before, with Rose when she'd been on a desperate quest for a hat to match her taupe shoes, and the place had frankly terrified me with its fragrant, deep-carpeted swankiness, sneery assistants and eye-watering prices. However I was feeling quite flush that month and I hadn't spent any money on clothes for ages, and it felt quite glamorous and exciting to be pushing open the heavy glass doors and heading to the first floor to find the personal shopping department, where I'd arranged to meet Vanessa.

"So, Ellie," she said. "I've picked out a few pieces that I think will work for you." She was all bouncy and excited, and I could tell that, like me, she really loved her job, and I felt myself warming to her quite a bit. "I'm thinking some classic, timeless pieces for work, with some more directional bits and accessories to make them a bit younger and more fun, and then some great casual stuff that will make your weekend-wear look just a bit more pulled together." She smiled a bit pityingly at my black trousers and stripy top. I'd thought I was doing rather well by pinning a corsagey thing to my denim jacket and nicking another of Rose's scarves, but clearly she'd seen through me. "And one or two totally fabulous things for evening. And then when we're done, I'm going to send you downstairs to Martina who will sort you out with some decent bras – trust me, they'll make you look taller, curvier, the works."

I thanked her yet again for giving up her Saturday afternoon and going to such a huge amount of trouble, and said, "Right, let's get on with it then."

Vanessa ushered me through to a sort of super-cubicle – a room almost the size of my bedroom at home, with mirrors all along two walls, a squashy gold-coloured chaise-longue, a little table with a bottle of champagne in an ice bucket and a tray with coffee things and a plate of fancy chocolate biscuits. Knowing Black & White's clientele, I doubt many of those ever got eaten. Along the other wall stood a garment rail absolutely groaning with clothes.

"My god!" I said. "I'll never try all those on, I'll be dead of exhaustion."

"No you won't," Vanessa said in a steely tone that reminded me a bit of Rose. "Besides, once we get an idea of what suits you we'll be able to tell which of the things I've pulled out for you are worth you trying on and which aren't, and we'll discard the ones that aren't and I'll pop out and get some more styles I think will work on you. So – what's first?"

"Casual stuff, I suppose," I said, clinging limpet-like to my comfort zone.

"Casual? No, I don't think so," Vanessa said. "Come on, put this on." And she took a dress off the rail and held it out to me in the manner of a conjuror pulling a rabbit out of a hat.

I flinched away from it. "I can't wear that," I said. "It's pink." And so it was – a deep, almost lilacy pink like a peony. Looking at it, I realised that almost every single garment I own is either black, white, grey, beige or denim. "And what's more it's got a hole in it." It did too – a massive great cut-out bit across the shoulders at the back.

"Nonsense," Vanessa said firmly. "This colour will be amazing on you. And this is a really versatile piece – perfect for going out in the evening in the summer, daytime parties, even for work with a jacket over it. Now try it, please, just for me?" And such was the magnetism of her personality that the next thing I knew I was looking at myself in the mirror, covered from collarbone to knee in pink. I looked amazing. The dress lengthened my legs and made a waist magically appear where no waist had been before. The colour made my eyes look a brighter green and my skin look rose-petal perfect. And when I turned around to look at the back, no trace of bra strap showed in the hole.

"Wow," I said. "You're good." I couldn't stop smiling.

"See?" Vanessa was grinning like a maniac too. "Now we'll put that in the 'probably' pile and move on."

My admiration for Vanessa's skill increased to something approaching reverence as the afternoon wore on and I tried on jeans that made my arse look all pert and tiny; suits that actually fitted rather than bulging out in all the wrong places; tops that had random tucks and frills and drapes that made them flattering and interesting instead of just tops. She'd even brought a few scarves in different sizes, and showed me various clever ways to tie them so they looked... right, somehow, not like I'd just wound them round my neck because there was a bit of a nip in the air. "But you're not buying these here," she said, "You'll go to the high street, where scarves are three quid, not fifty like this one. They're fashion pieces, you change them every season to update your look."

I nodded obediently. By this stage we'd finished the champagne and we'd both flopped down on the chaise longue, exhausted, and started on the biscuits, and the rail full of clothes had been sorted into a big pile 'yes' section, a smaller 'maybe' section and a very small pile of 'no's, most of which I'd rejected because my conscience simply wouldn't allow me to spend more than fifty quid on a top.

"Well," Vanessa said, "that's what I call a good afternoon's work. I've missed doing this so much, although the buying side is great fun too."

So I asked her about her career and she told me how when she stopped modelling at twenty (she'd got too big, she said, and looking at her I realised that although she's tall, athletic and far from fat, Vanessa's actually not skinny: she just wears clothes that fit her and really, really suit her figure), she'd worked her way up from folding garments on the shop floor (another surprise), and eventually done a couple of years' stint in the personal shopping department before training as a buyer. And she said that far from going off to be a Lady Who Lunches if she and Tom had children, she was planning to cut short her maternity leave and hire a nanny and go back to work as soon as she could, because she felt her brain would atrophy otherwise. She told me a bit about the shop's background – how it was formed when an old-fashioned draper's shop called White's had merged with an old-fashioned corsetry shop called Black's, and for ages it had sold gloves and parlourmaids' uniforms and bloomers and suchlike to well-to-do Mayfair ladies, and then in the 1950s it had started to import ready-to-wear fashion from Paris, and the rest was history. Well, it was all history, of course, but you know what I mean.

Then she said, "Actually, I was chatting the other day to one of my colleagues, Barri, who's head of marketing, and he mentioned that he's looking for a press and communications person. You wouldn't be interested, would you?"

I said it depended on various things, and although I was very happy where I was one keeps one's eyes open for opportunities, and then she told me the salary and I gulped and said I'd think about it and maybe send a CV, and took this Barri guy's email address. Then we went and paid for everything and even with Vanessa's discount it was eyewateringly expensive, and there were so many bags – how is it that clothes can be so heavy? They don't feel heavy when you're wearing them – I decided to take a taxi home, which made me feel like the indulged daughter of some Middle Eastern potentate. But of course, as is always the way, there were no taxis to be had, and it began to rain – a thin drizzle that had everyone putting up their umbrellas and trying to shelter under awnings and generally making the crowded streets even more rammed than they'd been before. I pushed my way on to a side street and headed south, hoping my luck would improve. But the drizzle intensified, and soon it was proper, full-on rain, and the only taxis I could see had their lights stubbornly off, and one of them drove too fast through a puddle and sent a sort of junior tsunami over the pavement, soaking my trousers so they stuck damply to my calves with every step.

"Fuck," I muttered. One of my carrier bags was soaked too, and the thick, expensive paper was disintegrating into mush. I didn't feel glamorous at all any more; I just felt like me, caught in the rain on my way home to spend a Saturday night on my own. I ducked into a doorway to squash the clothes from the bag that had got soaked into one of the intact ones, and realised I was right outside Gilbert's, a wine bar where Claire and I had been a few times before she had Pers. I'd go in, I decided, and dry my hair under the hand dryer and have a glass of wine while I waited for the rain to stop.

A few minutes later I was ensconced at a table in the corner, sipping Sancerre and trying to look aloof and mysterious, not like the kind of tragic loser who drinks alone on a Saturday night, or, worse still, like I'd been stood up. I wished I had a book with me, but instead I used the Black & White Spring/Summer catalogue to hide behind while I checked out the other people in the bar. There were the usual crowds of tourists, wearing those see-through rain cape things that no Londoner would be seen dead in, and poring over huge maps, soggy from the rain. There was a table of girls who looked like they were on a hen night, although it was hard to tell because, this being Mayfair, they were all terribly well dressed and glamorous and there wasn't an L-plate or cock-shaped deely-bopper in sight. And there were loads of couples on dates: a silver-haired man with a much younger blonde woman who certainly wasn't his daughter, judging by the way he was pawing her thighs; two teenagers who looked barely old enough to have been allowed in, staring at each other in shy, tortured silence; a couple sitting next to each other at a banquette with their backs to me, her dark head and his lighter one almost touching at they talked intently. Then the girl stood up and slid out of the booth and the man followed and held her coat for her while she slipped it on, and she lifted her sheet of silky hair out of the collar and it swished down her back, and before she'd even turned round I'd recognised her, and him. Claire and Ben.

I felt a flood of heat rush over my face, and held the Black & White catalogue higher, praying that its oversize format would obscure my face. But they wouldn't have noticed me; they wouldn't have noticed anyone. It was like they were surrounded by an invisible bubble of intimacy made for two as they moved easily through the crowd towards the door, Ben's hand sort of hovering over Claire's back, so her hair occasionally brushed against it. He held the door open for her and the wind whipped her hair over her face, and I imagined I could hear her laughter, and then Ben put up a big black umbrella over them, and they walked off together, their shoulders touching.

Chapter Ten

Every day the next week when I walked into the office, Duncan and Ruth and whichever of the volunteers were around looked at me and went, “Swit swoo!” and made me give them a twirl and tell them what I was wearing and what label it was, and although by Friday I’ll admit it was starting to get a bit old, I was actually really pleased. Of course, their being so lovely made me feel even guiltier about the fact that I was spending my lunch breaks polishing my CV, and that by Thursday it was winging its way to barri.doherty@blackwhite.co.uk, the email address of Vanessa’s head of marketing. I’d been working with Ruth and Duncan for four years by that stage, after leaving my previous job as a lowly press officer at Amnesty International, and I’d grown really fond of them, and of course I loved YEESH and everything it stood for. However much I told myself that everyone had to advance their career somehow, they’d find someone to replace me really easily, and that a stint in the private sector would do my CV no harm, I still couldn’t stifle the sense that I was betraying them, but I consoled myself with the thought that I was a dead cert not to get the job, given that I was neither an ex-model nor dating anyone whose name Barri would recognise.

So it was quite a relief when the week was over. Rose and I were both home that Friday night – she was still giving

Oliver the silent treatment, as far as I could make out, which seemed a bit harsh since several weeks had passed since his Commitment-related transgression, but that's Rose for you. We were sitting in the living room, me watching telly and picking at a jacket potato in a desultory sort of way; Rose painting her toenails. I've always wondered, when the women's magazines go on about 'pampering yourself', exactly who they think they're fooling. As far as I can tell, nothing could be further from pampering than the stuff like manicures and pedicures and eyebrow shaping and face masks that Rose spends so much time on. It's boring repair and maintenance, necessary if you're not going to let yourself go altogether, but it's about as close to pampering as cleaning the kitchen floor – a task Rose approaches with as much enthusiasm as I do manicures.

"Rose?" I said.

"Mmmm?"

"You know Ben and Claire?"

"Like, durrr, obviously. Why? What's up?"

I paused. I was torn between wanting to tell my sister, and knowing that as soon as I did, I'd have to stop pretending that what I'd seen in the bar last Saturday hadn't happened. All week I'd been trying to stop my thoughts lingering on them, how they'd looked together, Claire happy and laughing, Ben solicitous, almost tender as he held Claire's coat for her, opened the door, covered her with his umbrella. How had they got together, I wondered? I'd imagined a moment of revelation in which Ben removed Claire's glasses and said, "Why, Miss Jones, you're beautiful!" (except Claire doesn't wear glasses, and she always looks beautiful). In my head, imaginary conversations between the two of them played on an endless loop. They went pretty much like this.

Ben: Darling!

Claire: My darling!

Ben: There is only one thing standing between us and perfect happiness.

Claire: Yes. Ellie.

Ben: We will have to tell her eventually, darling.

Claire: Yes, darling. But not just yet. She'll be so hurt.

Ben: Poor Ellie. It's hard for her, being overshadowed all the time by Rose. And of course by you, my darling.

Claire: Poor Ellie. It's not her fault she's plain and awkward and, well, a bit dull really.

Ben: Let's not talk about her, darling. Our time together is too precious.

Claire: My darling!

And so on.

"They're going out," I said to Rose.

"Ben and Claire? No way! When did they tell you?"

"I saw them together," I said. "I haven't talked to either of them for ages. They've shut me out. It's not like when Ben got together with Nina, and he couldn't stop gushing about it."

Although, I realised, I felt a bit the same as I'd felt when Ben got together with Nina. Quite a lot the same.

Ben first told me about Nina on what looked like being a perfectly ordinary Tuesday night down the Latchmere. We used to do the pub quiz there, before the Duchess cleaned up its act and started having one too, with a slightly lower standard and more generous prizes (a less vinegary bottle of Pinot Grigio for second place, which was usually the height of our attainment). I'd got there at seven as usual in order to bags us a table, get a drinks order in, peruse the menu and make the tough decision between the vegetarian platter and the mushroom burger and chips. I'd polished off a pint of Stella and was sending 'don't even think about it' looks at other quiz-goers who had designs on the six chairs I'd appropriated, wondering whether Alex or Tim would be first to show up, when Ben sort of floated into the room on a cloud of happiness, with a gormless beatific grin on his face. Of course I knew straight away that something was up.

"Pint," I said, shoving his glass across the table. "Now tell me why you're looking like a spaniel puppy that's just won Best in Show. Lotto jackpot? Surprise nomination to a safe seat in Islington? Collision en route here with a van carrying Krispy Kreme doughnuts?"

"Oh my God, Ellie," Ben said, "Do you believe in love at first sight?" No word of a lie, he did.

I sparked up a fag – you were still allowed to smoke then – and in between puffs I told Ben in no uncertain terms that love at first sight was a load of delusional bollocks, in common with love of any other kind, but that it was better out than in, and the sooner he told me what the fuck was going on, the sooner I could cure him of this madness. And quite uncharacteristically Ben, who's normally restrained to the point of constipation about his feelings, spilled the beans.

"I've met a Pre-Raphaelite angel, Ellie," he gushed. "My dream woman. Beautiful, original, ethereal. And I have her mobile number!"

I told him to get a grip and start from the beginning, and he duly did, after a few more asinine burblings about her remarkable beauty and charm, which made me lose all enthusiasm for my coleslaw.

He'd been on the Victoria line, it turned out, on his way from Highbury and Islington station to Green Park, where he would change on to the Jubilee line to go one stop to Westminster and work. At King's Cross the goddess had fought her way on to the rammed train, along with the hordes of tourists that blight the lives of Londoners using the station. He'd been impressed by the naked aggression with which she'd elbowed aside a group of German students, Ben said, nabbing the only seat in the carriage and flopping gleefully into it with – and here he went all misty-eyed again – her violin case nestled in her lap.

"It's a Strad, Ellie," he said, "Although I didn't know that then, I only found out later."

"From the top, I said, Benedict," I told him sternly, and he apologised and returned to the back story.

So this girl – he didn't know at the time that she was called Nina – had sat down opposite Ben, and he'd immediately noticed her not only because of her seat-obtaining skills and her violin case, but because she was wearing a black evening dress at nine in the morning, and because she had waist-length rippling hair the colour of autumn leaves, according to Ben, and skin like a pearl, and the body of a gnome. Or he may have said a fairy, I'm not sure – anyway, she was evidently small but perfectly formed. So Ben did what all men do when a girl they fancy gets on the Tube and sits opposite them: tried to check her out whilst appearing indifferent. As luck would have it, the bloke sitting next to Ben had a copy of that day's Independent that Ben ought to have read himself before work, so he sort of craned his neck and scanned the leader column over this man's shoulder, whilst surreptitiously checking out the red-haired girl across the aisle.

Before long, he realised that he wasn't nearly as subtle as he'd thought, and that the ginger goddess had realised she was being checked out and was pissing herself laughing at him.

"She just radiated joy, Ellie," said Ben. "Do you know how unusual it is to see a person smile on the Tube at nine in the morning? She wasn't just smiling, she was properly corpsing, leant over her violin case with her hair cascading down on to the floor like she didn't even care if someone's old chewing gum got caught up in it." And he looked momentarily distressed at the idea of such desecration befalling the copper locks of wonder.

"Oh, for God's sake," I said, "Less of the mooning, more of the story. What did you do?" I needed him to hurry up, because the quiz was due to start in fifteen minutes and soon our other friends would turn up and then Ben would be sure to lose the narrative thread.

"I froze," he said. "I met her eyes and froze like Odysseus tied to the mast when he heard the Sirens sing." And he sighed a ridiculous, wafty sigh. "But then the train pulled in at Green Park and I saw that she was getting off at the same stop I was and I knew that this was my chance. So I spoke to her."

"Great!" I said. "And you got her number?"

"I did," Ben said proudly, "and it only cost me twenty quid."

"What?" I squeaked. "There's a name for people who do that, you know, and it's..."

"Busker," said Ben. "She's studying at the Guildhall and plays her violin in Tube stations sometimes to make extra cash. I listened for about half an hour, I was late for the morning briefing because of it but I just couldn't leave. I gave her a fiver and then another, and then she told me her name – Nina," his voice fell to a reverential hush, "and then her number. 074..."

"Stop!" I said. "Stop right now! You might be stalking her but I'm not ready to add her to my address book just yet."

"But you will, Ellie," Ben said, "because she's coming here tonight. Here! Tonight!"

By this point my veggie platter had lost all its appeal, and I muttered something along the lines of, "Oh, wow, great," and then Erin turned up and Alex and the rest of our mates followed shortly afterwards, and we got another round in before the quiz kicked off. Then, right in the middle of a critical question about Middlesbrough's FA Cup record, which we'd normally have relied on Ben to crack, he totally zoned out and gazed, mesmerised, at the door.

"Nina is here," he declared, and stood up so quickly he almost sent twenty quid's worth of perfectly good lager crashing to the floor.

At first I couldn't see Nina as she walked into the pub, but that was because she was so tiny – even in her retro cork-soled clogs, the rest of the Latchmere's clientele towered over her dainty five foot nothing frame. But Ben had clocked her straight away, by some sort of radar, and he fought his way through the milling crowds and ferried her back to our table with the same gloating pride I've since observed when Winston brings a limp, half-chewed squirrel in though the cat flap.

"This," he said, "is Nina."

There's no pretty way to say it, she reminded me of an insect. An exotic, highly coloured wasp, perhaps, with her fragile limbs and filmy, fluttery clothes, but an insect none-theless. And there was something faintly repulsive about the way she alighted on each of us in the group – Alex, then Erin, then Tim, then me, bestowing little kisses on us with her crimson proboscis – and saying how lovely it was to meet us and how much Ben had told her about us. I told myself that Ben and I were just friends, just fuck-buddies, that I had no right to be jealous. But still, I loathed Nina on sight.

"But you must have known he'd get together with someone else sooner or later," Rose said, snapping me back to the present. "Or did you think maybe you and he…?"

"Not after Nina," I said.

"I've often wondered about that," Rose said. "I mean, it was ages ago, and he's been single ever since. It's weird."

"He doesn't talk about it," I said. And I realised that, in spite of our closeness, there was a side of Ben that I never saw any more: the side that waxed all poetic over Nina's hair, the side that brought me tea and toast in bed, the side that was a great shag. I'd congratulated myself on our unique friendship, but really Ben had only let me know a fraction of himself. And now he was sharing the rest with Claire.

"Perhaps it won't last," Rose said, "and you'll get another chance."

"It's not that," I said vehemently. "It's not. It's… well, I was there first. They're my friends, not each other's."

Even as I was speaking, I could hear how bratty and petulant I sounded. But Rose didn't say anything about that. She reached over and gave my hand a squeeze, and said, "You know, Ellie, you're looking so stunning at the moment."

I said thanks, but a bit warily, because I knew she was trying to steer the conversation around to something else, in the subtle way she has that's actually totally unsubtle. Sure enough, she said, "You should go and see Gervase."

Rose's mate Gervase – he of the spectacular handlebar tache and affair with the married man – is also her hairdresser. Rose has been following him around from salon to salon for about eight years – he started doing her hair when she was at university in Edinburgh, and I suspect Rose may have been partly responsible for persuading him to up sticks and import his talents to London. Anyway, after all this time they've become friends as well as stylist and client, and I dread to think what will happen if one day Gervase fucks up Rose's foils or cuts an inch too much off her ends or something – World War Three I expect. But so far he has kept a clean sheet and every time Rose comes back from seeing him she looks swishy-haired and happy.

"Just a few highlights," she said, "And maybe some layers through the front. My treat. You'll look amazing, you'll see. When I'm down about something, Gervase always makes me feel better, every time." And before I could frame an objection, she'd whipped out her phone and texted Gervase, and informed me that he'd had a cancellation and could fit me in the next morning at ten.

Chapter Eleven

As I stood in the salon the next day, being swathed in a kind of nylon raincoat affair by one of Gervase's much-pierced minions, I started to feel sick with nerves, and remembered why it had been so long since I'd darkened the doors of a hair salon. I'm sure it's not only me who feels this way. Every time – every single time – you say you want just a couple of centimetres off, or a subtle colour to give it a bit of gloss, you get a pitying look, and end up leaving with hardly any hair, or bright ginger streaks, or a mullet. If the worst that happens to you is a bouffy blow-dry that makes you look like Kim Kardashian, you've got off lightly. My hair's nothing to write home about – in fact its natural state is limp, mousy and either crackling with static or flat with grease – but at least I know where I am with it.

"Now," said Gervase, once he'd given me a kiss on both cheeks, which felt a bit like being snogged by a fur coat, and sat me down in a chair and ordered another minion to bring me a cappuccino, "just look at yourself, Ellie. Look!" And he grabbed my jaw and angled my head towards the mirror. I was reminded of yet another reason why I hate hair salons – surely the only people who can bear to spend an entire morning gazing at themselves in a mirror are the deeply self-obsessed and the extremely short-sighted?

"The first time I met you," Gervase went on, "I thought, my god! Those eyes! Those cheekbones! This girl has something special! I've been waiting years to get my hands on your hair, Ellie. Let's find your inner goddess!"

I muttered something about taking just a few centimetres off the ends, but Gervase was having none of it, and because he's Rose's friend and such a sweetheart, I found myself meekly agreeing to highlights, layers, a conditioning treatment, a blow-dry and all the rest. Then I took a deep breath and immersed myself in *Vanity Fair*, forcing myself to read all the features, even a pretentious over-long one about Hilary Clinton that did that ridiculous and annoying 'continued on page 148' thing. It took three hours, but finally Gervase finished whisking around me with canisters of spray and dragging huge round brushes through my hair, and said, "There!"

I looked at myself in the mirror and gave my hair an experimental swish. Instead of flopping around my face like a spaniel's ears, my hair framed it, making my eyes look bigger and my jawline cleaner. It had gone from a dull lightish brown to a lovely honey gold, and it was straight and shiny but somehow springy at the same time. I looked like me, only fabulous, and I happily paid the extortionate price and gave Gervase a twenty quid tip, trusting that he'd pass it on to the minions, because he probably earns more than I do.

I walked out into the street and stood there for a while, wondering what to do. It seemed a shame to take my lovely hair home and waste it on the flat, so I decided – just on a whim – to get on the Circle line and go all the way around to Moorgate and see what was on at the Barbican and perhaps have coffee there. It was an awfully long way to go just for a coffee but, to be perfectly honest, I wanted to put myself into Oliver's orbit, just for a moment. Since the last time I'd seen him, when he'd been so wonderful to Pers and me, I'd been... I won't say stalking him, but sort of keeping myself aware of him, reading his posts on Facebook and on Twitter – although they were still mostly incomprehensible to me, concerning the Markets and the cricket – and thinking and thinking about him: his face, his voice, the way his arms had felt around me, the smell of his skin. I haven't had much experience of unrequited desire, but I suspect that it's hard to keep it alive without encouragement – it would probably wither and die, like a bunch of roses left in a vase without water or that weird blue gel stuff florists use. Thankfully, in these enlightened times, people in my position are able to follow – okay then, stalk – the object of their desire via social media, thus keeping the flame of passion burning as strongly as when it was first kindled.

I was thinking all this as I trundled around the outskirts of zone one on the Tube, marvelling at my ability to channel the love-struck heroine of some bodice-ripper romance and occasionally giving my hair a swish to see if it still felt lovely, which it did. Pathetic though my sentimental ramblings were, they made the journey to Moorgate pass incredibly quickly. But by the time I got there, my idea of doing an Oliver-themed tour of London – an 'in the footsteps of', as if he were Samuel Pepys or someone – no longer seemed so clever, just childish and pathetic and even a bit psychotic. I was on the point of turning around and ducking back into the carriage and letting the train take me all the way on round to Victoria, but the doors made their insistent beeping noise and slammed shut behind me, so I let myself be swept along by the crowd to the stairs, and as I emerged into the relative brightness of the cloudy day, I heard running feet behind me and a familiar voice saying, "Hey! Rose!"

I stopped and turned around and there was Oliver, jogging towards me on the grey City street, and the tourists who'd got off the Tube with me had all scattered away and it felt like he and I were the only two people in the world. Except of course it wasn't me he expected to see, it was Rose, and when he realised he had the wrong sister he skidded to a halt and said, "Ellie. My god, I'm so sorry. I thought you were..."

I said, "You thought I was someone else. Sorry I'm not."

He just stood there, looking at me in a rather puzzled way, like Serena told me Dad did for about five days after she stopped wearing contact lenses and got her glasses – something about her was different, but he couldn't quite figure out what it was. Serena and I laughed about it for ages when she told me the story – she told me it proved something about how men see the world as opposed to how women do, which I have of course forgotten and now wasn't interested in because Oliver was staring at me quite intently, and he said, "Actually, I'm not sorry at all."

We stood there for a bit, looking at each other. It was one of those blustery days you get towards the end of winter, and gusts of cold air were eddying around us, sending empty crisp packets and discarded travelcards skittering along the pavement and making my hair whip around my face and stick to my lip-gloss.

Then Oliver said, "Were you on your way anywhere?"

I said, "I've just been having my hair done. I thought I'd wander along to the Barbican and see if there was anything good on – I've been so busy at work I've been neglecting my cultural enrichment programme." And I gave a little smile so he'd know I wasn't as up myself as that.

"We certainly can't have that," Oliver said. "But there's not much on at the moment – just some weird experimental jazz thing and an exhibition about James Bond, but I've seen that so you'll have to wait for another day – you may live twice but I only visit exhibitions once."

I laughed and rolled my eyes at his cheesy joke, but felt a little flutter of joy inside, because whatever we were going to do, we were going to do it together.

Then he said, "Is feeding ducks cultural enough for you?"

"Ducks?" I said.

"Amphibious birds that quack," said Oliver. "You'll like them."

I laughed. "All right then, lead me to your ducks."

We walked in the direction of the Barbican and Oliver started talking about how one of his favourite things to do on weekends was to sit by the pond in the central square and throw bits of bread for the ducks. He'd just been to the organic shop on Moorgate to buy the special seedy rolls that were their favourite, he said. He explained that it was almost like a meditation, and that however crap a week he'd had at work, after sitting and watching the birds get all enthusiastic and eat his seedy bread, he felt better, soothed and sort of healed inside. Frankly it was the most bonkers thing I'd ever heard in my life, but it was also quite sweet, and of course I was so smitten by Oliver he could have said his favourite way to relax was train-spotting or potato-printing or something, and I would have gone 'awww' and thought it was wonderful.

After fifteen minutes or so I realised he had a point. There was something terribly cute and calming about how the ducks started this almost murmury quacking when they saw us, and came swimming over and started fishing the crumbs of bread out of the water with their beaks, and a couple of the braver ones even got out of the pond and came and milled around our feet. Oliver and I didn't talk much, we just said asinine things like, "Look at that one with the blue feathers," and "What are those black and white things then?" (They were coots. So shoot me – I read English, not zoology.)

But by the time the bread was finished and the birds had swum away – a little lower in the water than when they'd started; the cavalier way in which they'd stuffed themselves made me understand how foie gras happens – I realised my jaw was slightly sore from smiling so much, and I felt relaxed and lighthearted, but very cold.

"Okay," I said, "you're right. I now see the appeal of ducks. How did you discover this form of therapy? GP referral? I haven't done it since I was a kid."

"I used to bring a kid here," Oliver said. He suddenly looked stricken with sadness, and I remembered Rose mentioning his ex-girlfriend, the one that got away. I longed to ask him more about it, but something about his frozen face made me decide not to.

Then he said, "Fancy some lunch? Or tea and cake? It's almost three."

I realised I hadn't eaten all day and I was properly starving.

We wandered through the deserted streets, and as we walked Oliver chatted about the City, the Wren and Hawksmoor churches and how you could tell the difference between them, the old layout of the streets and how the basic structure had changed over the years. It made me realise that although I'd lived in London for ten years, I'd more or less confined myself to the bits along the river, and that there were great swathes of the place about which I knew nothing. But mostly I was just enjoying listening to him talk, the lovely resonant quality of his voice, the way every now and then he looked at me and smiled, and I smiled back.

After a bit he stopped outside a little restaurant with white walls, and tables and chairs of various shapes and sizes crammed anyhow into the room.

"This do?" he said. "Not much is open around here on weekends, I'm afraid I normally survive on microwaved stuff from Waitrose."

I said it looked fine to me, and it was true – I'd have been happy to go just about anywhere at that point, I was so elated to be with Oliver.

We sat down and both ordered coffee. I could feel that my stomach was about to make a loud and embarrassing rumbling sound, but I also felt stupidly shy and awkward, and looked at the menu and felt as if there was nothing on it I could order without looking greedy or gauche. But Oliver said to the waiter, "We'll have a triple chocolate brownie, a piece of lemon cheesecake and a piece of carrot cake, please." He grinned at me. "The carrot cake's so we get one of our five a day."

I laughed. "And the lemon's so we don't get scurvy?"

"Correct."

The waiter brought three plates absolutely heaving with cake and we picked up our forks, and Oliver said, "After you?"

I said, "No, after... damn, this looks too good to be polite about it." And I dug in.

The cake was gorgeous and we finished it in record time, and then Oliver said, "I know it isn't considered the done thing in the middle of the afternoon, but I think a bottle of champagne would go down rather well, don't you?"

I said that now he mentioned it, it did seem like the sensible way to proceed, and he caught the waiter's eye and ordered one, and soon we were sipping away, and it felt so deliciously decadent I wondered why I didn't drink at teatime every day of my life. Well, I never would of course, because that's the start of a slippery slope that ends with cans of Special Brew wrapped in blue plastic bags on the bus on the way to work in the morning, but you know what I mean – it was rather fabulous.

Oliver asked after Pers and Claire, and I said that they were both well, because I didn't want to mention Ben, so I steered the conversation on to more neutral topics and we chatted about books we'd read and films we'd seen, and who was going to win *Masterchef*, and to be honest it felt just like a first date – one that was going a lot better than my first dates usually do. I kept catching myself gazing at him, trying to commit to memory the way his long, smooth hands looked as he lifted his glass, the way his lips had a sort of half-smile even in repose, the way he lifted one eyebrow when he was being ironic. I tried to do that once, practising in front of my bedroom mirror for about half an hour before I gave up because it was too difficult and made me look ridiculous. I suppose it's one of those things like wiggling your ears, which you either can do or you can't.

I asked him about living in the Barbican, and he said that obviously it was convenient for his office in the City, where he often worked insanely late hours, but that he loved the architecture, the slightly alien feel of the place, and the fact that he was living in what had started out as a bit of a social experiment.

Then he said, "I love music, too, that's another thing. When I first moved here I used to go to concerts and recitals a lot, but I've more or less stopped now."

That pained, shadowed look had crossed Oliver's face again, so I muttered something anodyne about pressure of work, and how hard it is for anyone to get time to themselves.

"I do miss green spaces, though," he went on. "Hence the ducks, I suppose. I have a place in the country, which I suppose makes me one of those evil second-home owners proper country people complain about, but it was my grandmother's and I can't bear to sell it. I don't get out there as often as I'd like to."

I realised that must have been where he was at Christmas, when he came to pick Rose up after her horrible outburst over lunch, and I was abruptly reminded that this was Rose's boyfriend I was sitting with, drinking champagne with and gazing at. Rose's boyfriend whose ankle was pressing against mine under the table. I hastily moved my leg away.

By this stage it was dark outside and the waiters were moving around the room putting extra knives and forks and glasses on the tables and lighting candles. Oliver looked at his watch, and poured the last of the champagne into our glasses, and I felt my heart sink, knowing that he was about to ask for the bill and our afternoon together would be over. But he didn't.

"I know it's a Saturday night and extremely short notice," he said, "but if you don't have any other plans, would you like to have dinner with me?"

I wanted to say yes. I wanted to drink more wine with him and pick at my food and flirt and meet his eyes in the candlelight across the white paper tablecloth. I wanted the spell of intimacy that seemed to have been cast around us to remain unbroken, and eventually to hear him ask me softly if I'd go home with him, and to walk back through the silent streets and past the pond where the ducks would wake up and quack drowsily at us, and up to the dizzy heights of the thirty-fourth floor, where he'd said his flat was, and make love to him with the lights of London spread out below us the way he'd described them. More than anything, I wanted to say yes. I remembered Rose's stupid, bratty outburst to Dad and Serena, and how she'd been deliberately ignoring Oliver – almost as if she didn't really want him. But then I thought about her careful control since their row, or whatever it had been, and how much effort she'd been putting into staying bright and cheerful, and how she shared everything with me: her thoughts, her clothes – but surely not her boyfriend. I looked down at my hands, clumsily pleating the tablecloth, and my voice sounded all croaky when I said, "Oliver?"

"Mmmm?" he went.

"What's going on with you and Rose?" I asked.

His face sort of closed up, and he said, "You need to ask Rose that."

I shook my head, and stood up and said, "I'm sorry, I think I'd better go. Thank you, it was a lovely afternoon." I put thirty quid on the table and ignored Oliver trying to make me take it back, and ignored him asking me to wait, and I walked out into the street feeling tears stinging my eyes. I hadn't been concentrating when we'd walked to the restaurant and the area was unfamiliar, so I shambled around for ages stopping to check the maps on bus stops, but eventually I found a bus going towards Waterloo and got on it, and then I got the train home. By the time I reached the flat I was feeling dry-mouthed and headachey – maybe afternoon drinking isn't such a great idea after all – and I had a tight, sore feeling in my throat from not crying. It was after eight and I thought the chances of Rose not being home were pretty good, but she was.

She was all dressed up to go out, in a cream-coloured cashmere dress and slouchy boots with high, high heels, and waves of scent and happiness were radiating from her as she put on her coat and tucked her keys and her mobile into her squashy gold bag.

"Ellie!" she said. "My god, your hair is stunning! You look great! I didn't realise you were coming home, otherwise we could've gone out to celebrate."

I muttered something about being quite tired anyway, and Rose said, "Guess what? I decided to forgive Ollie. I've just spoken to him and I'm off to meet him now. Aren't you pleased?"

Chapter Twelve

"No," said Ruth. "No, he's away on holiday in Sardinia. He might be able to do it via his mobile. No good? Let me see if I can arrange something else. Yes. Yes, I'll ring you back. Twenty minutes. Okay. Bye." She crashed her phone down on to its cradle. "Shit," she said. "Shitshitshitshitshit."

"What's up?" I asked.

"BBC News is up," Ruth said. "They want to do a segment on our new ad campaign – apparently it's caused some controversy in the right wing press, and bloody Duncan's on bloody holiday and they want to record an interview with someone this afternoon, and I said I'd take Chessie to ballet because Diana's got her AGM."

"Can't Leda do it?" I asked. Leda's one of the medics who man the minge bus – she's super-glamorous and photogenic and does quite a bit of our media stuff when Ruth and Duncan aren't available.

"She's up in Aberdeen." Ruth started frantically scrolling through the numbers on her phone.

"Can't Ellie do it?" piped up Russell, our newest and most hapless volunteer.

"Yes!" said Ruth, at exactly the same moment as I said, "No!"

"Now, Ellie," Ruth began. Back in the day, she used to be a primary school teacher, and every now and then you can hear that 'quieten down, children' note in her voice. Clearly there is a large part of me that is still six years old, because it has an almost mesmeric effect on me. "Please give this some thought. It's only a ten-minute piece, they say. You've done radio for us before and you come across ever so well, and you've just had your hair done."

"Go on, Ellie, you'll be brilliant," Russell said, clearly loving the drama. It must've made a nice change from updating our press contacts spreadsheet.

"Ruth, I..." I started to object, but then realised I didn't really have any choice in the matter. With Duncan away and Ruth committed to taking a rare afternoon off to ferry Diana's daughter around, and Leda up in Scotland going round to schools talking about the HPV vaccine, there really was nobody but me who was available to go on telly and talk about the 'What have you picked up' campaign. I was going to have to man up, stop acting like a wibbling baby, and do it. The alternative was YEESH missing out on precious free publicity.

I've done a few radio interviews for YEESH, as Ruth pointed out, and that's been fine. But I have an absolute horror of lots of people looking at me. I first realised it at school, when I'd beaten all other comers to get the coveted role of Juliet in the annual Shakespeare production. The real prize was not so much the part as the opportunity for endless on-stage snogs with Peter Barclay, the fittest boy in the sixth form, who'd inevitably been cast as Romeo, despite the fact that great swathes of his lines had to be cut because he could only remember about a dozen words on the trot. I rehearsed to within an inch of my life and was fitted for the costume department's finest trailing gowns (some Classical and some Victorian in style, but I didn't care). I knew my lines backwards and if I say so myself, I'd been pretty good in all the rehearsals. I'd even been nurturing a little dream of going to RADA after school and having a dazzling career on the London stage before taking Hollywood by storm. So on opening night I wasn't even particularly nervous. Then my first cue came and I walked out on stage and looked at the sea of expectant faces in the front rows, and thought about all the people in the darkness beyond, hundreds of eyes on me, and I froze. I couldn't say a word. I opened my mouth and nothing came out – not so much as a squeak, and certainly not, "How now! Who calls?" Fair play to the people playing Lady Capulet and the nurse who carried on without me, and maybe if you didn't know the play you'd have thought I was supposed to be being virginal and demure. What felt like about five hours passed, during which a wave of heat swamped my entire body and my hands felt the size of watermelons. I suppose it must only have been a few seconds, because by the time it got to "It is an honour that I dream not of", I'd recovered myself enough to speak. But for the rest of the evening the same thing happened over and over – each scene I was in, I dried completely and couldn't get my first lines out. It was awful. I was mortified and Peter Barclay was furious to have been shown up, and later on at home I cried so much I was nearly sick, and the next day I pleaded a throat infection and Mandy Simms took over.

Obviously that was the end of my fond ambitions about being an actress, and I've even thought that if I ever get married, I'll have to ask all the guests to close their eyes when I walk up the aisle, because otherwise the experience will be too terrifying. So since starting the job at YEESH, I'd dodged any suggestion that I might like to represent the organisation on 'national television', as it's always called.

"It won't be so bad," Ruth said. "They're happy to send a camera crew round to the office, it's not a live audience or anything like that."

"Go on, Ellie, you'll be brilliant," said Russell again, a one-man cheerleading squad.

"Okay," I said. "Tell them I'll do it."

"You're a lifesaver." Ruth reached for the phone and I finished my coffee and felt sick.

Of course I got no work done while we waited for the appointed hour to arrive. Ruth and I wrote a few sound-bites and printed them out, and once she'd gone off to collect Chessie I got Russell to pretend to be the interviewer and I rehearsed them over and over until I was word perfect. Then I dashed off to Boots and bought a load of makeup and troweled it on.

When I got back to the office there were wires trailing everywhere and lights being set up. Russell was standing in front of the camera holding a piece of A4 paper up next to his face and looking important. "Here's Ellie now," he said. "We're just checking the white balance." Bless him – clearly he was wishing he was going to be on telly as passionately as I was wishing I wasn't.

"I'm Karen, the producer," said a pretty, dark-haired girl in a navy-blue suit. "And Paul's our cameraman. Now if you don't mind just stepping over here," she ushered Russell out of the way and I noticed him give a last, longing look at the camera, "we'll get started. Could you say your name so we can check the sound levels?"

I opened my mouth and a strangled squeak came out. I cleared my throat and tried again. "Ellie Mottram." My voice sounded thin and high.

"Thanks Ellie," said Karen. "Okay to go, Paul?"

"Okay," said Paul.

"Great. Ellie, just relax and try to address your answers to me, not to the camera."

I nodded, feeling as if my mouth was stuffed with cotton wool.

"Ellie, YEESH's recently launched campaign to raise awareness of the increasing rate of STIs in young people has been labelled offensive and scaremongering. How would you respond to that?"

I swallowed and took a trembly breath. I could feel cold sweat springing out on my palms. "The campaign has attracted some negative comment," I squeaked, and cleared my throat again, "but they say there's no such thing as bad publicity. And although it's been criticised in some sectors, there has been a huge amount of praise from others, particularly from some influential medical bloggers."

I was starting to relax. Imagine you're talking to Rose, I told myself firmly.

"And even if people don't like the message," I went on, "the fact remains that it needs to be heard. Rates of infection are increasing in young people at a rate higher than at any time since..." And I was off. All the words Ruth and I had prepared were neatly lining up in my head, waiting for their turn. I could hear my voice returning to more or less its normal level as I trotted out the statistics and figures. Karen asked a couple more questions about the funding of the campaign and I answered them easily.

"Great," she said, "I think we have enough now. You'll be on at six and ten this evening provided nothing huge comes up."

She thanked me, and Paul packed up all his wires and lights, and they both left, and I collapsed into my chair.

"How was I?" I said needily to Russell.

"Fab," he assured me. "Brilliant. Like you did it every day."

I couldn't face watching the news that night, but my Twitter feed was full of friends saying kind things about how well I'd come across, and when I checked my email there was a message from Vanessa's boss Barri.

"Saw you tonight on BBC1 – very impressive. You are a highly credible candidate and project the image we're looking for at Black & White. I'd very much like to see you for an interview later in the week. My PA will be in touch to agree a convenient time."

There was no message from Ben, nor Claire, nor Rose. But Oliver had written on my wall on Facebook. "Congratulations – just seen you on the box and you were brilliant. You were as dazzling as you were compelling. Hope to see you soon." He'd finished the message with a couple of kisses, and – oh my God – invited me to his thirty-fifth birthday party in six weeks' time, along with Rose and about forty other people whose names I didn't recognise. His birthday was a week before Pers's first, and I couldn't help feeling that that must be some sort of omen, although of what I couldn't say.

I don't want to give you the idea that my work at YEESH was one long round of fabulousness, all being on the telly and getting to buy new lipstick on expenses – nothing could be further form the truth. In fact, just two days later, I was up at five in the morning to catch the first train into the office and there load up the minge bus with about a ton of information leaflets, posters, medical supplies, our rather festive 'You're the boss of your body' bunting and a gross of condoms, and head off to a college in Enfield for one of our mobile clinics. Duncan was back from holiday (looking ridiculously tanned in contrast to everyone else's February pallor) and Leda back from Scotland, so I'd offered to stand in for Ruth as meeter and greeter and let her hold the fort at the office and have a lie-in for once.

By the time we'd set ourselves up in two empty classrooms, arranged all the literature about the HPV vaccine and the contraceptive implant and 'No means No' and all the rest on a table and baited it with bowls of mini Mars bars, it was nine thirty. The punters were already beginning to loiter about, the boys kicking the floor and turning up the music on their MP3 players and trying to look like they knew it all already; the girls stood in little giggling groups, nudging one another and going, "You first, Kaylee." "No, you first, Lily." I sat down behind the table, ready to direct the boys one way to Duncan and the girls the other way to Leda, and braced myself for the onslaught.

After eight unrelenting hours of saying, "Hi, my name's Ellie. Would you just like to grab some brochures or would you like to chat to someone?" and explaining that I was totally unqualified to answer any questions and they'd have to wait, and dealing with the odd smart arse trying to embarrass me by saying, "Miss, my mate's bust his wrist. If he wanks with the other hand, will it feel like someone else doing it?" and smiling nicely and saying I was sure Duncan would be able to help, I felt like I never wanted to see a teenager again.

Alongside the brash, confident, sassy kids were so many sad, shy ones in shabby clothes who looked like they had no one at home to listen to their problems or give them advice, and who couldn't meet my eye as they whispered why they were there. Such were Duncan and Leda's tact and skill that they all walked out looking less frightened, bewildered and embarrassed than they had walking in, and it was honestly quite humbling to think that in the few minutes they spent with each boy or girl, they might be making a real difference to their lives.

At last five o'clock arrived and we drove in silence back to the office, where we performed the morning's routine all over again in reverse – the bunting folded up, the much-depleted stocks of condoms and brochures returned to the stationery cupboard, the stocks of the Pill and the MAP and all the rest placed back under lock and key. Leda and Duncan headed wearily home, and I said I'd just send a few emails then lock up. But as soon as all was quiet, I sat at my desk, took out my mobile and called Ben.

"Oh, hi, it's me," I babbled as soon as he answered. "I'm sure you're terribly busy but I'm passing through north London" – well, the minge bus had done so, about two hours before – "and I wondered if you fancied a drink?"

There was a pause, then Ben said, "I'm sorry, Ellie, but I don't think I can."

I waited for him to say, "Until later..." or "Tonight, because..." or suggest meeting up another time, but he didn't. He stayed quiet. And the next thing I knew, I was blurting out, "Ben. Is this about you and Claire?"

There was another long pause, before Ben said, "Ellie, I'm not free to meet you tonight."

I felt almost as if I'd been hit. Tears pricked my eyes and I struggled to catch my breath, and when I did my voice sounded all croaky. "Okay," I said. "I guess we'll talk sometime. Bye." I ended the call and stared for a few seconds at the blank, unhelpful screen of my phone. I looked around the shabby, cluttered office of YEESH, and thought of the job offer from Black & White that had arrived in my inbox that afternoon, and I found I had made a decision. I needed to move on – from my job, from Ben, towards a future that held different things and perhaps even a different me.

You know what it's like when you get a new job. For about the first week you're figuring out where the loo is and where to get decent coffee, and eating your lunch at your desk like Billy No-mates, and not saying much in meetings because you don't want to say the wrong thing, and mixing up Jackie from accounts with Lauren from HR, and all that stuff. Then all of a sudden you start feeling like part of the furniture and you can start doing some proper work. That's what it was like for me when I started at Black & White, anyway.

It felt really weird on my first day, getting the train into Victoria instead of Waterloo, making my way through Mayfair to the splendid Regency building and going round the back to the staff entrance instead of pushing through the imposing glass doors. I had to sign in and be given a temporary pass, then wait at security watching various motorbike couriers dropping off and collecting important-looking parcels, waiting for Barri to turn up. When eventually he did, he was even shorter, camper and more Australian than I remembered. Ever since I was old enough to devote much thought to important, abstract things, I've known that prejudice is bad and wrong, but I'm sure we all have little corners of our minds where ideas and assumptions that really don't belong there lurk in little dust-covered heaps, and every now and then something happens to make you realise they are there, and meeting Barri made me realise I had stereotyped Antipodeans in my head as being macho and tall.

Instead, Barri was a plump little man of about five foot three, with expensively cut hair and expensively cut suits that he wore just a bit too padded about the shoulders, and his hand when I shook it was as soft as a child's. He ushered me up to the marketing department's sumptuous office, which had a deep dove-grey carpet on the floor and was lit by huge black chandeliers, and showed me to a sleek white desk in the middle of a row of other, identical sleek white desks.

Nine thirty came and the other people in the department started to drift into the office, and honestly it was like watching a fashion show. One after another they pushed open the door, paused to make an entrance, then sashayed towards their desks, carefully putting one foot directly in front of the other as they walked, so their hips swayed elegantly and their legs looked very, very thin. One after another they came up to me and offered cool, soft hands for me to shake, and introduced themselves.

"Isla, creative services."

"Odette, e-commerce."

"Daisy, events management."

"Piper, copywriter."

And so on and on, a seemingly endless parade of posh, groomed girls. In my head I nicknamed them the Barriettes. Finally in bustled one boy, who looked plump and harassed and barely old enough to be out of school, and he was, "Torquil, admin bitch." And so my first day began with me feeling lumpy and out of place – although not badly dressed, thanks to Vanessa. But as the days went by I realised that Piper was actually quite a good laugh, and that no one liked Daisy so it didn't really matter that I thought she was totally up herself, and, as I say, gradually I stopped feeling quite so much like the new girl. I even managed to push to the back of my mind the horrible guilt I felt about letting Ruth, Duncan and my friends at YEESH down, especially as Barri had wanted me to start ASAP, so I'd taken some of my outstanding holiday in lieu of part of my notice period. But what with all the settling in, and a few evening functions I had to go to, I didn't have much time to think about anything but the new job for a while.

On my second Friday there I was surreptitiously looking at my phone, wondering whether I should text Rose to find out what she was up to and guiltily noticing a missed call from Dad from three days before that I hadn't returned, when it rang, and Ben's brother Alex's name flashed up on the screen. That's literally how I have him saved on my phone – "Alex (B's bro)". Although I've known Alex for ages, almost as long as I've known Ben, we've never made a habit of ringing each other, because we've always been in touch via Ben, so I knew he must have vital intelligence to impart.

After we'd exchanged a few random pleasantries, Alex said, "Ellie, I fear the phantom menace has returned." He's a bit of a sci-fi nut, is Alex – I've sometimes thought this may be why he doesn't have a girlfriend. I knew straight away what he meant, though.

I said, "Nina?"

Alex said, "Yes."

I said, "How?"

He said, "Facebook."

I said, "Shit."

My first thought was of Claire. I had no idea how her relationship with Ben was panning out, not having spoken to either of them for almost a month. Well, I'd spoken to

Claire once, but told her I was terribly busy in my new job and would call her back, but I hadn't. Thinking about that made me feel as sick with guilt as remembering Dad's missed call did, so I was trying not to. But if Nina was back on the scene, Claire was going to need my friendship like she never had before. She stood no chance against Nina, who would suck Ben into herself like some sort of dark matter, consuming him just like she did six years before.

When Ben and Nina got together, Ben and I had been in a routine of seeing each other two or three times a week. We'd meet up for drinks or go and see a film or I'd go round to his and scrounge dinner – even back then, he was a much better cook that I've ever been. Occasionally we'd sleep together, but I told myself I wasn't in the market for a relationship, I was young and free and had no intention of settling down, and we were friends, companions, partners in crime. But then Nina came along, and all that stopped.

After that first evening at the Latchmere, there had been no convivial nights out with Ben and Nina. There was a night in at Nina's flat, but that proved to be anything but convivial. I was invited, and Alex, and a couple whose names I can't remember, although the rest of the evening is branded on my memory. They were musician friends of Nina's, and they both wore trailing back clothes and sat silently together the whole night holding hands. She smoked Sobranie cigarettes in a long silver holder and he wore an outsize velvet beret thing that flopped down over his forehead, and a more pretentious pair you couldn't hope to find. So I wasn't too put out by their silence, as I'm sure it was preferable to whatever wanky and annoying things they might have had to say for themselves.

The evening began awkwardly, with all of us standing around in Nina's basement flat in Camden, which smelled of incense and sex and was dimly lit and rather grubby. Nina handed round little glasses of absinthe mixed with water – of all the vile things – and we all pretended to drink it (I ended up tipping mine into an unfortunate pot-plant, and thirsting for a G&T). There was a CD of some sort of plinky music playing, and when I asked Nina what it was she said it was an Alpine zither player. I kid you not. I kept catching Alex's eye and trying not to collapse in a giggling heap, so after a bit I went through to the kitchen to find Ben slaving away over a vat of consommé, which he was trying unsuccessfully to clarify with beaten egg.

"I don't want to let her down," he said frantically. I suggested that giving everyone drinks they could actually drink and relying on the subterranean gloom was probably the most sensible way to deal with not-quite-clear soup, and Ben agreed and eventually we all sat down, perched around a table with a lace cloth on it, and Nina produced a bottle of sherry and poured tiny glasses of it. I watched Nina taste her soup, then put the spoon down with a little clink that I can only describe as meaningful. She didn't eat any more and when she and Ben cleared away the plates I heard her in the kitchen, hissing, "It wasn't clear! It wasn't properly clarified, Benedict!" and Ben murmuring something soothing back. Then there was an absolutely sickening crash and Nina screamed, "It wasn't clear!" and there was another crash. Alex and I leaped up and went to see what was going on, and there was Ben dripping with soup and Nina twatting the bowls, one by one, against the wall. It should have been funny but it wasn't, it was actually quite frightening, and even now looking back I can't seem to laugh, I just remember Ben looking baffled and shocked, and Nina's rage, which almost immediately dissolved into hysterical tears. Pretty soon after that Ben suggested we all leave, and we didn't need telling twice.

So after that night I wasn't in a hurry to make Nina my new best friend, and it soon transpired that not seeing Nina meant not seeing Ben either. He and I made arrangements to meet up several times, but each time he cancelled. Nina was ill. Nina had a recital the next day and she needed Ben there to calm her nerves. Nina's grandmother had died. Nina's other grandmother had died. Nina's pet snake was shedding its skin and couldn't be left. I'm not making this up.

Anyway, after a few months of this Alex rang me and said he needed to see me, and I knew that it was about Nina and Ben, so I cancelled my Pilates class (I'd only been to about three and, come to think of it, I never went again, which is pretty typical of my track record with exercise classes) and met him at a bar in the City near his work. When I arrived he was already there, halfway down a pint of Guinness and looking depressed.

"We've got to get Ben out of that relationship," he said, before I'd even sat down.

"I know she's a bit bonkers," I said, "But don't you think Ben will realise it eventually for himself?"

Alex shook his head. "Ellie, she's more than a bit bonkers. I'm worried. They had a huge row the other night and Ben turned up at my flat and he had massive scratches down his face. She went for him with her nails."

I thought of Nina's blood-red talons and winced. "Jesus," I said. "What happened?"

"Apparently she thought he'd been looking at some other woman on the bus, and she went ballistic."

"Jesus," I said again. "Why did he go back to her then?"

Alex rolled his eyes. "He's in love with her. Sometimes when I see them together they seem really happy. Her music's a massive thing for her, and she's really good at it, apparently, really talented. I think Ben likes all that – you know him, he's always been more into watching the footie on the box than anything cultural and he probably thinks she's broadening his mind. Plus of course she's dead hot."

"Really?" I felt a stab of jealousy. "She's all skinny and ginger and annoying."

"Girls never know when other girls are hot," Alex said. "Take Keira Knightly, for example. Girls are like, 'Oh my god, she is so annoying,' but blokes know bloody well that she is the sexiest thing ever. If we got the chance we totally would."

"Nina's nothing like Keira Knightley," I said. "Apart from the annoying part."

"See? That proves my point." Alex took another gulp of his drink. "Besides, she's all fragile and vulnerable. Ben thinks she needs him."

From what I'd seen, Nina was about as fragile and vulnerable as a malaria-carrying mosquito. "Really?" I said again.

"She was one of those child prodigies," Alex explained. "Been playing the violin since she was four. Loads of pressure. Going to be the next Vanessa-Mae, apparently. When she goes off on one, it's normally when she's stressed. She's got Ben convinced that she needs him to keep her calm and help her achieve her potential."

"What other times has she gone off on one?" I asked, horrified but fascinated.

"Once when she wanted Ben to listen to her play and he was checking emails, and she threw his work laptop at the wall and totalled it," Alex said. "And she disappears. Goes AWOL for days at a time, doesn't answer her phone, ignores his texts. And then when he's decided she isn't coming back she turns up again and it's all emotional reunions and shagging each other senseless."

"Stop!" I said, covering my ears. "I don't want to hear any more."

"So, yeah," Alex said. "Treat 'em mean, keep 'em keen. Looks like it works, because he's still completely nuts about her."

We talked around the issue for a while, but we couldn't decide what to do for the best, so we just had a few more drinks and felt helpless, and in the end Nina kind of resolved the situation on her own. Ben rang me up on a Sunday afternoon a few weeks into the new year, totally unexpectedly.

"Want to come round?" he said. "I've got something to show you."

Part of me was furious with him for ditching his friends for some psychotic redhead – not that I'd been jealous of Nina, of course – but mostly I was so pleased to hear from him that I said I'd be at his flat in half an hour.

When I got there he opened the door, and there was this little black and white ball of fluff mewing around his feet.

"Meet Winston Purrchill," Ben said. "I adopted him from Battersea this morning. He was left there in a box with his mum and his brothers and sister. Apparently the mum was only a teenager when she had them – he's a broken Britain kitten." Ben scooped Winston up and held him next to his face and the kitten broke out into a thunderous purr – really quite remarkably loud for such a small cat. Ben had the same soppy, smitten look on his face that he'd had when he first met Nina, and you didn't have to be an expert in human psychology to work out that Ben had replaced waif A with stray B, so to speak. I sat down and Ben put the kettle on and made tea, and I waited, making admiring sounds about Winston as he shimmied up my jeans with his tiny claws, and eventually Ben told me what had happened.

"I went round to Nina's on Wednesday night, just like we'd arranged," he said, "but she didn't answer the door. I didn't have a set of keys because she'd thrown them out of the window a couple of days before." A shadow of pain passed over his face. "I was panicking in case she'd... done something stupid. So I broke down the door. The neighbours called the police and everything – we'd had a few rows recently and I guess they were just fed up with all the noise. But she wasn't there. All her stuff was gone, her violin and her books and CDs and Monty the python and everything. I tried to phone her and left loads of messages, but she never called back and after a few days the number came up as unobtainable. I don't have her parents' number or any of her friends' – you just don't, do you?"

"No, I suppose not," I said.

"I rang the Guildhall and tried to talk to her tutor or someone, but they won't tell me anything because of the Data Protection Act. God, Ellie, I just wanted to know that she was okay."

I refrained from pointing out that as far as I could tell Nina had never been okay. "I understand," I said.

"Then yesterday I got this." Ben reached into his pocket and took out a mauve envelope. How typical of fucking Nina, I thought, to write a letter when anyone else would have emailed or texted or whatever. He pulled out a flimsy piece of paper, and I swear, the room was instantly filled with the horrid, heavy scent Nina used to wear. If it wasn't actually Poison, it should have been. He passed it to me, and I shuddered when I touched it.

"Dear Benedict," I read, "It is over. I don't have the words to say this without causing you pain, but there is someone else. Another man. Betraying you has broken my heart, and I know that my leaving will break yours. But there is nothing I can do – our love is too strong for me to control. Perhaps one day we will meet again and you will understand, even forgive me. But for now all I can do is say goodbye, and ask that you try not to hate me, and remember all the good times we had together. Nina."

I can't remember the precise words, but trust me, it was melodramatic tosh along those lines.

"So now I suppose it's just me and Winston," Ben said, and then he put his head down on the kitchen table and full-on sobbed, like a little boy.

I instinctively moved to wrap my arms around him and offer what comfort I could, but there was something about his desolation that made me hesitate. It felt like he was in a private place, where I wouldn't be able to reach him – and wouldn't be welcome if I tried. I stood up, touched the back of his hand gently, and put the kettle on again. When it had boiled I made tea – the bright orange builder's stuff Ben likes, that will strip the enamel off your teeth if you don't swallow fast enough – and once he'd had a few sips he stopped crying and we talked about Winston for a bit, then I went home. There didn't seem to be room for me.

Ben seemed to get over Nina after a while. People do – broken hearts don't stay that way (unless you're Leona Lewis, of course. Moany cow). But he didn't seem quite the same, and the way we were together certainly wasn't. I was conscious of the gap Nina had left in his heart, a dark, empty place that I couldn't imagine ever being properly filled by anyone else. We stopped having our delicious, drunken nights together that were supposed to mean nothing, but meant so much. Nina had changed Ben in some fundamental way, and I'm not exaggerating when I say that I truly, truly hated her for it. Maybe what I really hated was that she'd changed me, too.

All this was a long time ago, of course, and Ben and I had become just friends, without the benefits, and I honestly didn't think about Nina very often at all. Perhaps it would be different now, I thought, now that Ben had Claire and so much time had passed. Perhaps he could finally get over it all, properly. If anyone could banish the ghosts Nina had left in Ben's heart, it would be Claire. But I still felt sick thinking about it all, and I said again to Alex, "Shit."

Alex said, "Yeah, shit. But it gets worse."

"What?" I said, feeling a sick jolt of fear.

"She's got a kid," Alex said. "He's called Benedict."

Chapter Thirteen

As soon as Alex's call ended, my phone rang again. I didn't want to give my new colleagues the impression that I was the sort of slacker who spends their Friday afternoon gossiping with their mates, so I almost didn't answer. Then I saw that the caller was Dad, and remembered his missed, unreturned call from the other day, and hastily pressed accept.

"Serena's in hospital," Dad said without preamble.

"In… is she okay?" I asked. "Are the babies okay?"

"She's okay for now," Dad said. "But they don't know how things are going to turn out over the next few days."

With a frightening, shaky note in his voice, Dad told me that Serena had been up on a ladder painting a mural on the wall of Rose's old bedroom, which was going to become the nursery (apparently she and Dad had had words about her doing DIY in her condition, but Serena had told him not to be such a silly old fart, and that she was pregnant, not ill, and a happy mum means a healthy baby), when she'd suddenly felt faint and overbalanced and ended up in a heap on the floor, surrounded by brushes and pots of Farrow & Ball and her stencil of smiling, chubby dragons and unicorns and wizards. This had been three days earlier, when Dad first rang me. I felt absolutely wretched with guilt.

"She said she felt okay, just shaken up," Dad said, "but then yesterday she started having pains and bleeding, so we thought she'd better go in and get checked out. We told each other we were probably over-reacting but we were both worried as hell."

"What did they say?" I asked.

"They say it's placental abruption," said Dad.

"Placental what?" I pressed the phone against my ear and started typing the phrase into Google, the way you do when you hear about medical stuff, even though no good ever comes of it.

"The placenta's threatening to detach," Dad said. "Normally they'd deliver the babies but twenty weeks is way too early and because they're twins they're small anyway. So they're keeping her in hospital, flat on her back, basically."

I quickly scrolled down my screen, and horrible words like haemorrhage and still birth jumped out at me.

"Shall I come?" I said. "I can get the train tonight and stay for the weekend? I won't be able to do anything much but I could keep you company."

Dad said, yes, please, and then he said, "Please will you let Rose know? I left her a message too but she hasn't come back to me yet."

"Of course," I said. "I'll be there about eight, okay? I'll text you when I'm on the train."

Dad said thanks and rang off, and I shut down my computer, glad to switch off the horrible words on the screen, exchanged the usual Friday formalities with my colleagues and headed for home.

How monstrously unfair it was, I thought, that poor Serena should be going through this, at risk of losing her precious, longed-for babies, while bloody Nina had not even rated the birth of her child as important enough to let his father know. Then of course I realised how silly and unreasonable it was to think that way, when Nina, vile as she was, presumably loved her son dearly, because mothers always do, don't they, even when they're deeply unpleasant people otherwise, or they've had the misfortune to give birth to one of those unattractive, pudding-faced babies you sometimes see. Just because Nina had treated Ben appallingly, didn't mean she wouldn't be a wonderful mother, I told myself – but I wasn't convinced.

On the train I quickly tapped out a text to Rose, telling her what had happened and that I was on my way home, and she would probably want to pack a bag as well, but she didn't reply.

If I'm being honest, I was quite relieved by the prospect of a weekend back at Dad's with him and Rose. Although one's supposed to relish the challenge of a new job and all that stuff, it's actually a really isolating time. I was missing Ruth and Duncan and Russell and all the motley crew back at YEESH – the glossy denizens of Black & White were lovely enough in their way, but they were taking a lot of getting used to. I also hated the distance that had opened up between me and Claire and Ben. I wanted the two of them to make a go of things, I really did, but I was beginning to think that leaving them to it hadn't been the best idea. And I'd restricted myself to checking Oliver's posts on Facebook only once a day, and that hadn't actually been all that difficult to stick to, as there is only so much emotion to be gleaned from reading about the FTSE 100, grain futures and the Ashes. I missed Rose most of all. It's not like we'd made a habit of cosy sisterly evenings together with Eastenders and massive slabs of Fruit and Nut, the way sisters who live together carry on in books (as if! Rose would rather eat her own hair than a slab of Fruit and Nut). But over the years I'd sort of got used to her getting home at about ten each night and telling me about the glamorous time she'd been having at whatever launch or party or sale she'd been at, and her friends turning up for kitchen sups, and all the rest of it. Of late, she'd barely been home at all, because, I supposed, she'd been at Oliver's. Thinking about them together left me with a hollow, sick feeling inside, so I avoided doing it, but, for probably the first time in my adult life, I was lonely. I didn't like it one bit. I'd even thought about getting a cat, but Rose is allergic to them and the fallout that would ensue if she arrived home and found the flat full of allergens and fur on her black dresses didn't bear thinking about. We'd go together to Dad's, I decided, and rally round him in a sisterly way and we'd be a family again. I was imagining making and freezing loads of batches of veggie lasagne and stuff, and with a mad rush of blood to the head I even wondered if I could learn to crochet, and make little booties for Serena's babies. Then I remembered my spectacular lack of success with Pers's Camelduck, and I shelved that plan.

Anyway, I was feeling quite eager and positive when I fought my way off the train and hurried to the flat. I ran up to my bedroom, retrieved my overnight bag from the top shelf where it was languishing, and stuffed in a random assortment of pants and tops and toiletries. Then I took off my work suit and hung it carefully away in the cupboard. I put on a pair of the skinny jeans I'd chosen with Vanessa, and a plum-coloured cashmere jumper that I'd never worn before because it was dry-clean only, and I was standing in front of the mirror brushing my hair when I noticed there were two reflections of me. Two blonde-haired girls in designer jeans and dark, fitted tops.

For a fleeting, disconnected second I wondered if I was hallucinating from stress, or if we'd suddenly acquired a resident ghost. Then of course I clocked Rose standing behind me in the doorway. With my new hair and new slimness, we were looking more alike than we ever had. Ghost or no ghost (and obviously there are no ghosts, and anyone who thinks there are is sadly deluded) it was really quite unsettling.

"I didn't realise you were here," I said. "Are you ready to go? We can get the six twenty train if we hurry."

"I'm not coming," Rose said.

"You're not – what do you mean?"

"I'm not coming," she said again, quite coolly.

"Look, Rose," I said, trying hard to sound calm and reasonable, "I know you find it hard to get on with Serena. I know it must seem like a massive climb-down after what happened at Christmas. But think of Dad. These are his babies, they're our half-sisters or brothers. He needs us there. Serena could die, she could literally bleed to death, or they could lose both the babies. If that happens and you aren't there, think how terrible you'd feel."

"Ellie, I said I'm not coming, okay? I'm not changing my mind and nothing you say is going to make me. I'm not a hypocrite and I'm not going to have some emotional hospital-bed reconciliation with Serena. I don't like her, I never have and this hasn't changed my feelings. She's in hospital, she's being cared for by professional people who know what they are doing, and my being there or not won't make any difference to the outcome."

"But it would make a big difference to Dad," I pleaded. "And it would make a difference to me."

"Sorry, Ellie." Rose turned around and walked back into her bedroom.

I'm quite a level-headed person usually. I rarely lose my temper and I absolutely hate rows, but I'm afraid I lost it with Rose then. I stood in her doorway and shouted all kinds of horrible things at her – about how she never thought of anyone except herself, she was a cold-hearted, selfish bitch and if anything happened to Serena it would be her fucking fault. By the time I finished Rose was crying, but I didn't care. I picked up my bag and walked out of the flat. I didn't even miss the train.

"It's bloody Victorian," fumed Serena, lying back in her hospital bed, surrounded by her laptop, her Kindle, her phone, her iPad and her Wii – all the high-tech, streamlined gadgets I'd come to regard as as much a part of her as her spiky hair and sleek spectacles. In addition to all this, though, there were things that were totally alien to Serena's character: bouquets of flowers, cards with a preponderance of pink and even a full-on fruit basket. "I thought that in the twenty-first century pregnant people could just get on with being pregnant, but evidently my stupid body and that wobbly stepladder thought otherwise, and so I'm stuck here for the foreseeable, and so are our babies. At least I hope they are." Then the clean, elegant lines of her face sort of smudged and her clear skin was suffused with a horrid flush, and she let out a noise that sounded like, "Hnnnggg," and started to sob. Dad said, "Angel, don't upset yourself," and Serena said between sobs, "Watch what you say, Luke, or you'll fucking upset me," and I thought it was about time I went for a walk.

It was weird, I couldn't escape the sound of her weeping even when I stepped beyond the curtains surrounding Serena's bed. She and Dad could easily have afforded a private room for her but, as Dad had explained to me in the car on the way to the hospital, Serena insisted that she and the babies would get no better care privately than they would on the NHS – or "our NHS", as Dad told me Serena had described it. He was unable to keep a note of pride from his voice at Serena's commitment to the welfare state, even in extremis, and I have to admit I shared it. Anyway, I walked down the ward a bit and thought I'd try and find somewhere where I could get a decent cup of coffee – fat chance, the NHS is wonderful in almost all respects, but Flat White it is not. So I walked towards the exit, a long, long way it seemed, with my heels clicking on the supposedly sound-deadening flooring. But I could still hear those awful, desperate sobs. I paused, wondering why I couldn't make out Dad's soothing voice any longer, and then I realised that the sound of women crying was happening in stereo, or whatever the version of stereo is when there's many, many more than two sources of it. From behind each of the curtained-off cubicles came the sounds of women's sadness – some whimpering, some quietly moaning, one actually keening in pain or fear: each voice expressing its own terror of loss.

Reader, I legged it.

I sent Dad a text saying that I'd see him back at home – he'd given me a set of keys – and I'd be around the whole weekend, but for now I felt there wasn't much I could do. Then I dived into a taxi waiting outside the hospital door and asked the driver to take me straight to the local pub. In fact, I may even have said, "The Rose and Crown, my good man."

I ordered a G&T, necked it in double quick time and ordered another. By then I'd calmed down a bit, so I took a look around to see if there was anyone I knew in the pub. The Rose and Crown's a real local local, where you can happily sit on your own and have a drink and read a book without people thinking you're there to get picked up. But generally you won't be on your own for long, because you'll bump into someone you were at school with or a mate of Dad's or the woman who runs the Oxfam shop, or... It's that kind of place. And sure enough, within minutes I was chatting away to Max the bartender, who'd somehow found out about Serena being in hospital and wanted an update. I left out the gory details, but told him that for now she was okay, although not out of danger. Then I ordered another G&T and a packet of cheese and onion crisps, because I hadn't had any dinner and was suddenly feeling almost crazed with hunger, and just as I was ripping open the packet a voice behind me said, "Ellie Mottram!"

I was really glad I hadn't had the chance to eat any crisps yet, because there, leaning in for a kiss, was Peter Barclay, the fittest boy in the sixth form, and he'd lost none of his fitness. He was tall – over six foot – and kind of rangy, with a slight gangliness about him that I remembered from school – you know how it is when boys suddenly shoot up and don't quite know what to do with their hands and feet? Even though it was barely spring and still freezing, he had a bit of a tan, so I guessed he must ski or play golf or run or something. I hoped it wasn't golf. He had lovely, even white teeth, his blue eyes were as smiley as I remembered, and his dark blonde hair still stuck up a bit on one side.

Anyway, I noticed all this in about a nanosecond, before we started saying the usual things about how long it had been, and what had brought us back to the old manor. I told Peter about Serena, and he made sympathetic noises, which reminded me that in spite of being the fittest boy in our year, he'd also been really, really sweet and kind, although of course such was his fitness that he would still have had all the girls after him even if he'd been an utter dick. He, it turned out, was home from London where he worked in IT, for his sister Jess's wedding the next day, and she was indulging in a bridezilla strop of such epic proportions that Peter had elected to leave her, her five bridesmaids and their mum to it, and decamp to the Rose and Crown for a bit of peace and quiet.

By the time we'd caught up on all this we'd finished our drinks and my crisps, and Peter bought another round and a packet of peanuts, and we carried on chatting away as you do when you haven't seen someone for ages, catching up on all the news about how Mandy Simms and Ewan Miller are married with triplets, and Charlie Armitage is in prison for embezzlement, and Alice Chambers was killed in a road traffic accident, and you're so busy going, "Wow, really?" and "Always knew he was a wrong 'un," and "Oh God, how awful," that there's no room at all for awkwardness. We were chatting so much and laughing so much I barely noticed that we'd had two more drinks and I was beginning to feel decidedly squiffy, and I realised that we were flirting with each other.

We'd moved to a sofa – the Rose and Crown has lovely worn leather Chesterfields – and the cushions sort of dipped a bit in the middle, so we kept being slid towards each other, and our thighs kept touching, and every time they did Peter looked at me and I looked at him, and our eyes locked on to each other for a second before we looked away and carried on chatting. After a while I stopped moving away and let my leg press closer and closer to his, and a few minutes after that I felt the warm pressure of his hand on my thigh, and a delicious little jolt of desire went through me, and I knew we were going to end up in bed, and that everything that happened between now and then would just be a kind of formality. Max called last orders at half eleven and we had a final drink and I went to the ladies' and looked at myself in the mirror to check that my mascara wasn't smudged and I didn't have peanut skin on my teeth. I didn't, thank God – in fact I looked all glowy and excited, and even quite pretty. I went back to Peter and he took my hand as we walked out of the door. It was one of those really cold but beautiful nights you sometimes get when the sky is crystal clear, and there was a new moon and a dusting of stars. We paused for a bit, looking at the night and each other, and then there was that amazing moment when you know you're about to kiss someone but haven't yet. I've sometimes thought it's the best part of sex – when you don't know if they're going to be a rotten, slobbery kisser or suck on your nipples like a baby or have a fugly stunted cock like a button mushroom, or any of the other things that can lead to woeful disappointment. Anyway, there we were in the cold night, our breath clouding around us, Peter's hands on my shoulders under my hair, and I felt this wonderful sense of freedom and anticipation, and of course I was already as turned on as hell. I smiled up at him and closed my eyes and waited for him to kiss me, and when he did it wasn't disappointing in the slightest. His lips were warm and soft and dry, and his tongue gently questing, and I could feel that he was smiling while we kissed, and I was too. I could feel the roughness of his jumper under his coat and the hardness of his back, and I could tell from the erection pressing into my hip that his cock was going to be neither mushroom-like nor stunted.

We moved apart after a long, long time, and grinned at each other in the moonlight. "Your parents' place or mine?" Peter said. "Yours is closer," I said, and we ran down the road together, holding hands and giggling like teenagers, every now and then stopping to snog each other. We got to the driveway of Peter's parents' house, which was a great, red-brick pile of a place, and walked as silently as we could over the gravel. The house was in darkness, and Peter made a silent 'shhh' face at me as he fitted his key in the lock (after a couple of unsuccessful attempts; clearly he was also a bit pissed). He took my hand and led me up the dark staircase and into his bedroom, which hilariously looked exactly as it had when we'd lounged around in it as teenagers, smoking illicit fags and listening to Radiohead CDs, even down to the block-mounted Arsenal posters on the walls. It was really strange and actually incredibly erotic, because of course all those years ago I had longed and longed to be kissed by Peter, but it had never happened because he was the fittest boy in our year and I was the geeky girl who was good at English.

He closed the door but left the curtains open so the room was flooded with moonlight, and I could see the smile that never seemed to leave his face, and the amazing length of his eyelashes as he took me in his arms again and we carried on kissing, now sort of snatching at each other's clothes as well. I unbuckled his belt and started to undo the buttons of his shirt under his jumper; he rather expertly undid the clasp on my bra with one hand and his warm fingers found my breasts. I heard myself give a little gasp and my hips bucked towards him; he gasped too, and we pulled apart again and both went, "Shhh," and started giggling madly. I sat down on the bed and pulled off my boots and socks –

there's no elegant way to do this, is there? – and Peter sat next to me and did the same, then he pushed me back against the faded denim-coloured duvet and kissed me on and on and on while he unbuttoned my jeans and explored me with gentle, skilful fingers until I came. I looked at him and grinned again, and he rummaged around in his bedside drawer and found a condom, and we took off the rest of our clothes and he put it on – I remember hoping fleetingly that it wasn't 2001 vintage like the rest of the room – and then we had the most amazing fuck. Every now and then we'd sort of pause and look at each other and laugh, because it was just too random and so nice, and our bodies worked together so well, with just enough skill and a total lack of self-consciousness. Then the pace increased and we moved more frenziedly together, and I could feel sweat on his back and I kept my eyes open so I could see his face when he came, and it looked and felt so fantastic I came again too. We lay in each other's arms in the single bed, whispering and giggling, until we fell asleep.

I jolted awake the next morning from a horrible dream in which I turned up for a meeting with Barri with no clothes on, with a sense of having forgotten something important. It took me a few seconds to realise where I was. Peter had already got up, and I realised I'd better hurry and make myself scarce and get back to Dad's. My phone had died so I had no way of knowing what time it was, but the sun was shining brightly outside and I knew it was late. I dragged my clothes on and picked up my bag and tiptoed out, hoping that I'd be able to sneak away unnoticed and find my way home, but there at the bottom of the stairs was Peter's sister Jess in a huge white meringue of a dress and about a zillion pretty bridesmaids in teal satin shifts, and Mrs Barclay in coral with a massive hat. I thought about turning round and bolting back to Peter's room but it was too late, they'd seen me. I had no alternative but to carry on my walk of shame down the stairs, going more and more slowly as more and more eyes turned towards me, and honestly, I have never been so mortified in all my life.

Chapter Fourteen

When I got back to Dad's, he wasn't there, and once I'd charged my phone I got a text from him saying he'd spent the night in the hospital with Serena. I was hugely relieved – partly that she was still okay, obviously, but also that Dad hadn't found out about my dirty stop-out behaviour. He would have been terribly worried and then probably had a complete wobbly and grounded me, like he used to do when I was fourteen. So I spent the rest of the weekend being a model daughter: I did actually make a couple of dishes of veggie lasagne and put them in the fridge, telling Dad he needed to keep his strength up, and I baked a huge batch of chocolate brownies (the one and only thing I can actually bake), and took them round to the hospital for Serena, along with a stack of copies of *Wired* and *Macworld* and *Computer Arts* magazines. She was really pleased, and immediately ate about three in rapid succession – brownies, obviously, not glossy IT-related publications. For such a tiny woman, Serena can put away an incredible amount of cake. According to Dad, the doctors were feeling quite positive about the chances of the babies hanging in there for a few more weeks – the idea apparently was to fill them with steroids and get them to grow as quickly as possible, which sounded a bit freaky to me – I imagined two monster twins expanding and expanding inside Serena and eventually splitting her open like something out of a horror movie, but then I've always been a bit squeamish about childbirth. Evidently if they could get the babies to around thirty weeks' gestation they were almost certain to be okay, so it was now just a question of keeping our fingers crossed and hoping that Serena wouldn't go completely off her head with boredom lying flat on her back for another ten weeks.

Anyway, I stayed with Dad on Saturday and Sunday nights, and went straight in to the office on Monday morning, partly, I'll admit, because I wasn't in the mood to see Rose. She hadn't even texted me to find out what was happening, and every time I thought about her I felt a cold twist of anger and worry. I was furious about her selfish and uncaring attitude towards Serena. Despite all my resolutions to the contrary, I'd ended up being the good, dutiful daughter, again. I knew that what I'd done was the right thing, but even the memory of my night with Peter, which brought a smile to my face and a flush of remembered pleasure to my body, was cold comfort.

Most of all, I was genuinely puzzled by Rose's behaviour. Although she's sometimes thoughtless, she is a genuinely kind person, and it seemed unlike her to sustain such a horrible attitude for such a long time, especially if she was all loved up and happy herself. It really made me sad that Rose wasn't going to be the first person to hear the story of my night with Peter and my walk of shame the next day – she would have pissed herself laughing. But I didn't want to talk to her about it, or indeed about anything else, really. I don't believe in telepathy or any of that nonsense – obviously – but all our lives I've felt a sort of connection with Rose, almost as if she's been a second presence in my brain, and every so often I'm able to see her face or hear her voice and know how she'd react to whatever I am doing or saying at the time. Now that wasn't there. I had absolutely no idea where Rose was, what she was doing or thinking or feeling. I didn't even know when I'd next be seeing her, although of course I assumed that she'd be among those present at Oliver's birthday party. There was an empty, yawning space that had opened up between us, and thinking about it almost made me cry, on the crowded commuter train just as it was pulling into Paddington, which would have made me look like a right mentalist.

I pushed my worry about Rose to the back of my mind as I made my way to the office, which wasn't actually too difficult as I had a busy week ahead and some stuff on the go that I was really quite excited about. I'd put together a story about how our new Spring/Summer collection, which was hitting the store that week, was a microcosm of worldwide trends outside of fashion – talking about environmental issues and technology being deployed for the greater good and people's sense of themselves as global citizens and all that stuff. It was all touchy-feely, calculated to assuage any guilt Black & White's customers might feel about the fact that essentially what they were doing was spunking enough cash to feed a family in Somalia for about five years on their new season's wardrobe. Anyway I was really pleased about it, and I knew that a lot of the style journalists I'd made contact with would use it, and I might even have a shot at getting on to some of the hard news pages too. This would be a massive coup, and one I badly needed, because I was beginning to realise that Barri was not the easiest person in the world to work for. He was capricious, inconsistent, demanding, and appeared to make pets out of some of the members of his team, changing them on a whim and leaving whoever had been the last flavour of the month wondering what on earth she'd done wrong. Just the previous week, Odette had been in tears because Barri had given her a particularly humiliating public bollocking and then whisked Isla out to lunch. Deride and rule appeared to be Barri's modus operandi, and I neither liked nor respected it.

Anyway, dodgy management style or no, it was Monday morning and the only way to begin the week as far as I'm concerned is to ease into it gently, so I switched on my computer, sipped my coffee and ate my rather grim but allegedly low-fat, low-sugar porridge while I checked my emails, and then I logged on to Facebook and straight away up pinged a message from Claire.

"Ellie! Where have you been?"

Avoiding you, I thought. And perhaps you've been avoiding me, too. "Hey," I typed. "What's up?"

"Loads!" she messaged back. "Big weekend! Huge!"

Shit, I thought. Ben. Are they getting married? Surely not. It had only been a few weeks. Moving in together? A knot of tension formed in my stomach, but I forced myself to type a cheery, "Tell all!"

There was a pause, and I imagined her typing frantically away. Then her message appeared on my screen.

"Your god-daughter has only started cruising!! Before her first birthday!! How super-advanced is she? She zooms around the place holding on to walls and furniture like a little monkey, it's so cute and clever but I wasn't expecting her to start for ages so I had to spend the entire weekend Pers-proofing the flat. She is nattering away like mad too – I'm sure on Saturday she tried to say 'Camelduck'. How cool if that was her first word?"

"Bless her, the clever sausage!" I replied, my heart melting. "When can I see you both? It's been ages."

"We must make a plan," Claire said, with maddening vagueness. Once again, I imagined her and Ben together, talking pityingly about me and my single status and wondering how they were going to reveal their new-found love to me. Well, I wasn't going to ask, but I was going to let them know that they weren't the only ones having wild, passionate sex. "So... you'll never guess what?"

"What??" said Claire.

"I only shagged Peter Barclay," I said. I'd regaled Claire in the past with the sorry tale of Peter and the school play, but just in case she'd forgotten I added, "Romeo? Fittest boy in the sixth form?"

"Waaaah!" went Claire, "Fabulous! What happened?"

I quickly updated her on the Serena situation, then told her the story of my night in the pub with Peter and sneaking into his bedroom, and how I'd woken up the next day and been confronted with the bridal party and had to stand there and be introduced to all of them, absolutely desperate to get out of there and dying for a wee and conscious that I simply reeked of sex.

"Can't... breathe..." Claire typed. "OMG, Ellie, only you. That is so funny. You've made my day. So are you going to be seeing him again? Would be so romantic if the two of you got together, hey? Romeo and Juliet revisited."

"Will have to wait and see," I typed, then added a few random smilies for good measure.

I took a sip of my coffee and realised it was stone cold, and that I'd been typing away to Claire for the best part of half an hour, and I could see Daisy giving me a look from across the office that said, "You aren't really typing press releases at ten o'clock on a Monday morning," so I said to Claire, "Am being watched. Must go. Will update you on all news when I see you. Big love and cuddles to Pers from her proud godmother."

"L8r xxxxx," said Claire, and I shut down Facebook – after quickly checking to see if Oliver had updated his status over the weekend, but he'd only posted a link to some story in *The Economist* about quantitative easing. I actually found myself reading it all the way through, impenetrable and dull as it was, because doing so made me feel somehow a bit closer to Oliver, and I imagined the next time I saw him being able to say something intelligent about the UK economy and him being impressed. Which is proof if proof were needed that unrequited love makes idiots of us all.

Anyway, Monday wore on and I fired off a few emails, put the finishing touches to my press release and had a meeting with Isla to select the images that would accompany it, and then I went out and bought a sandwich and a pair of shoes, the way you do, and when I got back to the office there was a massive bunch of yellow roses on my desk.

"Who put these here?" I demanded. "Who are they for?"

"Torquil put them there, obviously," said Piper. "And, obviously, they're for you. Isn't there a note? How cool – do you have a secret admirer?"

I located the card in amongst all the flowers and opened the little envelope, and felt myself blushing absolutely scarlet as I read.

"Ellie – I just wanted to say sorry for leaving you in the lurch on Saturday. I was summoned to take our mad Nan to the church and stop her throwing Polo mints at the guests. I didn't want to wake you – you were like Sleeping Beauty. But I suppose I should have done, because I heard you made quite an entrance. Anyway, it was an incredible night and I'd love to see you again. You know where to find me. Peter x."

I was wearing skinny petrol-blue jeans, a grey mohair jumper, grey and plum outsize scarf tied in one of the intricate knots Vanessa had shown me, a silver aviator jacket and fringed, grey suede boots. It certainly wasn't the sort of outfit I'd have chosen for Sunday lunch followed by a walk along the canal six months ago; it's what Rose would have worn, and I would have teased her for wearing. It did, however, look pretty good, and I felt my first actual date with Peter warranted making a bit of an effort. I'd even been, for the first time in my life, to have my eyebrows properly shaped at a salon, and a highly shaming and painful experience it had been too, particularly the bit in the beginning when Anya the eyebrow girl limbered up her tweezer hand and said, "We start in the middle, yes?" I mean, it had been a long time and everything, but it's not like I'm Frida Kahlo. Cheeky mare.

I'd arranged to meet Peter in Camden, in a pub near the market, which would never have been my first choice because I know how hellishly busy the area gets on weekends, and as soon as I walked in I knew that my worst fears were justified – the place was rammed with hipsters and tourists. Thankfully Peter had had the foresight to book a table, and the waitress led me to it, and there was Peter, immersed in the sports pages of the *Sunday Telegraph.* (Call me shallow, but I did cringe a bit when I saw his choice of reading material.) The last time I'd seen him, he'd been wearing ordinary jeans and a jumper, but today he'd clearly made a special effort with his appearance. He was working the grandpa-chic story that was one of the big trends of the season, with a tartan scarf looped around his neck over a tweed coat with leather patches on the elbows and a chunky cardigan, and when he stood up I could see he was wearing red corduroy trousers that ended at the ankle, revealing argyle socks. I wondered hopefully whether the copy of the Torygraph was just an ironic addendum to the look, and then it struck me that it was possible none of it was ironic, and this was his normal Sunday attire. My fashion radar simply wasn't finely tuned enough to tell. Anyway, when he kissed me he smelled and felt so nice that I remembered our amazing night together, and felt better and forgave him for the socks. And the red trousers.

I sat down and Peter asked me how my week had been and how Serena was, and I told him, and asked him about how Jess's wedding had gone, and he told me, and then we ordered our lunch – roast chicken for him and nut roast for me, and a bottle of red wine – and then a bit of an awkward silence fell, which I filled by chatting away about the other people in the pub.

"Look at that family there," I said, indicating a couple and their perfectly behaved, Boden-clad offspring. "I bet you they're both barristers, and they live in Highgate, and coming here for lunch is their version of slumming it."

Peter laughed. "I live in Highgate," he protested, but joined in the game anyway. "And over there, the bloke with the dreadlocks with the blonde girl. He's her bit of rough, she's only going out with him because her parents would be so shocked if they knew, except she's wasting her time because she'll never have the bottle to introduce him to them."

I resisted pointing out that the dreadlocked man was quite hot enough to shag on his own merits, so to speak – I so would, anyway – and instead said, "Those two in the corner. Food bloggers. Look, she's got her camera with her and they're going to photograph every single dish and analyse it to within an inch of its life, and actually they're hoping that the management will realise that's what they're doing and comp them things or give them a discount."

By this point our own lunch had arrived and we started eating – actually, I was more kind of picking at my food, because I wasn't particularly hungry and was feeling a bit shy and clumsy still, aware that what this was really about was me and Peter deciding whether we liked each other enough to sleep together again, and after that we'd have to decide whether we liked sleeping together enough to see each other again, and it's a rather nerve-wracking situation to be in, more like an audition or a job interview than a date. I took a gulp of wine and looked around the room some more – it was one of those cavernous, contemporary places, all metal struts and expanses of glass and exposed brickwork – and I became conscious of a bit of a commotion by the entrance, and said to Peter, "Oooh – what's going on there?"

I heard a child's bell-like tones exclaim, "I'm not eating in this dump." Immediately the volume of conversation in the restaurant dropped as everyone turned their attention to eavesdropping on the drama, the childless ones with horror as they vowed that if they ever had kids, they'd never, ever behave that way in a public place; the parents with relief that, on this occasion at least, it was someone else's offspring kicking off.

"I want to go to MacDonalds," said the child, its voice piercing the sudden silence of the room. There was a little murmur of embarrassed laughter, and as if encouraged, the kid continued, "I don't want to have my lunch here. It stinks. It smells of bumholes."

There was a pause, presumably while the child's parents tried very quietly to persuade it to shut the fuck up and stop showing them up in public, and then the voice rang out again, "I won't, and you can't make me! Bumholes! Runny poo!" Another pause, then fresh inspiration struck and the child piped up, "Foreskin!"

Oh, how I regretted having my back to the door, so I was unable to appreciate the drama to the full, without craning rudely around for a look. I was giggling helplessly into my nut roast, but Peter was looking a bit shocked and disapproving. "I'd never have been allowed to get away with behaving like that," he said.

"Poor parents, though," I countered, "You don't know, maybe the kid's a perfect angel normally and this is just a blip. Can you see what they're doing?"

"Trying to reason with him," Peter said stiffly. "It doesn't appear to be working."

"Bumholes!" said the child again. "I bet the food tastes like poo! Poo and vaginas!" he finished triumphantly, and I could no longer resist twisting in my chair to catch a glimpse of the little sod and its unfortunate parents. I tried to glance discreetly around, but then froze and simply gawped, for there in the doorway, on either side of the child, a boy of about five wearing a Batman costume, complete with hood, were Ben and Nina.

My first thought was that Nina looked exactly the same, with her long, bright hair and vivid, floaty clothes. She was still tiny and insect-like, even more so because she was wearing huge retro sunglasses with bright blue lenses. The child – Benedict – was nothing like Ben or her at all: he was a plump, compact, dark-haired kid with beetle brows that could have done with a bit of attention from Anya the plucking lady, and to be brutally honest, he reminded me of the little boy in *We Need to Talk About Kevin*. Because I've been so close to Ben for so long, I generally have a fairly good idea of what's going on in his head at any time, a bit like I do with Rose, but you wouldn't have to know him to tell how he was feeling then, with about a hundred people all staring at him with varying degrees of pity and scorn. He looked bewildered and embarrassed, as if he'd like nothing more than to disappear beneath the reclaimed sanded floorboards, and totally unprepared for the realities of parenting this spawn of Satan.

"Shall we go to MacDonald's, then, sweetheart?" Nina cooed. "Is that what Mummy's little man wants?"

"Yes," said the child, only he sort of stuck out his lower lip while he was saying it, so it came out like, "Mwuss."

Nina flicked her filmy tangerine-coloured scarf over her shoulder, apparently totally unfazed by the attention they were attracting, and said, "Come on then, my darling. Mummy will take you there, and you shall have a banana milkshake for a treat. Come on!" she sort of snapped at Ben as an afterthought, and the three of them turned around and left, and everyone gradually returned to their food, sorry that the show was over but glad they had a topic of conversation that would last them all through their lunch and probably a good few dinner parties too.

I was considering telling Peter that I knew Ben, and filling him in on the whole sorry story, but he'd already launched into a bit of a diatribe about parenting techniques, and how laissez-faire, neglectful mothers and absent fathers were contributing to the moral decline of society and had been linked to the London riots last summer. He even quoted an article by Melanie Phillips that he'd read in the *Daily Mail* recently. Honestly, it was as if his body had been taken over by aliens. I wanted to say, "Who are you and what have you done with the bloke I fancied?" And in short order thereafter, "It's not you, it's me," immediately followed by, "I'll always love you as a friend." But then I thought about Oliver's birthday party in a couple of weeks' time, and turning up looking like the loser girl who couldn't get a date. And I thought about Ben and Claire (or Ben and Nina), Rose and Oliver, Vanessa and Tom, Simon and Khalid – basically everyone I knew in the whole world being part of a couple, like Noah's sodding ark. And I'm ashamed to say that I went home with Peter and shagged him, just because I didn't want to go home on my own.

Chapter Fifteen

The next week, work started off vile and grew steadily viler. It began with Barri's Monday morning breakfast meeting. This little brain-child of his meant that instead of starting at the relatively civilised hour of nine thirty, we were all expected to be in the office for half eight, and would gather around the meeting room table for a post-mortem of the previous week and some 'blue-sky strategising' about the week to come. Sadistically, Barri always arranged for a huge platter of pastries to be delivered from the food hall, so we sat there staring at the buttery croissants and sticky blueberry muffins and custard doughnuts, all absolutely determined not to be the first to cave in and eat one. Alongside the platter of shame was a bowl of fruit: bananas, which I detest, and a few rather sad-looking apples and clementines. The first time I'd attended one of Barri's Monday meetings I had been unaware of the unwritten rules surrounding the pastries and, because I'd got up at six for a run and had no time for breakfast and was starving, I'd casually reached for a croissant and started eating it, and everyone around the table fell silent. There was even a little gasp from Isla, and Barri stopped talking about forecasts and gave me a look that practically took the polish of my nails.

"Wow, Ellie, you're a lucky girl," he said.

"Sorry?" I said, bewildered.

"I bet we'd all like to be able to eat naughty food like that, and keep our weight… Oh." And he gave me a sort of sneery, dismissive look, and suddenly I didn't feel hungry any more in the slightest, and left the rest of my croissant drying out on the plate, and by lunchtime I'd been quite lightheaded with hunger.

I'd realised now that the pastries were simply another weapon in the arsenal Barri used to intimidate his team, and like so much of his management strategy, its effect was subtle yet deadly. The previous week, after particularly trenchant critique of her design for the cover of the Autumn look-book, I'd walked into the kitchen for a coffee and found Isla hunched over the breakfast platter, crumbs on her chin and tears in her eyes. When she saw me she turned scarlet, muttered, "Just clearing up," and tipped the rest of the pastries into the bin before legging it out of there as if she'd been caught doing something dreadful. And when I'd gone to the loo a few minutes later, I'd heard retching and sobbing coming from one of the cubicles. The two events may of course have been totally unconnected, but I'm just saying, those pastries were used manipulate our morale to quite lethal effect.

But now I'd been at Black & White for several weeks and I was wise to Barri's little ways, so I calmly sipped my coffee (black, one sweetener) and peeled a clementine and ate it, one segment at a time, even managing to leave three segments behind on the plate to prove that I was totally in control of my vile, base urge to ingest calories in order to sustain my body's essential metabolic processes.

"Odette, an update on the style blog, if you don't mind," Barri said.

"Of course." Odette smoothed a lock of poker-straight blonde hair back over the shoulder of her coral-coloured jacket, and moved a turquoise-nailed finger over the trackpad of her laptop. "We had four posts go live last week. An exposé of Peaches Geldof's changing style, a piece by Delta Hughes, the celebrity stylist, on how to wear bustles, a round-up of the new neons, and," she paused and looked around the table rather smugly, "an interview with Bliss Newham. Bliss, as you know, was very much the face of the fashion weeks this season. She walked for Givenchy, Balenciaga, Chanel, Dior and many others – in fact, she made a record seventy appearances on the catwalk. So we were delighted to have a blog by her – which Piper ghosted, of course – in which she reveals how her meteoric rise to stardom hasn't affected her down-to-earth attitude, how she keeps her incredible figure through exercise and good genes, and loves burgers and chips, and how she has met so many warm, beautiful people in the fashion world, who she knows will be life-long friends."

I tried not to be a little bit sick in my mouth, and pulled my shorthand notebook towards me and wrote, "Bliss Newham, unspoiled beauty," for something to do, and so that Barri, who was sitting next to me, would think I was concentrating really hard and thought Odette's revelations were of great significance.

"Excellent!" Barri said. Odette looked even smugger.

"Our new collections have gone live and are selling well," she said, and trotted out some figures, which I noted down for a press release.

"Now, Daisy," Barri said, "How's the planning going for the polo in May?"

Daisy banged on for a bit about all the celebrities she'd managed to get on the guest list for this shindig, which was apparently a huge deal for Black & White. Every year the store was one of the main sponsors of an international polo tournament, the kind of thing that gets described as a 'glittering event' and a 'highlight of the social calendar', at which loads of celebs and trust-fund babies turn up in inappropriate clothes and get plastered. Daisy was organising the hospitality in the VIP marquee, where those in the inner circle of fabulousness would be spending the day being fed vast amounts of free food and drink, watching the action on the polo field and then 'dancing the night away at a star-studded after-party', as my press release put it. Rose had been with Vanessa a few years back, when she was dating Danny the polo player, and she apparently had a fabulous time and was introduced to Prince William, who Danny had known at Eton. She didn't shut up about it for ages, I remember.

When Daisy had said her piece, Barri moved on around the table. Poor Torquil was savaged over some samples that had gone missing – it was almost certainly not his fault, and they'd been appropriated by some venal journalist – but he blushed a livid shade of puce and sweat broke out on his acned brow, and he looked at the plate of apricot Danishes with a kind of crazed desperation. I made a mental note to take them to the kitchen and throw them away immediately after the meeting in order to save Torquil from himself. When Isla's turn came, she was clearly terrified, stammering and stumbling over her words, but she got off relatively lightly, because, as far as I could tell, every shred of originality had been stripped from her design and it was a bland, slavish reflection of The Brand.

As far as Barri was concerned, I was learning, The Brand was gospel. He held dear to his heart a weighty document (if something which only existed on the company intranet could be said to be weighty – its megapixels were legion, anyway) called the Brand Guidelines, which set out in minute detail what fonts, colours and words were to be used in all company communications. The English language took rather a battering – Barri had apparently declared a unilateral war on the humble comma, and the word 'that' was never to be used. Even the geography of London came under fire in the Brand Guidelines – the street on which the store was located could only be referred to as 'Bond, W1S'. I'd been forced to read the entire tome from cover to cover during my first week, and with every page I'd felt a fresh surge of annoyance at its triviality.

Isla finished speaking, then Piper briefly summed up what she'd been up to the previous week – mostly writing blogs pretending to be fashion models – and then it was my turn.

But Barri said, "That's it for this morning, ladies and gent. Get out there and make the magic happen!" And everyone got up to shuffle back to their desks, limp with relief and exhaustion, although it was only nine in the morning. "Oh, Ellie. A moment, please." And Barri – I'm not making this up – stuck his tongue out of the corner of his mouth, ran a finger theatrically across his throat, and allowed his head to drop dramatically backward. So, I was in for assassination.

Part of me just felt wearied by his histrionics, and conscious of how poor a manager he was to be treating people this way. But mostly, I'm afraid to say, I felt small and scared. Vindictive and petty as I was beginning to realise Barri was, he was my boss and ultimately I needed the job, and everyone wants their employer to think well of them. So I sat back down and pulled my shorthand notebook back towards me, despising myself for the tremor in my hands, smiled brightly and said, "Yes, Barri?"

"What," he hissed, "is this?" And he produced from his powder blue leather Smythson document holder a copy of the previous day's *Sunday Mirror* colour supplement. I realised with a slight sinking feeling that I'd been so busy shagging Peter, then eating pizza in bed with him before dashing home to get a load of washing on and snatch a few hours' sleep, that I'd neglected my usual perusal of the Sunday papers. Barri flipped the magazine open, and there was a six-page spread based on the press release I'd sent out the previous week, all about globalism and ethics in fashion. It looked great – Nadine, the junior fashion assistant who I'd got hold of on the phone and befriended after we'd realised she was going out with James, the guy on their news desk who I used to chat to when I was at YEESH, had really pulled out the stops.

"Wow," I said to Barri. "That's quite a lot of coverage."

"Ellie," he spat, "It's coverage. In. The. *Sunday. Mirror.* Have you not read the Brand Guidelines?"

I felt sick. "Of course I have. There's nothing in them about the *Mirror,* is there?"

Barri smiled a nasty smile. "No," he said, "there isn't. There's also nothing in them about how we don't get graffiti taggers to spray our brand on railway arches, nor have tramps model our clothes when they're dossing in Trafalgar Square, nor employ feral cats to piss our signature scent on walls." All of these struck me as rather innovative ideas with quite a lot of potential, actually, except maybe the one about the cats, which while inspired would be tricky to bring to fruition. But clearly Barri thought otherwise. "I thought I had spelled out in our Brand Guidelines that Black & White is upmarket, Ellie. Was that not clear to you?"

"Of course it was," I said. "But isn't this great publicity? It's worth about fifty grand, in terms of the space."

Barri leaned towards me, so I got a sickening waft of his aftershave, and could see the careful powdering-in of the gaps in his eyebrows. "We're upmarket, Ellie. Up-fucking-market. That means *Vogue*, or *Tatler*, or *Harpers*, or *Elle* at a push. We associate our brand with high-end titles and high-end titles only. Now what I want you to do is stop smearing our image all over the gutter press, only send out releases that have been signed off by me personally, and only send them to approved contacts in approved media – I'll get Torquil to compile a spreadsheet and talk you through it. Now go back to your desk and start making calls to our approved journalists asking them if they are free to attend our polo event in May. You'll report in to Daisy on that one. Clear?"

If Ruth or Duncan had asked me to do something so ridiculously counter-productive, I'd have looked at them and gone, "What?" and we'd have argued the toss until either they came round to my point of view or I understood the method in their madness. But I wasn't sure it would work that way with Barri. To buy myself some time, I carefully wrote on my notebook, "*Vogue, Tatler, Harpers*" then, in brackets, "(*Elle*)." Then, "Polo."

Then I said, in what I hoped was a calm and reasonable tone, "But, Barri, I really feel that…"

"No, Ellie." He held his tiny, manicured hand up in front of my face. "Remember this. The Brand is sacred. We cannot allow our individual egos to interfere with The Brand. And another point. There's a very wise thing I often find myself telling my girlies when they first come on board and do something a little bit off-message, and I feel you might benefit from bearing it in mind."

He had a sickly sweet smile on his face. I bit back my rage and tried to look attentive, and picked up my pen.

"Ellie," he said, "hear this: there is no 'I' in 'Team'."

I looked down at my notebook, and carefully wrote, "There is no 'I' in 'Team'." I looked up at him, smiled nicely and said, "Thanks, Barri, I'll remember that." And, slowly and clearly underneath, I wrote, "But there is a 'U' in 'Cunt'." Then I got up, taking the plate of pastries with me, and went to the kitchen and ate the lot, then was sick and cried in the ladies'.

When I'd finished crying and splashed cold water on my face (why does one bother doing this? It makes no difference at all, except that instead of looking puffy-eyed and blotchy, you look puffy-eyed and blotchy with wet hair), I went back to my desk, attracting various sympathetic and curious looks from my colleagues. When Piper saw me she discreetly slipped a pack of witch hazel eye pads over to me, and then made me a cup of tea, bless her, which of course made me cry again.

I sat hiding behind my monitor, waiting for the lump in my throat to subside and my eyes to stop burning. I was smarting with hurt and injustice, and when Peter sent me a direct message on Facebook at lunchtime asking how my day was going, I couldn't resist pouring out the whole story to him.

"He sounds like a total dick!" Peter typed, loyally.

"He is," I said, beginning to feel a bit better, the way you do when you've offloaded on someone who you feel is well and truly on your side.

"Want me to send the boys round?" said Peter.

"No," I said. "Barri v gay, would love that."

"I see," said Peter. There was a pause, then he said, "Want me to hack into his Grindr profile and edit his personal info to say he is short and fat?"

I giggled in spite of myself. "Good idea," I typed, "Except he is actually short and fat."

"Okay," Peter replied, "in that case we need a better plan. How about…" there was a pause, then I saw him start typing again. "I take you out for cocktails and dinner tonight to cheer you up? Will you feel a bit better after that?"

I thought how lovely he was, and wished I wasn't having increasingly grave misgivings about our relationship – if you could even call it that after two shags (three if you counted round two on Sunday). "It's working already," I typed.

I spent the rest of the day on the phone to Daisy's press contact lists, trying to persuade them that what they really wanted to be doing on a Saturday in May was not enjoying time with their families, mowing the lawn, spending the day in bed with their partners, catching up on work, going to Tesco, or any of the billion other things that normal people do with their weekends, but attending Barri's 'star-studded' polo day, and then writing about it. Needless to say, a lot of them said, "Let me get back to you," and I knew they never would, and I'd have to chase them and chase them and they would end up automatically ignoring my calls and deleting my emails, which would make my job a lot harder when I was trying to get in touch about a story they might actually want to use.

So by the time five thirty came, I had well and truly had enough, and I shut down my computer and picked up my bag and walked out, even though there were only three names on the list left to call and I could easily have got through them before I left. I went to Selfridges, where I found a gorgeous black lace top to go with the grey pencil skirt I'd worn to work (even with my staff discount, I wasn't going to give Black & White and by extension Barri a penny of my hard-earned salary that day), and impulse-bought a cute little T-shirt with a bee on it for Pers and a new Dior nail polish for Rose. Then I put on some red lipstick and went to meet Peter at the Connaught.

Within minutes of walking into the bar, I could feel my shitty day fading into the background. The room was so glamorous and fabulous, I felt pretty fabulous myself in my new top and flattering skirt and shiny lipstick, and Peter let me bitch about my horrible day and made me laugh and bought me a proper grown-up martini with an olive in it. I sipped my drink and looked at his tanned skin and smiley eyes and long legs and all the rest, and tried to feel lucky to be going out with him. But no matter how hard I pushed the part of me that was saying, "If only it were Oliver here, not Peter," deep down inside myself, I couldn't stop hearing it.

I know a lot of men who subscribe to the 'treat them mean, keep them keen' school of thought, and believe that every compliment you give a girl should be sort of countered with a dismissive comment; who'll check out other women in the room on the basis that it's going to make you more anxious to please them; who'll try not to let on that they like you lest you fail to like them back enough and bruise their poor, sorry egos. Peter, bless him, wasn't like that. All through that evening, he told me again and again how beautiful I looked, he laughed at my jokes, he reassured me that everything at work would work out fine, and even if it didn't, it didn't matter because someone as brilliant as I was would find another job just like that, recession or no recession. He bought us another cocktail and dinner in a posh bistro that had loads of vegetarian options on the menu, and by the time we'd finished and he'd insisted on paying the bill and found a taxi with impressive speed and skill, I was feeling so grateful for his niceness, and of course a bit pissed, so I asked him to come back to the flat.

After I'd fumbled my keys out of my bag and opened the front door, Peter lifted me up in his arms and carried me up the stairs to the flat. I can't tell you how many times I've wished that someone would do that to me, but to be totally honest when Peter did it I realised that, although romantic, it is rather over-rated. My head bashed against the ceiling light bulb, he almost tripped over my handbag, and I was worried that he was going to put his back out. So it was a bit of a relief when we got inside and collapsed on the sofa. Peter cupped his hands over my breasts in my new black lace top. "God, you're sexy," he breathed, and I closed my eyes and kissed him again.

"You, too," I lied.

We pulled off our clothes, and I was lying back against the sofa cushions, Peter kissing the inside of my thighs, moving his mouth gradually upwards, when I heard footsteps on the stairs. "Shit!" I pushed him away. "Quick, into my bedroom. Rose is home." We grabbed our clothes off the floor – or most of them, anyway; I found my bra draped over the telly the next day, God only knows how it got there – and legged it into the bedroom, slamming the door behind us just as I heard Rose's key in the lock, and her and Oliver's voices as they entered the flat. I heard Rose say, just as she had the first night I met Oliver, "Whisky, Ollie?" but this time he said no thanks, he was rather tired and would just as soon go straight to bed.

Peter and I were lying on my duvet, giggling at the ridiculousness of the situation. “Come here,” he whispered. “I’m not going to be put off my stroke just because your little sister’s home. I might even like the idea.”

I pushed him gently away. It was no good, I realised – I couldn’t have sex with him, especially not with Rose and Oliver in the next room. It made me feel all knotted up and a bit guilty, as if I was cheating on Oliver by sleeping with Peter, and somehow deceiving Peter too. The idea made me curl in on myself, away from Peter, and I turned over and drew my knees up to my chest, wrapping my arms around my knees.

“I can’t,” I whispered to Peter.

“What do you mean, you can’t?” he said, and I said, “Shhh,” but neither of us laughed.

“I just can’t,” I said softly, “not while Rose and Oliver are next door.”

“But you must have done before.” Peter looked baffled and annoyed.

Well, of course I’d had sex any number of times with Rose asleep – or awake, I have no idea and don’t really care – in her bedroom. But I couldn’t say that to Peter, so I just said again, “Pete, I can’t. I’m sorry. Next time we’ll go back to yours and…”

But Peter was already getting up off the bed and pulling his clothes on. “I think I’ll go back to mine now, actually,” he said, rather huffily, “And please don’t call me Pete,” and of course I said, “Go, then, Pete,” and that was it – our evening together was well and truly spoiled. I got under the duvet and lay there, numb and silent, while Peter finished putting his clothes on and checked his pockets for keys, mobile and so on.

Then he said, "I'll ring you," and walked out.

I turned off the light and lay in the darkness with my eyes closed. It took me a little while to realise that I was straining to hear any sounds coming from the rest of the flat. I thought I could hear the murmur of voices but I wasn't sure. Then, very clearly, came the sound of Rose's bedroom door opening and closing, and then the front door slamming again, considerably harder than it had done when Peter had left.

Puzzled, I got up – I needed to clean my teeth and take my make-up off anyway, I told myself – and walked downstairs to the living room. Rose was on the sofa, her feet curled up underneath her. She was wearing one of the pretty lace camisole and knickers sets she sleeps in, and she was crying.

"Rose?" I said. "What's the matter?"

"Oliver's gone," she said. "He didn't want us to have sex and when I tried to talk about it he walked out."

I sat down next to her, suddenly wanting to laugh. "You're not going to believe this," I said. "Pete – Peter's just stormed out into the night in a massive strop because I wouldn't have sex with him."

Rose looked at me and I looked back at her, and I put my arms around her and felt her delicate shoulder blades under my hands as I have done countless times over the years when I've hugged and comforted my sister while she's cried, and her hair tickled my nose the way it always has, and a tear trickled down her cheek and into my ear, and I shook my head to get rid of it and met her eyes, and we both started to giggle helplessly. We ended up tangled together on the sofa, laughing so much we couldn't stand up, until eventually I calmed down enough to make us a pot of tea and Rose found a box of chocolates one of her admirers had given her, and we had a bit of a midnight feast, and for a while it felt as if we didn't need anyone else as long as we had each other.

Chapter Sixteen

Rose held her long hair in a bundle on top of her head while I pulled the zip up her back, and then let it fall. We stood next to each other in front of the mirror. She was wearing a metallic silver bandage dress, strappy at the top and coming about halfway down her thighs, and on just about anyone else it would have looked tarty and OTT, but Rose was so slim and delicate – even slimmer than usual, I noticed – and her makeup was so subtle, she looked elegant and perfect. I'd borrowed a plain black shift dress from her, and was feeling decidedly smug because I'd never been able to fit into any of Rose's clothes before, but now I could, and I looked pretty good myself.

"Not bad," I said.

"I think we'll do," said Rose, and we picked up our handbags and went downstairs to ring for a taxi.

I don't know what I'd expected Oliver's birthday dinner to be like – when Rose had explained that it was going to be champagne followed by dinner at an Italian restaurant I suppose part of me expected it to be a bunch of mates meeting at a bar somewhere before going on to Pizza Express for some food, like my friends' birthday parties generally are. But then Rose had explained this was an Italian restaurant run by a celebrity chef, with a plate of risotto setting you back forty quid, because it came with shaved white truffles (I checked out the menu online), and all the women would be wearing designer frocks, and Rose had bought Oliver a painting (a painting! My mates were lucky if their girlfriends bought them a bottle of wine and a DVD), so I dashed out and bought him a present too, spending ages trying to choose between dozens of pairs of almost identical, equally expensive pairs of cufflinks. Rose and I had taken two hours to get ready, and she had that nervous, fluttery look about her that made me suspect she was hoping for great things to come of the evening. While we waited for our taxi she changed her shoes from black stilt heels ("I always think black makes you look like you've only got one pair of shoes in the world," she said) to red stilettos, but then those got rejected also ("Too obvious,") in favour of a pair of silver sandals, until she decided they didn't work either ("Too matchy-matchy,") and she went back to the black, which of course had been the right choice all along, and I sat and waited not very patiently while she faffed about. I'd texted Peter the day before, after three days' silence from both of us following our row, and apologised for behaving weirdly, and checked that he was still coming. I was genuinely sorry we'd had a row and I felt bad about hurting him, but also part of me, the shallow, shameful part I'd rather forgetten existed, wanted Oliver to see me with a good looking, suitably smitten boyfriend in tow. So I texted Peter again to make sure that he knew the address and tell him we were going to be late, and at last, when the cab had been waiting almost ten minutes and I was fretting that the driver would get fed up and leave, Rose was ready.

There was something about Rose that evening, I thought as we scrambled into the back of the taxi. She'd lost weight, as I'd noticed when I zipped her into her dress; her slenderness was bordering on fragility, I was worried that she hadn't been eating properly. But she was sparkling with nervous excitement, almost manic with it, opening her bag and checking her face in her compact mirror, applying fresh lipgloss, fiddling with her hair. I wondered what Oliver had done to crack the veneer of indifference that Rose had so carefully preserved over the past few weeks.

"So who else is going to be there tonight?" I asked.

"Well, Ollie, obviously," Rose said, "and us, and Peter, and Ollie's friend Algy from work, and some other colleagues of his, and various art people. Simon and Khalid. Jamie Cunningham."

"Who's he?" I asked. The name was vaguely familiar.

"Honestly, Ellie, do keep up." Rose smiled. "He's an artist. Ollie bought a couple of his paintings recently, and we've got one in the flat – the little drawing on the landing?"

I'm not like Rose – I don't mind art, but I don't particularly notice it either, so I had to close my eyes and mentally transport myself back home so I could picture what she meant. It was a small charcoal sketch of a cat, and I liked it because it reminded me of Winston, Ben's black and white moggie, and every time I looked at it I thought of Ben and that made me happy. I hadn't been looking at it much recently, though.

"Cool," I said. "Is he nice?"

"He's all right," Rose said with careful indifference. "A bit shy. He keeps saying he wants to paint me. I think he'll be out of his depth with Oliver's crowd."

I thought, but didn't say, that I was likely to be out of my depth with Oliver's crowd too, and I was really glad that at least Peter would be there, and he'd talk to me even if none of the bankers and art people did. I thought fleetingly how nice it would be if, instead of being on my way to a smart restaurant where I'd have to be appear my sparkling best and talk to strangers without being gauche and shy, and not embarrass Rose, and impress Oliver, I was on my way to meet Ben or Claire for a pizza. But I swallowed the knot of trepidation in my throat, and said to Rose, "Are you sure I look okay?"

"You look amazing, Ellie," she said. "You always do." But she was anxiously inspecting her own face yet again, so I wasn't sure I could believe her.

"Seymour Street, madam," said the cab driver, and we paid and piled out.

The entrance to the restaurant was almost blocked by a crowd of about fifteen men in jeans and boots and padded jackets, and I thought how odd it was that a group of homeless people would congregate outside an expensive restaurant in Mayfair, and then I noticed that they were festooned with cameras, most bearing long lenses that would probably cost more than our entire dinner.

"Smile!" Rose hissed, as a fusillade of flashbulbs exploded in our faces.

I smiled determinedly, and fought the urge to hoik up my bra strap, which was slipping down my left shoulder, and we made our way to the entrance, looking a lot more poised than I felt.

"Christ," I said to Rose while we waited to be shown to our table, "What was that about? Surely Oliver's not that important?"

Rose laughed. "Not quite," she said, "but Madonna comes here quite often. They were probably hanging out in the hope that she'd appear, and we might do in a pinch."

Rose has had her photo on the diary page of *Hello* a few times, and she pretends it's awkward and embarrassing, but I suspect she's secretly terribly gratified by it. And once when she was in *Tatler* she really struggled to hide her delight, and I found the cutting in the kitchen drawer several months later when I was looking for the Royal Taj Mahal menu, although when I asked her if it was okay to throw it away she acted terribly casual and said yes, of course, she couldn't think how it had got there.

Anyway we made our way to Oliver's table, and there he was, wearing another of his impeccably cut suits, with a shirt in a sort of amethyst colour, open-necked with no tie, and there was a bit of designer stubble on his face, so I supposed he had dressed down for the occasion. I just stood there for a bit, rooted to the floor as they say, and not just by Rose's patent McQueen heels, which were pinching my toes like mad. I was so transfixed by Oliver that I barely noticed Peter standing next to me, holding two glasses of wine.

"Hello, gorgeous," he said. "You look fucking incredible. I incredibly much want to fuck you."

"Shhh," I hissed. "Hi. So glad you could come." I kissed him, aiming for his cheek, but he turned his head strategically so I ended up kissing his mouth.

Comparisons are odious, everyone knows that, and I'm ashamed to say I was odious too, as I weighed Peter up against Oliver and found him wanting. Oliver was so polished, so at home in this environment, among these glossy, important, moneyed people. I tried to kindle the desire I knew I ought to feel for Peter, but it was like trying to light a fag with a lighter that's flint has gone – just a dull scraping, and no spark at all. I couldn't help contrasting his perfectly nice, ordinary suit with Oliver and his friends' designer versions of the same thing; Peter's totally normal short hair with their proper, styled cuts; Peter's sweet, inoffensive Home Counties accent with their cut-glass tones. And when we all sat down for dinner and I found myself sitting on Oliver's left (Rose was on his right), I couldn't stop looking at his hands as he turned the pages of the wine list, listening to his voice as he ordered things without stumbling and faltering over any of the words as I would have done, admiring the slight crookedness of his smile and the huskiness of his laugh, I barely said a word to Peter for about half an hour.

On Oliver's other side, Rose seemed totally preoccupied too. She had her phone out on the table in front of her, and she was tapping it impatiently every now and then, and looking expectantly towards the door. I wondered if she was texting friends, speculating about whether Madonna was going to put in an appearance, but I didn't care much. When I felt a warm hand on my thigh, I almost melted in a puddle of delight, before I realised it was the wrong leg, and the wrong hand.

"Ellie?" Peter said, "Are you okay?"

"What?" I said. "Yes, of course, fine."

He lowered his voice. "I'm not sure I am," he said.

I turned to look at him. His face was furrowed and unhappy, and he looked all stiff and uncomfortable, surrounded by Oliver's laughing friends.

"What's wrong?" I said.

"Ellie, I think you know," he said. "I don't want to cause a scene at your friend's party, but maybe we should go outside and talk."

I pushed back my chair and stood up, ignoring the plate of risotto that had just been put in front of me. "Right," I said.

Outside, the night was warm and there was a thin drizzle falling. I thought how Rose would worry about her hair frizzing in it, and found myself worrying about mine.

"What is it?" I said to Peter.

"I think I may have got things wrong about us," he said. He looked utterly miserable, and a bit angry. "It's early days, but I really like you, and I thought you liked me. But I think there's something going on with you and Oliver, and I'm not comfortable with it."

I looked up at him and fixed a bright, sparkling smile on my face. "What do you mean?" I said. "Oliver's just a friend. He's my sister's boyfriend. I don't know what you're talking about."

But just then Oliver and a couple of his friends – the one called Algy and I think the one called Fabrice – came outside and looked at us, and moved discreetly away before lighting cigarettes, and my eyes were drawn irresistibly to Oliver, so much so that I barely heard what Peter said next.

"Ellie, I'm going to go home. I don't belong here, and you don't want me here."

"What are you talking about?" I said. "Of course I do." I could see Oliver looking in my direction, and I pulled Peter towards me and tried to kiss him, but his body felt cold and stiff, and he moved away.

"Don't patronise me," he said. "I might not have been to university, I might not work for some swanky Square Mile investment bank, but I'm not stupid. You have a think about things. If you change your mind about our relationship, call me, but as far as I'm concerned it's over."

"Pete, I..." I wanted to say, how could it be over – whatever it was, it had surely not even begun. But all I could manage was, "I'm sorry."

"Give this to Oliver," Peter said, pressing something into my hand. And he turned and walked quietly away into the damp night. I watched him for a bit, then went over and chatted to Oliver and his friends, and said that Peter had some work emergency, and it was only when we got back into the restaurant that I realised the warm wad of paper sticking to my palm was eight twenty pound notes, enough to pay for the wine we'd drunk and the food neither of us had eaten.

Raucously, the evening progressed. Oliver moved around the table talking to everyone, and Rose did too, although she seemed totally without sparkle. Algy and Fabrice ordered brandy and more champagne, and after a while Algy moved into Peter's place, and I chatted to him a bit but I couldn't summon up much enthusiasm for it, I couldn't eat anything, and I couldn't stop looking at Oliver on the other side of the table. Then Rose edged over into the empty chair on my right.

"Shall we go?" she said.

"No, no, it's fine," I said, "we can stay." But I was feeling sad and hollow and a bit cold without the glowing flame of Oliver's presence next to me.

"Let's go," said Rose. "You're upset because you and Peter have had a row. Come."

She put on her coat and picked up her bag, and both of us went round the table saying brittle goodbyes to people, and then we were outside again. The clouds had cleared now, and there was a bright new moon overhead. Rose, with the unerring skill she has in this regard, hailed a passing taxi, and held the door open for me.

"Off you go," she said, giving me a quick hug. "Will you be okay? I'm sorry, but I need to be somewhere else."

And she told the driver our address and slammed the door, and I craned my neck round as he was pulling off, to see if she'd gone back into the restaurant, but I couldn't, she'd vanished. When I tried to call her, her phone went straight to voicemail, and so did Peter's.

I said to the taxi driver, "I'm sorry, I've changed my mind. Please could we go the other way, to Highgate?"

It took almost half an hour to get to Peter's flat, but it wasn't long enough for me to decide what to say to him. When I rang his doorbell I was still unsure, and when he opened the door, wearing just a T-shirt and boxer shorts and looking cross and sleepy, I couldn't say anything for a few seconds. Then I sort of gulped, "I'm sorry."

"You'd better come in," he said, and I stepped into the hallway and leaned against the door.

"I won't stay," I said. "I just thought I should say that you're right, this isn't going to work. I've been really unfair to you and I wanted to apologise. I hope we can still be friends."

Peter gave a sort of crooked smile. "It's not me, it's you?" he said.

"That's right." I tried to laugh, and so did he. Then I gave him a hug, and said goodnight. The journey home on the night bus took even longer than it had taken to get there, I was cold and my shoes were mercilessly pinching my feet, but I didn't care – I felt lightheaded with relief.

Chapter Seventeen

"Question seven. Question seven, ladies and gents. The result of the annual prize for the most promising young British portrait painter is due to be announced in one month. Which great English artist does the prize commemorate?"

"Turner?" suggested Alex.

"What? No, you noodle, Turner painted landscapes, and anyway the Turner Prize is announced in March," I said.

"Oh." Alex looked a bit hurt. "It was just a suggestion."

"Well, it was a better idea than I could have come up with – I haven't the foggiest. I could text Rose and ask her? It's bound to be one of the ones whose stuff she values and sells all the time."

"No texting," Alex said. "Things may be bad, but they're not bad enough for us to cheat."

I'd forgotten that Alex shared Ben's ideas about morality and liked to play by the rules – all that sport at university, I supposed. Although if you look at the Pakistanis, maybe it's not such an ethical game after all.

We looked at each other glumly. Without Ben, our pub quiz team was looking rather threadbare. Alex is sound enough on questions about cricket and nature, and of course is the fount of all knowledge when it comes to *Star*

Wars, but there hadn't been any questions about that this week, and my expertise in Renaissance and Restoration drama hadn't been called upon either, funnily enough. We were buggered, and we knew it.

"And now for our music round! I'm going to play you a short burst of six songs, each of which has been covered recently by a contestant on *The X Factor*. Name the original artist and the *X Factor* hopeful, for one point each."

"Fuck," I said. "This isn't going to happen, is it?"

"Nope," said Alex. "I think we can kiss that bottle of cheap Pinot Grigio goodbye this week."

"Pint?"

"Go on."

I made my way to the bar and ordered two Stellas and a packet of peanuts. I'd hoped that the Tuesday traditional quiz night at the Duchess would take my mind off Oliver, and work, and feeling guilty about Peter. But it wasn't working. I felt depressed and preoccupied and I could tell Alex did too, so when I got back to our table and plonked down our drinks, I said, "So. Nina?"

"Ben reckons she's moving in with him," Alex said.

"She's what?"

"Moving into Ben's flat. With the kid."

"But... he's only got one bedroom," I said stupidly.

"Makes no difference to Nina," said Alex.

"Hold on," I said, "I know this track." The wonky sound system in the Duchess was blaring out 'Oooh, you make me live'. "It's Queen, isn't it?"

"Got it!" Alex scrawled on our answer sheet. "It's 'You're My Best Friend'."

"Top man!" I said. "Anyway, where were we?"

"Practicalities have never stopped Nina before," Alex said. "Apparently the kid sleeps in bed with her anyway."

"Eeuuw," I said. I mean, really. Pers sleeps in with Claire, but she's only tiny, and besides, she's gorgeous, not like Nina's horrible offspring. "But he's, like, five or something."

"Six," Alex said. "Ben says Nina believes he'll grow more independent when he's ready."

"Well, I'm sure he will," I said. I'm all in favour of attachment parenting and all that stuff, Claire explained it to me and it makes a lot of sense. "But in the meantime that doesn't exactly help Ben. Or Winston." I'm fiercely protective of Winston, whom I regard as a sort of god-cat (in the sense that I'm his godmother, obviously, like I am Pers's, not in the Ancient Egyptian sense) and he's always slept on Ben's bed.

"What is the common name for the grey, dove-like bird of the species *Cuculidae*?" intoned the quizmaster.

"Hang on," I said, "You know about birds, right? What was that?"

"Easy one, cuckoo," said Alex, and filled it in on our answer sheet. "Anyway, yeah, Nina's not keen on Winston. She reckons his fur aggravates the kid's allergies."

"What?" I fumed. "How dare she? What does Ben say about that?"

"Ben seems to have fuck-all choice in the matter," said Alex. "The little git thinks it's funny to pull his tail, and when he scratched him Nina went mental, and she's talking about getting him rehomed."

"No way!" I said. "Have you told Ben he needs to grow a pair?"

"Haven't had the chance," Alex said, "because he's gone into silent mode again. Not answering calls, not posting on Facebook, nothing. The only reason I know about the kid and the cat is because I turned up on his doorstep and saw the whole thing play out. It was like something out of *Child's Play* or *The Omen.*"

"I can't believe he's letting her do it," I said. "Swan back into his life after all this time and just take over."

"Yeah," Alex said. "But remember, Mum brought Ben and me up on her own after Dad pushed off, and it was really tough for her. Ben's always had a thing about absent fathers."

"And now, a film question." I was interrupted again by the quizmaster's mockney voice blaring out. "There's been a recent surge of interest in the forgotten art of elocution. Which Oscar-winning motion picture is believed to have inspired it?"

"*The King's Speech,*" Alex and I chorussed, and he wrote it down. "Anyway, what's up with Ben and Claire?" I said. "I thought they were seeing each other, and that's why Claire hasn't been in touch for ages. I assumed she was doing that loved-up eye-staring thing with Ben that she did with Ty, and I was leaving them to get on with it."

I knew when I said it that I sounded really resentful, and not happy for Ben and Claire at all. I was, really, it just felt a bit shitty that the two of them, my best friends, had got together and left me out. I should have been happy for them, and I'm sure that given time I would have got over myself and learned to be, but in the meantime I just felt... jealous. There, I said it.

"I honestly haven't a scooby, Ellie," Alex said. "Ben never said anything to me about what was going on with him and Claire, he just mentioned a couple of times when I wanted to meet up that he was busy, and seeing her. But what's with this bloke who changed his Facebook status to 'in a relationship with Ellie Mottram' a few weeks ago, then changed it back to 'single' on Sunday?"

"And now, a biblical question. Which of the twelve apostles mentioned in the New Testament was crucified under the emperor Nero, but at his own request had the cross placed upside down, because he didn't deem himself worthy of the same death as Jesus Christ? Which of the twelve apostles..."

"Peter, wasn't it?" said Alex.

"Of course it was," I said impatiently. "But listen, what the fuck am I supposed to do about Claire?"

Did she know? Had Ben told her? Was Ben seeing Nina behind Claire's back? Was Claire getting involved in some horribly messy menage à trois – or menage à six, I suppose it would be, if you counted Pers, Winston and Nina's ghastly child.

"Where is London's prestigious Guildhall school of music and drama located?"

"Barbican, isn't it?" Alex said, and I agreed, but I had a niggling sense that the question ought to have rung some sort of bell somewhere in my head. Slippery as a freshly-peeled lychee, the thought slid away.

"What is the former name of Hampshire County's cricket ground in Southampton, now known as the Ageas Bowl?"

"One for you, I think," I said.

It was the opening Alex had been looking for. "It's the Rose Bowl," he said, with a smug smile. "Which reminds me – tell me about your gorgeous sister. How is she? Come on, a nice, detailed description of her in her nightie would be great." Alex has had a massive, unrequited crush on Rose for ages.

"Bleurgh, pervert!" I said. "I will not provide you with verbal wank fodder based on my own sister. Now focus, we've a quiz to lose."

"What do the following words have in common: Reed, Stone and Twist?"

"Something about smoking spliffs?" Alex hazarded. "Inhale through a reed and you get stoned, or twisted?"

For God's sake. It was a pub quiz conspiracy. "Oliver," I spat.

The last thing I needed right then was to be reminded of him – but I didn't need to, really, because he was in my head all the time like an annoying, posh, handsome ear worm, interrupting my thoughts and my dreams and making me do little dances on the Tube. However hard I could have tried to make things work with Peter, I would never have felt the kind of dizzy passion I imagined Ben and Claire sharing, or the helpless desire I felt for Oliver.

It was all heinously complicated, like something out of the plot of a Shakespearean comedy, about which I would have been able to answer quiz questions effortlessly, had the uncultured git of a quizmaster bothered to ask any.

"I'll tell you one thing, though," I said to Alex, "Claire's the most gorgeous, fab person in the world, but if Nina's decided she wants Ben back, she's going to get him. It's like she's got some horrible power over him. I bet she keeps bits of his toenails and semen and stuff in a little bottle and dances widdershins around it and does incantations by the full moon."

"Don't!" Alex shuddered. "That's so gross. I don't need to think about my brother's spunk, thanks, never mind Nina harvesting it like something out of *Twilight*."

"Sorry," I said. "Let's talk about something else."

There was a bit of a pause, and then Alex said, "I've been meaning to say, you're looking pretty fit these days. Not that you didn't always, of course."

"Stop! You're only digging yourself deeper." I tried to sound severe, but of course I was quite flattered really.

"And finally, our literature round," said the geezer.

"Go, Ellie!" Alex hooted.

"Which Hans Christian Andersen story inspired the musical 'Honk'?"

"*The Ugly Duckling*," I muttered, and Alex had the grace to look a bit embarrassed.

"In which Shakespearean comedy," there was a chorus of 'awww' from the philistines in the pub, but I went 'yessss!' and did a little air-punch. "In which Shakespearean comedy does the low-born Helena seduce the noble Bertram through trickery?"

"Easy, peasy," I said, "It's *All's Well That Ends Well.*"

"Nice one, Ellie!" Alex said, and we high-fived each other across the table. But it was a lost cause – we only scored seventeen out of a possible forty points.

"When I see Claire on Saturday for Pers's birthday party, I really am going to have to talk to her properly," I said, as we shuffled out into the night, past the triumphant table of eight that had emerged victorious thanks to their superior grasp of the finer points of British art.

"If Ben and Nina end up together, we'll need to find more people for the team," Alex said, adding forlornly, "I don't suppose Rose would come?"

I said, "No chance." Then I saw my bus coming, and made a run for it.

Four days later, I was toiling up the grimy, narrow stairwell that led to Claire's flat, laden with carrier bags from Waitrose and a separate bag of presents. Before I could knock, Claire opened the door, and Pers came running towards me and threw herself against my legs. I picked her up and held her, and then, to my total surprise, I started to cry great splatty tears all over her perfect little head.

"Ellie!" Claire said, "Sweetie, you poor thing. Bloody Peter, the bastard! Shall we sew prawns into the hems of his curtains? Itching powder in his pants? Change the ringtone on his mobile to Pers screaming, and change the password so he can't change it back? Here, come in and sit down."

I carried Pers into the squalid flat and we all plonked down on the sofa, and for a bit I just kind of snivelled, then I managed to compose myself enough to start laughing, and say to Claire, "It's not Peter, not really. It's just that everything's so complicated. And Pers is one year old today, and she's so beautiful, and I love her so much, and I've missed you, and it's all just too much."

Claire said, "Sometimes I cry too, when I've put her to bed and I look at her asleep. Although often that's just relief that she's finally conked out and I can hit the gin."

"So," I said, once I'd more or less composed myself, "what's the plan then?"

"We've got about seven mums and babies coming," Claire said, "and I told them all that if it was a nice day we could meet in the park, and it is, thank God, because having them here would be social death for Pers, almost as bad as going to MacDonalds."

"Really?" I said. "Social death? But she's only one."

Claire looked darkly at me. "You won't believe it," she said. "The pressure's incredible. It's all about opportunity, you see – you might not necessarily want your child to be part of a particular circle, but you've got to put the effort in, otherwise you end up with the unter-mums."

"What do you mean?" I said.

"It varies from place to place," Claire said. "Here in Brixton, the Mummy elite are the attachment-parenting, baby-wearing, demand-feeding, lentil-knittery types, which is great for me because I kind of fit in with that style of doing things myself. A lot of us are single mums, or have partners who work in the media."

"Right," I said, not understanding a word.

"But in some other areas – in fact even a couple of streets down – there's a group of mums who are all Gina Ford-reading, early-weaning types with husbands who work in the city, whose kids are already enrolled in private schools and Mandarin classes. Their children wouldn't give Pers the time of day."

"Little bastards!" I said, enraged on her behalf.

"Ellie, they're only one," Claire said gently. "Anyway, you sort of decide which lot you want to be in, and then you have to go through their initiation rites: afternoons at soft play, baby yoga, playdates in the park, that kind of thing. This is Brixton – it's like wanting to join the Cherry Bloods or the Ghetto Crew, innit?"

"And what happens if you don't get in?" I said, fearing for little Pers's future.

"It doesn't look good for you." Claire sucked her teeth. "Not good at all. Your child doesn't get invited to birthday parties, not even by the children you've invited to yours. Or you invite children to your child's party and they RSVP no, even if it's somewhere really cool like the Science Museum."

"The Science Museum?" I said disbelievingly. "At one?"

"You bet," Claire said. "Pers and I have been to at least one party there, and one at the Natural History Museum, and one on the London Eye. That got a bit messy. But anyway, you don't need to worry about us. We're in the inner circle of the Acre Lane Hippy Mums. You'll meet the bedrin in a few minutes. Come on, let's pack the picnic."

Claire stood up and we went through to the kitchen together, carrying my Waitrose bags, Pers trotting behind us. I noticed that Claire was wearing a new dress, and it looked like it was properly new, not one of the charity shop finds she usually wears, and manages to look amazing in. This was a silk shift, printed in a cubist pattern in turquoise, coral and yellow, and it was gorgeous.

"Love the dress," I said. "The Acre Lane Hippy Mums will have some serious competition come the next election for Alpha Blud."

Claire grinned. "Fab, isn't it? It's only Topshop but it's such ages since I've had anything new, I thought I'd treat myself."

"Now," she said. "Let's see what we've got. Sticks of carrot and celery and cucumber, breadsticks and hummus," she piled Tupperware boxes out of the fridge and into a cooler bag. "Cherry tomatoes and grapes."

"No crisps?" I asked, horrified. "Not even Twiglets?"

"No crisps. Too high in salt, you see. Over on the dark side, at a Gina Ford, married-to-a-banker birthday party, you'd get crisps. Not here. Right. Hard-boiled quails' eggs, little sandwiches with goat's cheese, olives."

"Aren't those massively high in salt too?" I asked.

"Yes, but they're okay. The mums like to say that little Aneurin has loved olives since he was nine months old. Don't look at me like that, Ellie, I don't make the rules."

"I brought loads of champagne," I said humbly, "for the mums, obviously. And some biscuits – they're Duchy Originals, so they should be acceptable."

"Hmmm, a bit of an unknown quantity," Claire said. "We'll risk it, I think. I made flapjack, which is absolutely loaded with sugar of course, but evidently it's fine because oats are good for lactating mums."

"And cake?" I said, "Are they allowed cake?"

"Like, durrr, obviously," Claire said. "Check out the sugar and artificial colouring in this baby." And she whisked the lid off a tin containing the most beautiful rocking horse cake I've ever seen. "And," she whispered, "I've bought her a real rocking horse for her big present. It's so cool, she's going to unwrap it later. There isn't really room for it but we'll be moving soon so it doesn't matter."

Before I had the chance to ask for more details of this intriguing development – Claire's been dying to get out of her horrible flat for absolutely ages, and thought she'd never be able to spare the cash to move – she said, "Right, we must go – it would never do for the birthday girl to be late for her homies."

We packed everything up and Claire hoisted Pers into a new yellow sling that matched her dress, and put on a pair of absolutely beautiful sunglasses that looked new too, and they were either Prada or a seriously impressive knock-off. I picked up the heavy cooler bag in one hand and the picnic basket in the other and we left the flat, just as the downstairs neighbour fired up his first joint of the day and started playing Simply Red at full volume.

I was as desperate for Claire to get out of there and improve her life and Pers's as she was, and it looked as if things were finally turning around for them, with Claire's new clothes and Pers's rocking horse and the talk of moving. Was Ben funding this new lifestyle, I wondered? And if he was, what would happen now that Nina was back, trying to inveigle her way back into Ben's life and his heart with the aid of a child who, although infinitely inferior to

Pers, was Ben's own flesh and blood? You're going to have to talk to her, I told myself. You're going to have to ask what's going on, and tell her about Nina, no matter how hard it is.

But soon we'd arrived at the appointed spot in the park and Claire and I were too busy blowing up balloons (acceptable, in spite of their lack of eco credentials, apparently, as long as they were not the foil sort and blown up by the old-fashioned puffing method rather than using a helium canister) and spreading out picnic blankets and arranging food on plates (biodegradable ones made from sugar cane leaves) and trying to control a frantically over-excited Pers, to really chat. And then the friends started turning up – Ty with Olya; Abi and her daughter Calypso; Laura and her daughter Marina; Sally and her son Fabian; Cathy and her twins Harry and Hero; a little boy called Iskandar and his sister Zelide, accompanied by a gorgeous bloke called Ewan who was either their gay dad or their male nanny; Fran and her baby Zen, who was apparently being reared as gender neutral, and no one except Fran and her partner was allowed to know whether Zen was a boy or a girl. This pretty much silenced me for a while – I knew exactly what I wanted to say, of course, but knew it would result in Claire's expulsion from the inner circle of the Acre Lane Hippy Mums and social death for Pers, so I sat down on the grass and sipped my champagne and nibbled on some bizarre crunchy snacks made of dehydrated carrot and looked at the babies and their mothers.

It was so strange, I thought, that just a year or so ago none of these women had even met the people they now knew best in all the world. That's how it was with Claire and Pers, anyway. When she first brought Pers home Claire had literally taken to her bed for a week and cried and breastfed solidly, saying that she was never going to get her figure back or ever get a good night's sleep again or have a social life, and in between wailing and lamenting about all that, she sobbed about how she loved Pers so much she just wanted to lick her, and how could she ever be a good enough mother to this most precious and remarkable child. But within about three weeks, Claire had been changing nappies with one hand and happily breastfeeding Pers everywhere, even on the Tube, and identifying whether her crying meant she was hungry, or bored, or tired, or just wanted a cuddle. I wondered whether, if I ever had a baby of my own, I'd take to motherhood with the same ease. Somehow I couldn't see it happening, but it does seem to happen to most women, even those as patently underqualified for the job as I am.

I wondered what it was like for Ben, being presented with a child he hadn't even known existed for five years, and suddenly being expected to love it with the same intensity with which Claire, and to a much lesser extent I, loved Pers. I remembered what Oliver had said about the little boy he used to take to feed the ducks, and wondered what had happened to make him so sad. And I wondered about Nina. What could possibly have possessed her to deprive Ben of the chance to get to know his son for all those precious years, and deprive little Benedict of his dad? And I wouldn't have thought it possible, but I hated her even more than I had before.

By the time everyone had had some food and Pers had opened her presents – showing, of course, far more interest in the wrapping paper (recycled brown, tied with string) than she did in the presents, and the cake had been cut and some of it eaten, it was threatening to rain and most of the babies were threatening an afternoon meltdown, so everything got packed away again and we said goodbye to Claire and Pers's friends, and carried everything back up to Claire's flat and put it away. Then Claire got out Pers's rocking horse and she simply crowed with joy, bouncing up and down and laughing like mad. Then after she'd had her bath, when she was all dopey and grumpy and plainly ready for bed, Claire read her her story and she curled up in a ball and put her thumb in her mouth and she said, although it was a bit muffled obviously, "Rocking horse." Claire and I looked at each other, transfixed by her brilliance, and went, "Yes, darling, you have a rocking horse!" like a pair of hothousing loons, but Pers wasn't anything like as impressed by her precocity as we were, and she squirmed around a bit, getting comfortable, and then took her thumb out with a popping sound and said, "Angeruck." Claire said, "She wants her Camelduck!" and dashed off and got it for her, and we watched her fall asleep, clutching her silly knitted familiar, her long black eyelashes curled over her flawless cappuccino-coloured cheeks. Claire and I spent ages talking about her and her future, and then I told her a bit about what had happened with me and Peter, and by then it was half past eleven and Claire was yawning and looking discreetly at her watch, so I said I'd better go, even though we hadn't said anything about Nina or Ben.

Chapter Eighteen

"Ellie, have you updated the invite spreadsheet?"

"Ellie, have the caterers got back to you?"

"Ellie, have the Pimms people agreed to sponsor our welcome drinks?"

"Ellie, have you secured an interview in the *Evening Standard* with Diego Mendoza?"

"Ellie, have the Beckhams RSVPed?"

On and on and on Daisy went. It was relentless. I've always hated arranging events and this reminded me why. Until I came along Daisy had been the new girl, and she was clearly relishing the opportunity to throw her weight around a bit, which to be honest I could understand. Still, I was senior to her in every regard bar actual length of tenure, and her incessant demands for 'help', which actually meant me doing all the dull, impossible or generally shitty parts of the organisation of the hallowed Black & White polo day were really starting to piss me off. But without actually uttering the forbidden phrase "It's not my job," there was absolutely nothing I could do. And if I had downed tools and told her that I was supposed to be in charge of communications and not some glorified party planner, she would have been in Barri's office complaining about me faster than you could say 'bad attitude', so I just had to suck it up.

Every night for two weeks I was stuck in the office until stupid o'clock, putting invitations into envelopes, proof-reading menus, comparing samples of black and white ribbon, rejecting florists' designs on the basis that the flowers were insufficiently black and white. I wanted to scream, "There are no black flowers! And none of the ones that are white are truly white! What planet are you living on?" But I was stuck. Barri's intervention over my press release had ensured that the only thing my job involved was turning down image requests from publications that Barri felt didn't reflect our brand values, so I couldn't even claim that I didn't have time to play assistant to Daisy. And to add insult to injury, she kept me too busy even to comb the appointments section of the *Guardian* website and look for another job.

As the day of the polo tournament drew nearer, both Daisy and Barri became increasingly histrionic. Nothing was good enough. The guest list was insufficiently star-studded. The caterers were too expensive. The journalists who said they'd attend the 'exclusive' Black & White afterparty were too junior. The cocktails weren't exotic enough (Pimms said no in the end and Sainsbury's own-brand equivalent was deemed too downmarket, so we decided to offer a choice of White Russians and black coffee martinis, and I have to say that when I tried them at the official menu tasting, they were both absolutely disgusting). Fed up didn't begin to describe my state of mind by the time the big day dawned. My social life had been shelved; I'd barely seen Rose, been too preoccupied to devote any thought to the Ben and Nina situation, and when Claire asked me on Facebook how Peter was doing, I replied, "Who?"

Daisy and I travelled out to Berkshire to The Venue the day before The Event. I'd tried to subtly suggest that I might spend the night down the road at Dad and Serena's, now that she was home from hospital but still confined to bed, but this was met with a steely refusal from Barri and some more dark mutterings about Teamwork. So we ended up in a horrible corporate hotel, not that it mattered much, because we were too busy finalising the seating plan and assembling goodie bags (one box Black & White chocolate truffles, one little bottle Black & White signature scent, one rather tacky crystal-encrusted keyring from a jewellery supplier, one 'limited edition' half-bottle of Black & White house champagne… you get the idea). Except I ended up doing most of this myself, as Daisy announced at six thirty that she had an appointment at the hotel's spa to have her nails and eyebrows done. "I am hosting the event, so it's essential I look my best," she said, in tones implying that as a mere flunky, it didn't matter what I looked like, and in any case I was beyond help.

Despite what Daisy thought, I was aware that I'd be spending the day mingling with our glamorous guest list (a total of 150 journalists, minor celebrities and 'socialites', several of whose names I recognised from Rose's dinner parties). I set my alarm clock for half past five so that I'd have time to do my own nails, straighten my hair and put on a face-full of slap before convening with her at seven as arranged. The early start meant I'd look like death by the end of the day, but I supposed everyone else would too, thanks to the free cocktails and the sun, which was already blazing down. I put on the pink dress I'd bought with Vanessa, and in a nod to corporatism, black and white spotty sling-back wedges with a bow. They were as high as hell, and I knew I'd regret the decision to wear them, but I didn't want to let the side down.

When I saw Daisy, I realised that my choice of outfit was both stylish and relatively practical. I don't know what had been going through her shallow, ambitious little mind underneath the cropped platinum hair, but she'd elected to wear an extremely short, extremely tight white dress and gold stilettos that would sink into the grass and leave her unable to move, which would be no bad thing for me. She was also wearing knickers with orange butterflies on them – I could see them quite clearly through the dress. Furthermore, there was a long, pale streak down the back of her right thigh where she'd missed a bit while applying her fake tan. I didn't point this out to her though – call me a bitch, but I'd really had enough of her by that point.

We piled ourselves and the various boxes containing our place-cards, menus, goodie bags and all the rest into a taxi and set off. Daisy was frantically tapping away on her BlackBerry trying to look busy and efficient, but when I sneaked a glance over her shoulder I could see that she was texting her mates, egging them on to turn up towards mid-afternoon and avail themselves of some free food and drink.

"Now, Ellie," Daisy said in the annoying mistress-to-minion tone she had taken to adopting with me, "when we get there I need you to get straight on with laying out the stationery and gift bags on the tables. The florist will be there already, but you need to make sure that everything is placed correctly, according to the plan I gave you yesterday. You did print it out, right?"

"Of course," I lied.

"Now the gates open at ten, so we'll expect our guests to start arriving any time from then onwards. They'll be served white peach Bellinis or tea and coffee with pastries – make sure the caterers don't make the Bellinis too strong, we've only budgeted for two dozen bottles at that stage. After the first match, lunch will be served, then the main match begins at three. Make sure you are on hand throughout to mingle with the guests and answer any questions."

"Yes, Daisy," I said through gritted teeth. This was about the fifteenth time she had told me all this, and since I was the one who'd written the copy for the itineraries that were going to be displayed on all the tables, and printed them out, and mounted them in white cardboard folders and tied black ribbons around them, you'd think she would realise I could recite it in my sleep. But she was in full flow.

"Cucumber coolers will be served throughout the afternoon – and remember we had to fork out for real Pimms, so make sure they're heavy on the lemonade – together with red and white wine and sparkling water. Then we're serving more champagne with tea and cake at five, then cocktails will be served as the evening function kicks off at half six, and we're expecting it to finish at about eleven. Then you're free to go. Clear?"

"Yes, Daisy," I said.

"Now, I will be making sure our celebrity guests have everything they need, and I will need you to focus on the corporate tables." Typical Daisy, I thought – she was probably hoping to get off with some former boy-band star, or claim a supermodel as her new best friend. "There're the boys from McCarthy Robinson – bankers always know how to party – and the Rawlinson lot..." on and on she went. I managed to tune her out, and looked out of the window at the lovely green English countryside sparkling in the early morning sun. It felt like ages since I'd seen daylight.

"Here we are," Daisy said unnecessarily, as the taxi crunched on to a smooth gravel driveway.

I don't want to exaggerate, but the next two hours were purest hell. The marquee company had turned up late, which had had a knock-on effect on the furniture hire company, who had only just finished assembling the tables and arranging the chairs around them when we arrived, and still had to swathe each of the 150 seats in white covers and tie them with black chiffon ties. And until they'd done that, the florists couldn't do their thing because they'd be in the way, so they were standing around drinking coffee. The mobile mixology people claimed that there was a national shortage of cucumber, so people were going to have to be limited to one wedge per glass of weak Pimms. The caterers claimed the same, and said they'd had to replace the cucumber sandwiches with watercress, which meant the menus were all wrong. Plus they'd somehow managed to mislay a gross of avocado and crayfish tartlets, and had dispatched their most junior skivvy back to their HQ to rustle up a substitute, which meant that they were running behind on getting the breakfast pastries arranged on their platters. And Daisy discovered, as I could have warned her she would, that her heels immediately sank into the grass, severely limiting her mobility, so she was forced to stand in one place bashing out texts on her BlackBerry and shouting at everyone.

Eventually, against all the odds, the marquee was ready, and I must say it did look lovely. The tall vases of black and white calla lilies (the black ones were really a sort of dark maroon, of course, but they did look very nearly black, especially as the light wasn't very good), the snowy tablecloths laden with sparkling cutlery and glasses, the buffet table groaning with breakfast pastries – it was all really impressive, like a posh wedding. Even Daisy seemed satisfied.

"We've just got time for a coffee," she said, "Then we'll need to be on hand to greet our guests."

"Black or white?" asked a waitress, wielding a coffee pot, and I can honestly say I never wanted to hear those words again as long as I lived.

In due course the VIPs started parading in, the women in crotch-skimming skirts and high heels – Daisy's choice of outfit wasn't as outlandish as I had thought – the men in loud blazers and flannel trousers, and everyone in designer sunglasses. I stood at the entrance to the marquee with a smile fixed to my face, going, "Hello, so glad you could come, please help yourself to tea and coffee. Welcome, please help yourself to tea and coffee," on and on.

Then one of the loud-blazered men paused in front of me, took off his Bulgari shades and said, "There you are, Ellie!"

It was Oliver. "What are you doing here?" I stammered. "You aren't on the guest list."

"No, I'm not," he said. "But my mate Algie is, and when I heard you were going to be here I persuaded him that he had better things to do on a lovely sunny day like this. Will you let me in anyway?"

Of course I said yes, and went dashing off and found Algernon Stoke-Pemberton's place card and switched it with a hand-written one with Oliver's name on it, and he introduced me to a few of his banker friends, but we couldn't really chat because Daisy texted me and told me that Bliss Newham wanted Vitamin Water, and what Bliss wanted Bliss must have, so I rushed off to find some. Bliss, of course, was one of our VIP guests, and since she'd appeared on the front cover of US Vogue the previous month, and we were hoping to get her for our Autumn/Winter campaign, she needed to be kept sweet. As well as being extremely beautiful, with enormous turquoise eyes and black hair that she wore with the sort of brutally short fringe only those with perfect bone structure can carry off, she was known for being 'somewhat temperamental'. This of course was a polite way of saying that she was an absolute bitch, and when I returned with the hard-won Vitamin Water (none of the stalls around the polo ground sold it, and I'd been about to get into a taxi and travel the eight miles to the nearest Tesco Express to buy some, when I'd spotted a family unpacking their picnic, and lo and behold, it included several bottles of Vitamin Water, and I persuaded them to sell me one for a tenner. Cheap at the price, I thought, remembering to ask for a receipt to add to my growing folder of expenses) she told me it was the wrong flavour, and she'd just have a small glass of champagne instead.

By this time our marquee was heaving with VIP guests, all talking in loud voices and braying with laughter, and with the first polo match about to start, Daisy and I were faced with the task of herding them all outside, which we did. I don't know if you've ever watched a polo match. I hadn't, and I'd sort of assumed it would all be posh boys on horses cantering aimlessly about, a bit like fox-hunting only with a ball instead of a fox. I was broadly opposed to the idea in principle, both because it didn't strike me as a particularly egalitarian sort of sport, and because I'm uncomfortable with using animals in that way. But nothing could have prepared me for the speed and downright violence of the game. The poor horses were galloped furiously from one end of the pitch to the other, looking really tiny underneath the huge, heavily padded men who rode them, forced to crash into each other, their heads pulled around by vicious-looking bits and cruel spurs thumping into their sides. I stood and watched, feeling sick with revulsion and tension – but I couldn't tear my eyes away. Although every part of me thought how wrong and terrible it was, I was nonetheless captivated by the speed and excitement of it, even though I hadn't a clue about the rules and I couldn't really figure out what was going on or who was winning. I'm like that with sport generally, I'm afraid – Ben once tried to explain the offside rule to me and after about ten seconds I glazed over, and to this day I couldn't tell you what it is.

Most of the horses were various shades of brown – bay and chestnut, I suppose you'd call them – but there was one little grey one, even smaller than the others, that seemed to almost fly as its rider urged it after the ball.

"The field is six hundred feet long," said a voice next to me, "and they'll often gallop the entire length of it at forty miles per hour, several times in each chukka. That's why they have so many horses – they have to change them often, it's exhausting for them."

I looked around and saw Oliver next to me, and realised that I had been frantically clutching his duck-egg blue and magenta-striped arm. I loosened my hand with difficulty, and moved away, leaving a sweaty patch on his sleeve.

"Isn't it awfully cruel to the horses?" I said.

He shrugged. "Hard to say. It's better than it was – you used to see really excessive whipping and use of spurs but it's more tightly regulated now. It certainly isn't a game for wimps, human or equine."

I winced and grabbed his arm again as a huge brown horse crashed into the small grey one, sending its rider flying. "Jesus!" I gasped.

Oliver laughed. "This is just the warm-up game, the one this afternoon will be much faster and harder. Polo ponies are valuable animals – the riders don't take stupid risks with them."

"They look like pretty stupid risks to me," I said. "Do you play?"

"Can't," he said, "I'm left-handed and you have to be right-handed to play polo. If you had some clown like me waving a mallet around on the wrong side, it really would be dangerous." He grinned at me. "I hunt, though. Foxes, not just beautiful women."

"Oh, for god's sake," I snapped. "Could you be any more of a cliché?" But I smiled, and couldn't help feeling a spark of desire ignite inside me at the compliment, and the way he'd said 'faster and harder' had left me slightly breathless, as if I'd been doing the galloping. Behind my sunglasses, I stole a long look at him. Even in the ridiculous blazer, he was gorgeous – his lightly tanned skin, the long fingers holding his glass of champagne, the soft wing of hair falling over his forehead.

"You don't have a drink," Oliver said, "Can I get you anything?"

"I'm working," I reminded him. "I'd better go and chivvy the caterers – we're meant to be serving lunch in half an hour. I'm just the help here, remember, not an honoured guest like you."

"Promise you'll watch the match with me this afternoon," Oliver said. "By then everyone will be too pissed to care if you've deserted your post."

I looked around for Daisy, and saw that she was being chatted up by a spotty boy whose band had reached the *X Factor* finals – Daffyd Someone, I think his name was.

Anyway he was the crush du jour of women under twenty-five up and down the country, and I figured Daisy would be properly distracted for the next while.

"Maybe," I said. "I'll get back to you."

Thankfully the caterers seemed to have got their act together after their earlier blip, and were marshalling trays of tartlets, carving great lumps of rare beef and assembling rather twee nouvelle-cuisine style vegetables. There's something about the sight of a little bundle of carrot sticks tied together with a chive that always makes me imagine the cook biting off any rogue overlong ones, and the idea makes me feel slightly queasy. Anyway, they could bite away as far as I was concerned, as long as everything made it on to the tables on time. Not that much of it was likely to get eaten; very few of our guests looked like they'd had a square meal in several months.

On a sudden whim, I found my placecard at the table with our jewellery sponsors, the drinks people and a couple of the Black & White directors, and I found Daisy's, which was at the table next to Oliver's, and I swapped them around. Daffyd Whatsisname was at the table next to the dull corporate one where I'd originally been sitting, so I told myself I was doing her a favour. Then I brushed my hair and dusted on some face powder and bronzer and slicked a coat of coral gloss on my lips, and went to the bar and claimed a glass of champagne. After all, looking after the VIPs was work, and Oliver was a VIP, so I wasn't neglecting my duties in any meaningful way at all.

We spent the rest of the day together. When a plate of roast beef was plonked down in front of me, Oliver came over all authoritative and got the waitress to bring me a chicory Wellington instead. When Bliss Newham was spotted heading out of the Portaloos with a suspicious smear of white powder on her perfect, curling upper lip, Oliver distracted the paparazzi by pointing out that Daffyd and Daisy had disappeared together behind what he told me were called the pony lines. When the afternoon polo match got too hardcore for me to bear to watch, Oliver took me off for a wander round the grounds. And when the trophies had been presented to the winning team and the sun was sinking behind the polo field, the VIPs started stampeding back into the marquee for cocktails and yet more food, and the DJ fired up his decks, Oliver took me in his arms and said, "Please will you dance with me?"

"I don't dance," I said, elbowing him away. "Besides, I'm working."

The truth was, though, there was very little for me to do. I checked that the cocktail people had everything they needed, made sure the caterers were on track to produce sausages, fried onions and crusty rolls at nine thirty, instructed the DJ that he must wrap up by eleven, without fail, no matter what anyone said, because this was the countryside and we wouldn't be forgiven if the neighbouring sheep failed to get their beauty sleep. Then I checked my face and brushed my hair yet again. Thanks to some magic undercoat stuff I'd found in Rose's makeup drawer, my foundation was still in place and my eyeliner unsmudged. I looked poised and glossy, and even, in my pink dress, a bit glamorous. So I went back into the marquee and found Oliver, who had returned to his table and was drinking champagne, surrounded by his mates. I sort of hovered on the periphery, feeling like the fat girl at a school dance. But as soon as he saw me he stood up.

"Right," he said, "I'm leaving you lot to it and taking Ellie outside to look at the moon." And he grabbed a bottle of Black & White sparkling wine and two glasses in one hand and me in the other, and the next thing I knew we were outside the marquee in the warm and silent night.

"So are you still working?" Oliver asked, "Or have you stopped, and can you play?"

"I'm still working," I said. "Officially I'm on duty until eleven – that's more than two hours still to go. And when I've finished I expect I'll be too tired for anything except sleep."

"Pity," Oliver said, picking up a strand of my hair and twisting it around his fingers. "This is far too lovely a night to work. But I'm your guest, and a very important and demanding one, so I think you'll have to entertain me for a bit."

I laughed. "What kind of entertainment would you like? I can't do magic tricks or stand-up comedy or the dance of the seven veils, I'm afraid. I can recite the whole of Oscar Wilde's *Ballad of Reading Gaol*, but I think that might get a bit dull after ten stanzas or so."

"I can do magic tricks," Oliver said. He took a pound coin out of his pocket. "Here – when I count to three, grab the coin out of my hand."

He was as eager as a little boy, and I realised he was a bit drunk, so I played along.

"Okay, go on," I said.

He waved the coin around a bit, going, "One… two… three…" and of course when he got to three and I made a grab for the coin it had vanished.

"Impressive," I said.

"I'm not done yet," Oliver said. "Hold out your hand." I did, and the coin dropped from nowhere into my palm.

"How did you do that?" I asked, laughing.

"I'm a banker," Oliver said. "Moving money from place to place is what I do best."

"I know it's vulgar to ask," I said, "but are you incredibly rich?"

"Incredibly," Oliver said. "But not as rich as I'm going to be."

"Why?" I asked. "Are you plotting some evil scheme involving shattering the economy of third-world countries and sending commodities prices spiralling and making your fortune out of world famine, the way bankers do in books?"

Oliver laughed. "We're not that cool in real life," he said. "I'm going to get richer because that's what I do. I like money. I like manipulating it, and I like how it allows me to manipulate the world."

"Okay, now you sound like a Bond villain," I said.

Oliver put on a cod Russian accent and said, "Good evening, Ms Mottram. We've been expecting you."

I was just about to launch into a spiel about how that line doesn't actually appear in any of the films – a little gem of trivia I learned from Ben, who is a bit of a cinema nerd. But I didn't say anything in the end, because that was when Oliver kissed me.

The kiss seemed to go on for a long, long time, and everything about it was perfect: the still, moonlit night, the music drifting out from the marquee, the scent of crushed grass that still lingered around the polo field. Oliver himself was perfect too – his kiss had a breathless urgency that infected me, so I kissed him back just as fiercely, tangling my fingers in his soft black hair as I'd dreamed of doing for so many months, feeling the hard length of his entire body pressed up against mine, smelling the trace of some sort of aftershave or cologne or something on his skin – it smelled a bit of lime and a bit of leather and totally of Oliver, and left me reeling with desire.

Wanting to savour every moment, I opened my eyes, and saw that Oliver's eyes were open too, and we laughed and moved apart, suddenly awkward. I heard a sort of click in Oliver's throat as he swallowed, and there was a catch in his voice that I'd never heard before when he said, "Will you come home with me?"

I thought about my bag back at the hotel, and about all the sorting out and clearing up we'd need to do the next day, and the taxi that was booked to pick Daisy and me up at the end of the night – all the boring, practical reasons why I couldn't possibly say yes. I carefully didn't think about any of the other reasons, the real ones. And then I said, "Yes."

Chapter Nineteen

Oliver immediately became brisk and matter-of-fact. "Right," he said. "I'll ring my driver and tell him I'm ready for him. You collect your things and tell your colleague you've made other arrangements – although it looked as if she has, too. Don't worry about getting back here in the morning, Elliot, my chap, will take you."

I did as I was told. At that moment Oliver could probably have told me to jump off a cliff, or read a Jeffrey Archer novel, and I would have done it, such was the force of my longing for him. Feeling sick and trembly with nerves and desire, I ran to fetch my bag, checked that nothing disastrous was happening in the Black & White marquee and sent Daisy a text telling her I was going to spend the night at Dad's. Oliver was waiting for me outside when I emerged, and he took my hand and said, "Come on."

He opened the car door for me, and once he'd got in the other side he put his arm around my shoulders. The leather seats were slippery and squashy, and smelled of wealth and newness. I can't remember much of the journey – the car swished along empty lanes, and I got occasional glimpses of fields and trees and huge, ramparted gates – country stuff. We purred smoothly through the night, and I thought inconsequentially of the classic bit of copywriting from the 1950s, saying that the loudest noise in a Rolls Royce is the ticking of its clock. Oliver's car didn't have a ticking clock, but it was silent just the same. I didn't say anything and nor did Oliver. He held my hand, moving his fingers softly over my skin, stroking my palm and my wrist until I was almost writhing with lust.

"Here we are," he said at last, as the car's headlights illuminated the stone facade of the house. I remembered Oliver saying that it had been his grandmother's and he couldn't bear to sell it, but he hadn't mentioned that it was almost a mansion.

Oliver got out, and I waited for him to walk round and open my door for me, because I knew that was what he expected me to do. I thought, I must remember every second of tonight. I've longed and longed for this and now it's going to happen. Then I thought, shit, I've been standing all day and it's hot, I really hope my feet don't smell. What if he's a foot man? And what if he's a leg man? I'll disappoint him for sure. Then he opened the door, and took my hand again as I stepped out of the car.

"Thanks, Elliot," Oliver said to the driver. "Have a good night."

I hoped he wouldn't say something cringy and cheesy like, "Welcome to my humble abode," but he simply walked up to the front door and unlocked it, and said, "Come in."

The house was massive. Properly huge, and there were beautiful pictures on the walls, old ones in gold frames with dark varnish covering the paint and giving it that dark, glowy look, and modern ones in brilliant colours. My heels rang on the stone floor, before being muffled by a thick Oriental rug.

Oliver said, "Are you hungry? I'm sure you've barely eaten today, you've been working so hard. Or I could open some wine?"

I couldn't have eaten if you'd paid me, my throat was all closed up with tension, but I'd stuck to fizzy water almost all day, and realised I really, really wanted a drink. So I said that would be lovely, and then, feeling desperately shy, I said, "And where's the loo?"

Oliver laughed and said, "Come upstairs, I'll show you where everything is."

I could believe that the house had been Oliver's grandmother's – it clearly hadn't had anything new added to it for ages. The furniture, wallpaper and curtains were old and all their colours had faded to delicate, dusty shades of rose, jade and gold. On the landing we passed a chaise-longue with a massive tear in the seat, its stuffing oozing out. There were paintings everywhere – hanging on the walls, of course, but also propped up against them, some stacked three or four deep. And there was that smell old houses have, of dusty books and potpourri that dried out years ago, and a hint of damp. It was beautiful but it felt a bit sad, and frankly looked like it needed a good clean, especially the bathroom Oliver showed me to, which had suspicious stains in the bowl of the loo that might have been limescale or might not, peeling paint on the walls and only one scratchy, threadbare towel. I cleaned myself up as best I could, brushed my hair and put on more lip gloss, then went to find Oliver, leaving the plumbing clanking thunderously behind me.

He was in his bedroom, the one room in the house that appeared to have had anything done to it during the past hundred years or so. It was an island of bright newness in the shabby, neglected house. The floorboards had been polished, the wallpaper stripped away and the walls painted white. The bed was white too, covered in a think duvet like a cloud, and there was a huge painting hanging above it of a naked couple. It was quite modernist, all in shades of blue, and the proportions of the man and the woman were distorted, with her eyes located somewhere under her armpit and his feet for some reason enlarged to massive proportions, but I could still tell that they were enjoying sexual intercourse in the position which I believe is known as the reverse cowgirl. In front of the bed was a white sheepskin rug, and Oliver was sitting on it, drinking champagne, his legs stretched out in front of him. I joined him.

"What do you think of my Cunningham?" he asked.

"What?" I asked, wondering if this was some obscure reference to seventeenth-century erotic literature. "Your cunning what?"

"Jamie Cunningham." Oliver gestured to the painting above the bed. "Rose found that for me. Cunningham's not well known but he's going to be the next Marcus Brand. That painting was only finished two years ago, when he was experimenting with cubism, but it's already quadrupled in value. Although mostly I just like the subject matter." He handed me a glass of champagne.

I don't know if it was the mention of Rose, the stark, almost obscene eroticism of the painting, or Oliver himself, but the desire I'd felt for him was dwindling and I was uncomfortable and even a bit scared.

"What's wrong with his foot?" I asked.

Oliver laughed. "He must go through a hell of a lot of socks," he said. We were silent for a little while. I could hear the champagne fizzing in my glass and the sounds of a country night that are so soft they're almost silence: the hoot of an owl, the swish of a car passing on a distant road somewhere. "So, Elodie, here we are."

"Here we are," I said. I turned to look at him again, waiting for the familiar surge of desire his perfect profile and silky hair could ignite in me.

He pulled me towards him and kissed me, his lips pressing mine against my teeth with an intensity that was almost savage. His hands were moving over my body, eager and demanding, one squeezing my breast, pinching my nipple through my dress and bra so I gasped with pain and pleasure, the other snaking up my thigh. I heard the rasp of the zip of my dress being pulled down, and felt the sudden coolness of the air on my back, then Oliver's warm, dry hand moving over my skin. He pushed me gently back on to the rug and my head sank into the soft fleece. I felt a forest of goosebumps sprouting on my arms and legs. Oliver knelt between my legs, exploring my body, smiling down at me. I closed my eyes, and wished I could close my mind too, to the little voice that was getting louder all the time, demanding to know what the very fuck I thought I was doing.

"Look at you. You're lovely," he said.

I heard the rattle of buttons as he threw his shirt on to the wooden floor, and the metallic sound of his trouser zip, and my eyes snapped open again. Oliver was beautiful, as beautiful as I'd imagined him, his skin pale and smooth and flawless, stretched over a body so lean it was almost gaunt. He was staring at me so intently, his gaze felt as hot and demanding as hands. "Gorgeous girl," he said.

"I've wanted you for so long. I want to give you so much pleasure. You're the sexiest thing I've ever seen." He leaned over to kiss me again.

The voice was clamouring now, almost screaming in my head, "Does he say that to Rose? Surely there can only be one sexiest thing?" And that was it, like pulling the plug out of a sinkful of soapy water, my desire drained away, and I could see the detritus it had been hiding: that Oliver was cheating on Rose; that I was betraying my own sister; how horribly I'd used poor Peter and most of all, how disgusted Ben would be if he knew what I was doing.

"Oliver," I gasped, "Stop."

His face above me was flushed and bewildered. "What?" he said.

"Please, stop," I said. "I'm really sorry. But I can't do this."

"What's wrong?" he said, "Are you on your period? I don't mind, we can still…"

In spite of myself, I burst out laughing. "No. I'm not. I just don't want to carry on. It's not right."

"Jesus." He rolled over and found his jacket, where he'd thrown it on the floor, took a pack of fags out of the pocket, lit one and offered it to me. I shook my head.

"Jesus," he said again. "You might have said so earlier. This is going to bloody hurt." He gestured towards his still impressive erection.

"Sorry," I said, humbly.

"Do you mind staying here?" he asked. "Elliot's gone off for the night and I'm in no state to drive. I could ring for a cab for you but I doubt we'd get one to come out here at this time of night."

"It's okay," I said. "I'm sure you won't come and molest me in the night."

"You don't need to worry about that," he said. There was a pause, then he said, "You know, you've changed since I first met you."

"I know," I said, thinking of all those plates of salad and bowls of porridge, all the runs and the spin classes, the new clothes and the manicures.

"Not just the way you look," he said. "Everything. You were different from the other women I know. Less shallow. Softer."

"I suppose so," I said.

"I fancied you like crazy the first time I met you," he said.

"Really?" I remembered my ancient jeggings and shapeless hair.

"Sure. You seemed so passionate about things, so comfortable in your own skin. You were beautiful without trying. You're still beautiful, but now you're putting the effort in, and it makes you less... individual, I guess. Since you're not going to fuck me, I may as well tell you." He laughed.

I shrugged. "I suppose I needed to grow up a bit."

Oliver ground out his cigarette and lit another one. "You can still change your mind, you know," he said. "But you're not going to get another chance, after this."

"Why?" I asked.

"Because I've asked Rose to marry me," he said.

Oliver kept his word, and I slept unmolested in one of the spare bedrooms. Except I didn't sleep – I lay between the slightly damp-feeling sheets, turning over and over from my back to my side to my stomach to my other side to my back again, like a chicken on a spit. I tried to soothe myself to sleep in all the usual ways – counting slowly backwards from a hundred then back up again; imagining which famous people (alive or dead, real or fictional) I'd invite to my fantasy dinner party (my current list was Caitlin Moran, Oscar Wilde, Jim Morrison, Dorothy Parker, Marie Colvin, Nelson Mandela and Jacob out of *Twilight* – call me lowbrow, but you so would, wouldn't you?); the progressive relaxation techniques I'd learned from a long-ago yoga teacher. But nothing worked. My brain just wouldn't switch off and my body followed suit, and eventually I gave up and got my Kindle out of my handbag and tried to read, but that was no good either. I couldn't stop thinking about Rose and Oliver, Ben and Nina, what a horrible mess everything was, and how quite a lot of it was my fault.

At about seven o'clock I gave in and got up, feeling scratchy-eyed, achy and horribly cross. I had an unsatisfactory shower in tepid, rust-coloured water, with the pipes clunking and shrieking alarmingly above me, and got dressed again in my pink dress. There was no sign of Oliver, but when I went downstairs, Elliot, his driver, was sitting in the kitchen drinking tea. I blushed horribly when I saw him – how many women had he driven back here, I wondered, knowing they were going to shag Oliver and then be transported back whence they came the next day, like books being returned to the library before you've finished them, or clothes purchased online and found to be baggy around the arse, or something.

"Morning, love," he said. "Beautiful day."

I agreed, and said something about how it might only be April but it felt as if summer had properly arrived, and he said it would probably make for a soggy July, mind, and I said how lucky we'd been to have had such a mild winter, apart from the few snowy days around Christmas, and he said it made you think there might be some truth in all that talk about global warming, and I said yes, he was right, and realised we'd reached the point at which the subject was well and truly exhausted.

"Oliver mentioned that it might be possible for you to drive me back to the hotel where my colleague is staying,"

I said. "My bags are there and I was hoping to get back to London this morning."

"It's no trouble, love," he said. "Fancy a cuppa before we go?"

"No, thank you," I said, "but please do finish yours, there's no hurry." So I had to sit and look relaxed while he finished his tea and then had another cup, reading the sports section of The Times very, very slowly, occasionally making comments like, "QPR look to be staying up," and, "Sri Lanka are all out for 324 then," until I wanted to howl with frustration.

At last he slowly stood up, had a good old stretch, folded the newspaper neatly and put it in the exact centre of the kitchen table, and said, "About time we got going then," as if it was me who'd been keeping him waiting.

The lobby of the Swains Abbey Novotel smelled of coffee and bacon, and was crowded with bleary-eyed people with suit-carriers and hat boxes – evidently there'd been a wedding there the previous day. I made my way up to my room, changed into jeans and flip-flops, packed my bags, checked out, sent Daisy a text telling her I'd see her in the office on Monday, and got a taxi to the station, all with a sense of frantic urgency. It was only when I was on the train that I realised I was hurrying back to the flat to see Rose, and I had absolutely no idea what I was going to say to her.

"I wouldn't advise you to marry your boyfriend, because after being pursued by your sister for months he finally made a play for her," was something of a non-starter. "Oliver is a duplicitous shit who would have fucked your sister if she'd let him," wasn't brilliant either, as conversation-openers go.

Nor was I loving, "You would have to be certifiably bonkers to marry someone who cheats on you the second he's got a ring on your finger, because believe me, if he does it once he'll do it over and over again, and you'll end up as bitter and desiccated as one of those orange slices you hang on Christmas trees," even though it was true.

As is so often the way with train journeys when you are less than eager to reach your destination, there were no delays at all. Soon I was standing at our front door, fitting my key into the lock and praying, "Please let Rose be out, please let Rose be out." But she wasn't, of course.

"Hey, Rose," I called, walking into the hallway. I could hear the telly playing MTV – it sounded like Glee, which Rose absolutely adores. I dropped my bag on the hall floor and walked through to the kitchen. Rose was sitting at the table, surrounded by piles of paper. There was a ring on her left hand, a tasteful platinum band set with a single, huge diamond. She looked as if she'd been crying.

"Rose?" I paused in the doorway.

"Hi Ellie." Rose smiled a rather wan sort of smile. I went in and switched the kettle on, waiting for her to say something. It wasn't until it had boiled and I'd made a pot of tea and put it down on the table with two mugs, my Marmite one and Rose's Pantone Warm Grey one, that she did. "So, I'm getting married. Not in the morning, probably next year sometime. It took a while but we got there in the end."

Her face had its closed, calm look. She wasn't smiling at all anymore. I reached out and touched her hand, the one with the ring on it.

"You know this isn't really how you're supposed to tell me," I said. "You're meant to be shrieking and dancing and I'm meant to join in and then you ask me to be your chief bridesmaid and we scream some more. You're not doing this right."

Rose laughed, a soft, breathy laugh. "Sorry, Ellie. Of course I want you to be my chief bridesmaid. I'll work on going 'Oooh!' a bit, I promise. It's just that it takes a bit of getting used to, that's all."

"Rose," I said, "you do know that when someone asks you to marry them, that's when you're off-the-scale happy. Later on you can have rows about him having strippers on his stag night and whether his mother gets to choose the colour of your bridesmaids' knickers. But for the moment, you're meant to be really, really loved up and excited, and you aren't."

"You don't seem excited, either," Rose said.

"Well, no," I said. "I mean, it's not a surprise to me. I saw Oliver yesterday – he was at the polo with some mates – and he told me. I think he's a lovely guy, I think you and he could be really happy together. It's just... you don't seem sure, and to be totally honest nor does he."

"I'm as sure as I need to be," Rose said. "Oliver's got what I'm looking for."

"Which is?" I said.

"He's gorgeous looking. He's generous. He's well connected. And, Ellie, he's fucking rich. There, I said it. I need to marry a rich man and Oliver asked me and I said yes because if I don't I will be well and truly, totally fucked." And she swept her scattered piles of papers together in front of her and put her head down on them and started to sob huge, keening sobs.

"Rose, what the hell is this about?" I put my arm around her and reached for the roll of paper towels on the worktop. "Come on, what's going on?"

"Ellie, are you completely fucking stupid?" Rose said. "Do you know how much I earn?"

"How much you… no, of course I don't."

She mopped at her swollen eyes with a paper towel. "Well, I'll tell you," she said, and did.

I was shocked. Don't get me wrong, working as a press officer in the charity sector is not exactly the career you choose if you want to live in luxury, and although my salary at Black & White was a bit better, it was still far from huge, but it was still double what Rose said.

"Shit, Rose," I said, "that's not much."

"And do you know how many people apply for jobs like mine?" Rose said.

"No, I don't," I said.

"Hundreds. Every time Quinn's advertises a vacancy for a specialist. Hundreds. And every single fucking one has got a rich husband or gets an allowance from Daddy, so they can start their own art collection and dress the part and go to the right places."

"Shit, Rose," I said again.

"What did you think, Ellie? How did you think I bought all this stuff?" She sort of waved a hand at herself: her Paige jeans, her T-shirt, which looked like any black top with a sort of squiggly gold design on it, but I could see the design spelled out Moschino, her Mulberry bag on the floor next to her. "This top cost four hundred pounds," she said.

"Four hundred… Shit," I said again, uselessly.

"And Gervase doing my hair costs two hundred and fifty quid every month," Rose went on calmly. "Facials, manicures, pedicures, eyebrows, waxing – that's another two hundred a month or so. Skiing holidays, meals out, bottles of champagne in clubs – all charged as taken. It's what's called investing in one's future, and now the time has come for me to recoup my investment. Look at these."

She pushed the pile of papers over to me, and I saw that they were credit card statements. I flipped through them. I'm no financial genius but I'm used to working with budgets and I could see that things in Rose's world were badly, badly wrong. I quickly totted up the figures in my head and said, "You're ten thousand pounds in overdraft and you owe more than thirty thousand on credit cards."

"Correct," Rose said. "I can't even cover the interest. Let's say the credit crunch has not been kind to me."

I privately thought that the opposite was true, and the proliferation of easily available credit was what had been unkind to Rose, but I didn't think I should say so.

"I'm fucked, Ellie. It's getting so I won't be able to pay my share of the bills here."

"Okay, look, Rose," I said, "You've been so stupid I could slap you. But this is all fixable. It's only money. You don't have to get out of this mess by marrying someone you don't love. Dad would..."

"I am not fucking borrowing money off Dad," Rose said. "How do you think it would look? I behaved horribly, I know I did, I've known all along. I went there yesterday to tell him and Serena about Ollie, and I also told them how sorry I am. Maybe one day Serena will forgive me, I don't know. I hope so. But I'm not suddenly going to get all like, 'Oh Daddy, I know I was rude to your wife and wouldn't come and support you when you almost lost your babies because I was too insecure to spend a weekend away from my boyfriend, now please can I have forty grand?'"

"You were too..." I paused, thinking back, and I could remember all the opportunities Oliver had taken to make

Rose feel uncertain, to keep her on her toes. His lateness, his unreliability, and of course most of all his flirtation with me, which Rose could hardly have failed to notice. I felt sick with shame. "You don't have to do this, Rose, honestly," I said. "There's another way, I know there is, we just have to find it."

"You're so sweet, Ellie," Rose said. "But there really isn't. This is what I wanted, remember? What I've always wanted. A lovely big chunk of status, right here." She held out her hand and the diamond blazed in the morning sun. "I've made my bed and I'm going to lie on it, and it'll be a really comfortable bed, one with five hundred thread count sheets and goose down pillows."

"Rose, you can't. I can't let you."

"You can't stop me either." Her face was a smooth, serene mask.

I thought, yes, I can stop you. I could tell you about me and Oliver and what happened last night, and then surely you would change your mind. But by giving Rose the knowledge that would stop her making this stupid, life-shattering decision, I would risk losing my sister's love forever.

Chapter Twenty

Claire, Pers and I were eating ice cream in Brixton Village Market. I had a scoop of chocolate and a scoop of salted caramel, and bugger the calories; Claire had a scoop of mango sorbet and a scoop of vanilla, and Pers was having tiny bits of all of them, but not too much because although she loved the taste, the cold made her scrunch up her little face and look perplexed. As soon as Rose had left the flat – to go and meet Vanessa to share her news and no doubt get swept away on a ridiculous tide of plans involving Vera Wang frocks and receptions at The Sanderson – I'd got on the blower to Claire and said we needed to meet urgently.

"So, what's up?" she asked, offering Pers a micro amount of orange-coloured ice cream.

"Everything's gone completely and utterly fucking pear-shaped," I said. "Your genius plan certainly worked, but it's backfired."

"My genius what?" Claire looked bemused.

"Your plan. For me to get Oliver off Rose, remember?"

"Vaguely," Claire said. "You don't mean you… What did I say?"

"You said Rose was obviously Oliver's type, and as Rose's sister it would be really easy for me to make myself more like her, and be his type too. You said I could try hanging out at the places Rose goes, because I might see him there. You said I could do with spending a few quid on some designer clothes, and if I made more of an effort with Rose's friends they'd start inviting me to their parties and stuff, and I'd see him there. You said I could get a new job to impress him, and a boyfriend to make him jealous."

"Ellie, you... That's just bonkers. I can't believe you went and did all that stuff because of some stupid joke conversation we had. What were you thinking?"

"I really believed I was in love with him, Claire." I looked down at my ice cream. Suddenly it didn't seem so delicious any more, and I was feeling a bit sick. "I really did. Properly smitten, like a crush at school. I didn't mean it to happen, but it did. I just wanted to be around him, hear him talk, have him look at me. All that bollocks."

"But you're not any more?"

"I'm not any more." I told Claire about seeing Oliver at the polo, spending most of the day with him, and how glamorous and romantic and utterly perfect it had been, and how for those few hours I'd been able to imagine that he was my boyfriend, and forget altogether about Rose. I told her, my face absolutely flaming with mortification, how close I'd come to sleeping with him, but I'd brought proceedings to a screeching halt because it had felt so totally wrong on every level. I could see Claire longing to ask for more details, but wisely and kindly she nodded, put her arm around me and snuck a spoonful of my salted caramel ice cream.

"But you've come to your senses now, right?" she said. "You're over Oliver, Rose is bound to get over him soon too, and find someone lovely, and you can get back together with..."

"I am over Oliver," I said. "And I'm over Peter too. I should never have gone out with him in the first place, it was stupid. I should have left it alone after the first night, but I thought he'd make Oliver jealous. In fact I think I might be over men entirely. But Rose isn't. She's going to marry Oliver. And he's a lying, treacherous bastard and I can't tell her he is because then she'll know I'm treacherous too." A tear slid down my cheek and splatted into my ice cream container. I passed it over to Claire. "You may as well finish this," I said. "It's salty anyway." I explained to Claire about Rose's terrifying mountain of debt, how she refused to ask Dad for help and saw marriage to Oliver as her only way out of the mess she was in.

At that point Pers decided to make a bid for freedom and go toddling off towards the door, so Claire pursued her and left me gazing morosely at the rainbow of ice cream tubs behind the counter, remembering that in addition to all this doom and gloom about Rose, I was going to have to talk to Claire about Ben and Nina.

"So here's how I see it," Claire said when she returned, slightly out of breath, carrying Pers. "There are three things that could solve the problem. One, something happens to put Rose off Oliver. Two, something happens to put Oliver off Rose. Three, something happens that will solve Rose's financial problems and mean she doesn't have to marry Oliver. You've ruled out playing a role in option one, which you could do at any time, because you don't want to hurt Rose. Which is fair enough. You've also fallen at the last fence when it comes to potentially seducing Oliver away from Rose. And that leaves you with option three."

"But I can't solve Rose's financial problems," I objected. "I mean, I suppose I could go to Dad and tell him I needed money, and give it to Rose, but she'd know it was from him and refuse to take it, because she's feeling so bad about being vile to Serena."

Pers squirmed off Claire's lap and started to bleat a bit. "Come on, let's walk," she said, hoisting Pers up into her sling. We wandered out and headed towards the main square, jostling our way through the crowds of people who were taking advantage of the early summer sunshine and thronging the streets. There was the usual assortment of Brixton characters: the religious nutter with his megaphone, exhorting us all to find Jesus and repent; the Rastafarians playing drums and selling Jamaican patties; the beautiful young girls in impossibly short shorts; the dodgy geezers offering to buy used Travelcards outside the station. Normally I'd have relished it all: the vibrant mix of people, the sunny day, the company of my best friend and my gorgeous god-daughter. Today the sunlight and the summer fashion and smiling faces might just as well not have been there – all I noticed were the fag ends and splats of chewing gum staining the pavement, the newspaper and carrier bags that fluttered in the warm breeze, and the old bicycle chained up outside the station, its front wheel nicked long ago. I don't want to exaggerate, but I was honestly feeling swamped by hopelessness, that I'd never be able to make right the wrong I'd done.

Fortunately Claire never has much time for such navel-gazing. "Come on Ellie, snap out of it," she said, leading me through the entrance to the park and over to a bench, where we sat down and gave Pers her ball to play with on the grass.

"Rose needs another income stream," Claire said. "That's clearly going to be the solution. What's she good at?"

"Buying art," I said. "Being charming. Going to parties. Remembering people's names. Looking amazing."

"Hmmm, none of those are sounding particularly lucrative. Could she flog all her clothes on eBay?"

I pointed out that as it was partly Rose's wardrobe that had created her mountain of debt, selling it would only recoup a fraction of its cost.

Claire shook her head. "No marketable skills," she said. "That's the problem with young girls today. Look at me, on the other hand. I have marketable skills, and once I found somewhere to market them my problems were over. Did I tell you Pers and I are moving to a new flat next week? It's just down the road but it's lovely, with a little garden and a decent kitchen and a bathroom that doesn't have a small-scale penicillin factory on the wall, and everything."

"Claire, that's great," I said. "I'm so pleased for you. But, how did you... I mean, is this something to do with Ben?"

"Of course it is," said Claire. "It's all thanks to Ben. He introduced me to Lucille in the first place."

"What?" I said. "What's Ben's boss got to go with anything?"

Claire looked at me blankly. "I thought Ben had told you," she said. "I've been giving Lucille public speaking coaching. She needed to brush up on her speech-making and Ben recommended me for a few lessons. I used to do it before I got involved in teaching drama to kids. It's dull as hell but it pays quite well, and Lucille's recommended me to a few of her MP friends and now they're lining up around the block to have their As unflattened and their Hs undropped and their breath control sorted and stuff, and Pers and I can afford to live somewhere decent again."

"Hold the phone," I said. "Just wait one second. Are you saying that you and Ben aren't an item?"

"Me and Ben an item?" Claire said. "Ellie, you doughnut, what on earth gave you that idea? I mean, I like him and everything, but he's..." She stopped there, but I could almost see the words 'your boyfriend' forming on her lips.

"Ben wasn't my boyfriend," I said automatically. "But you and he were suddenly busy all the time, and I saw you together in town, and Ben didn't call me for ages and ages, and then when Nina turned up again I didn't know how to tell you because I thought Ben was seeing her behind your back." I blurted all this out, feeling tears sting my eyes.

"Wait, what?" Claire said. "What was that about Nina?"

I quickly filled her in on things with Ben and Nina, and the unspeakable Benedict, and Nina's plans to move herself and him into Ben's flat and evict poor Winston the cat.

"Blimey," Claire said. "I take my eyes off you for a few weeks and you don't just get yourself into an unholy mess, you let your family and friends get into one too."

I pointed out that it was hardly my fault that Nina had come back on to the scene – she was an unstoppable force of nature like a hurricane or a gas explosion or an epidemic of swine flu or something, and Claire had to admit that I was right.

"But it is your fault that Ben was available when she did manifest herself," Claire said. "Your fault entirely. Anyone can see that you and Ben are meant for each other. If you'd been being Ben's girlfriend instead of swanning off after Oliver and shagging Peter, Nina wouldn't have had a chance."

"That's just not true," I objected. "Ben fell for Nina like a ton of bricks when he first met her. One minute, happily single and occasionally shagging me, the next, totally deranged with love. He never felt that way about me." I sounded sad when I said it, I realised – sad and resentful.

Claire tossed Pers her ball. "That's because you never gave him the chance," she said. "That thing with Nina was ages ago, Ben was practically a child. And anyway, you were doing that daft thing of insisting you two weren't together when all your friends knew you were basically going out and mad about each other. He won't be feeling like that about Nina now, you just wait and see. You need to talk to him and find out the score. And I hope you've apologised to Peter for treating him so shabbily, because frankly, Ellie, you've been pissing about with other people's lives for long enough." She gave me a hug that took the sting out of her words. "There's nothing you can do about Rose," she went on. "Either she'll come to her senses about Oliver or she won't. Focus on the things that you can change."

Claire gets like that sometimes – all Zen and calm. I suppose it must be the influence of the Acre Lane Hippy Mums and all those Baby Yoga classes. But her serenity affected me – suddenly I became conscious again of the beautiful day, the sunshine, the blossom weighing down the branches of the cherry trees, Pers's little mouth pursed with concentration as she toddled across the grass after her ball. I felt my face break out into a huge grin.

"You say I need to talk to Ben?" I said.

I don't know what I'd expected, I thought, looking down at my hands as a fresh awkward silence descended, but it wasn't this. I suppose I'd imagined Ben and me slipping easily back into our old friendship, minus sex, of course, as long as Nina remained on the scene, but apart from that, everything being the same. The same shared jokes, easy companionship, and sense of being each other's most important person. But of course that isn't the way it works

– you can't be the most important person of someone who's been co-opted into the role of most important person to someone else.

Ringing Ben after so long had felt strange – I was used to finding his number in my phone's call log, where he was normally about the second or third on my recently dialled numbers. This time I'd scrolled and scrolled, all the way down, but his name wasn't there, and I'd had to look him up in my contacts list. It made me feel a bit sad, as if I'd lost or broken something important. But I told myself that everything would be fine, that all friends go through patches when they're in touch less often, and dialled. He didn't answer. I left a cheery message along the lines of, "Hey Ben, it's me. Just catching up. Let's meet soon for a pint – it's been too long! Speak soon. Bye." But he didn't respond to my message, nor the one I left the next day, nor the one the day after that. So in the end, in the manner of a desperate teenager stalking a boy who's dumped her and won't tell her why, I'd called him from my landline at Black & White, a number he wouldn't recognise, and then he'd answered. Which made me feel just brilliant, of course. But I forced the bright and breezy note back into my voice.

"Ben! Hi! Long time no speak!" I said, even though I have always been of the opinion that people who say 'long time no speak' are pseuds of the highest order and will be first up against the wall when the revolution comes, along with those who use the phrase 'the below' in emails and men who wear skinny jeans.

"Hi, Ellie," he said. "Sorry I didn't get back to you. Been very busy – only three weeks to Iron Man and the training's getting quite full-on. Work's hectic too." There was a pause, presumably intended for me to contemplate the busyness of

Ben's schedule and repent my selfishness in calling him. But instead I upped the brightness of my tone a few watts.

"Three weeks! Wow! You must be shattered!" I gushed. "But don't you get to do that thing soon, that you do before marathons? Starts with a T? Trickle? Means sitting on your arse eating spaghetti?"

"Taper." I could hear a bit of a smile in his voice. "Yeah, my last long session is this weekend. A hundred miles on the bike."

"Blimey!" I said. "Impressive! Knackering! Anyway! Let's meet up for a drink? Protein shake? If you can fit me in?"

Ben said a beer would be fine, and we arranged to meet in his local, the Bear and Bush, the next evening at eight.

And here I was, having spent three hours blow-drying my hair and putting on makeup and trying on and discarding clothes in a state of breathless excitement, as if I was going on a date or something, sitting opposite Ben, looking at the ice in my gin and tonic, in the middle of a horrible, uncomfortable pause.

First there'd been the awkward silence when he walked up to the table where I was waiting, which had come directly after he'd said, "Hi," and I'd said, "Hi." Then there'd been awkward silence number two, which had fallen as soon as he came back from the bar with our drinks and sat down. Then I'd gone off to the loo and checked that my face looked okay and brushed my hair, and gone to the bar as well and bought us a bowl of olives, and returned to our table just in time to catch the beginning of the third in a series that looked like it was set to run and run.

"You're looking really well, Ellie," Ben said, after what felt like about an hour. "Keeping up with the exercise?"

"Yes," I said. "You're right, it gets quite addictive. You're looking well too." He was, at that. Ben's always tended to be sort of lean and stringy, but there was a new tautness to him, a bit more bulk on his legs and shoulders and less around his middle, and I could see his belt was on an extra hole. I imagined how flat and firm his stomach would be underneath his stripy blue and white shirt. I imagined the clear outline of muscles that I'd see when he stretched his arms over his head, pulling the shirt off without bothering to undo the buttons, as he always did, and how his body would feel under my hands, ridged and hard beneath his warm, soft skin. And by that stage we'd got ourselves right in the middle of a fourth awkward silence.

"Another drink?" I said, scuttling off to the bar, barely waiting for his answer. I wished I still smoked so I could go and stand outside for a few minutes and compose myself, but then I told myself not to be ridiculous – this was Ben, my friend, and I was acting like a total loser. So I took our drinks and marched back to the table and sat down, and forced myself to make bright, cheerful conversation about my new job and the political issues of the day, and even the weather, for about ten minutes, hoping to break the ice. But Ben remained as frosty as ever, and as soon as my flow of bright chatter dried up, there we were – smack in yet another awkward silence.

Every topic of conversation I could think of trying to introduce was fraught with difficulty. I thought about telling him about Serena's babies, thankfully staying put and due in the next few weeks, but that would inevitably lead to the subject of Ben's own fatherhood. I wanted to ask him how Winston was, but again, that would lead on to the topic of ghastly Benedict. After a bit I said, "It was just Alex and me the last time I did the quiz at the Duchess. We were rubbish. We missed you."

Ben took a slow sip of his lager. His face was very brown, from all the running and cycling, I supposed, and it made his eyes look very blue. There were bleached bits in his hair, too, I noticed, where the dark brown, the colour of a polished conker shell, lightened to an ashy gold. Even his hands were tanned, with a sort of oval on the back of each of them, that I supposed corresponded to the holes in the backs of his cycling gloves. I reminded myself to tell him to put sunblock on his hands – you can't be too careful. I wished he'd smile, reach across the table and squeeze my hand – anything, just give me some sign that he still cared about me, and didn't hold me in total contempt. But he stayed sitting there, very still, apart from his hand slowly and carefully putting his glass back down on the table, precisely centred on a beer mat.

"Well, Ellie, maybe you should ask Oliver to come along next time," he said. "Or Peter. Or whoever your fucking status shag is this week." I don't want to exaggerate and say that he spat the names out, but let me tell you, it was close. I felt a horrid flush of hurt and anger creep up my neck and over my face.

"Ben," I said, "Please don't be like this. Please can't we just..."

But I could see he wasn't listening to me. His eyes had slid away from my face and were focussing on a point somewhere over my left shoulder, and a moment later I heard a voice say, "Sweetie, sorry I'm late. Ellie, it's been so long!" And there was Nina.

She was wearing a short shift dress in a sort of pistachio colour, and a trailing apricot and lilac chiffon scarf. Her shoes were cork-soled platforms that looked vintage, and she had a pair of outsize sunglasses pushed up on her head, holding back her mass of coppery hair. Her lips were painted the same vivid crimson she always wore, and I felt a stab of envy as I realised afresh how beautiful she was. Although she did have freckly knees – let it not be said that I don't see the silver lining. Ben stood up and kissed her on both cheeks, and after a few seconds I did too – it would have seemed churlish not to. Without asking if it was okay to join us, she slid herself on to the bench seat next to Ben, and put a possessive, red-taloned hand on his leg and gazed up at him.

"Would you like to have another drinkie?" she said, "Or shall we go? Vincent's on at the Jazz Café in half an hour."

One of the things that Ben and I have always shared is a healthy contempt for people who talk about drinkies and nibbles and use similarly cutesy diminutives – we even have a name for them: twee twats. Another is our dislike of jazz and the people who listen to it. I looked at him with a kind of bemused horror, but he was smiling fondly down into Nina's rapt face.

"I'm ready to go if you are," he said. "Unless you'd like another drink, Ellie?"

It was clear that I was not included in this invitation to an evening of wine and song – or rather, atonal hooting saxophones and bourbon, which has always tasted like cough mixture to me.

"I'd better head off too. I'm meeting Peter for dinner. Lovely to see you again, Nina," I said, lying on all counts.

Ben and I said a rather cool goodbye, and Nina fluttered about saying that we must arrange to meet up soon for a 'girlie catch-up'. I refrained from saying that I'd rather stick pins in my eyes, and told Ben I'd call him soon. Then I got on the Tube and spent the entire, long journey back to Battersea trying not to cry, and managed not to until I was at home in bed.

I know there's supposed to be nothing more cathartic than a good howl, but I've never really found that to be the case – crying just makes me puffy-eyed and blotchy-faced for about three days afterwards. So I snivelled into my pillow for a while, tried to fall asleep, and then got out my phone and had a look at my Twitter feed to cheer myself up. There was the usual assortment of random links to depressing news stories, tweets from various friends who were out doing glamorous things in fabulous places, and a few cute photos of cats. Then I noticed a tweet from @LucilleFieldMP – Ben's boss. "Really sorry I was a cunt to @EllieMottram. Miss her lots."

So, finally Ben had done the inevitable and posted by mistake from Lucille's account instead of his own. And he was sorry. I tweeted, "Epic fail by @BenedictTheRed noted and apology accepted," and fell asleep with the beginnings of a smile on my face.

Chapter Twenty-One

It was Saturday afternoon and I was sitting at our kitchen table, working. Since the apparently epoch-making success of the Black & White polo day, Barri appeared to have relented a little in his approach to my duties, so I was allowed to write proper press releases again and Daisy was one minion down. Unfortunately all the time I'd wasted colour-coordinating table napkins and evaluating the relative blackness of various types of olive meant that I'd missed a vital window to get press releases about our summer fast fashion line out to the weeklies, so I'd had to come up with a last-minute strategy for an e-campaign around the concept that we'd deliberately kept it all under wraps because it was so fabulous, hoping that all the media (okay, *Vogue*, which was the only medium that actually existed as far as Barri was concerned) would drop something and find space for us. Given that their high summer issues would have been planned and for the most part written, photographed, and laid out several months before, I wasn't too optimistic about our chances, but it was such a relief to be doing my real job again I was giving it my best shot.

I was working on variations on a headline around 'Summer's best-kept secret' when I got the feeling I was being watched. I turned around and there was Rose standing in the doorway, looking ever-so-casually at her phone as if she hadn't been loitering there for ages waiting for me to notice her.

"Oh, sorry, Ellie," she said. "Did I interrupt your train of thought?"

Well, she had, obviously, but I said, "No, of course not. What is it?"

"I was just wondering," Rose said, "if you're busy tonight?"

I said a fond farewell to my plans to finish my work, go to the gym, then spend the evening catching up on the new series of Mad Men while eating greasy takeaway pizza and drinking tea.

"No," I said, "I didn't have anything on."

"Great!" Rose said. "Because it's the Gainsborough Prize award ceremony tonight – you know, the portrait prize? It's like the Turner Prize except the artists have to enter one portrait only, and it's generally a more figurative work. It's all top secret, my boss is one of the judges and even I don't know who's won."

I wondered why she was giving me all this background information. "Sounds fascinating," I said, "but why would I want to go? You know I don't know anything about art."

"No particular reason," Rose said. "I just thought you'd have fun. There'll be lots of interesting people there. And I'll be working, so you can look after Oliver for me while I mingle."

Really? I thought. Oliver was surely able to look after himself, and as a keen art collector he was bound to know most of the people there anyway, and would probably be quite happy doing his own mingling. Rose was clearly up to something. Was she trying to set me up with some random single acquaintance, I wondered. But a look at her pinched, anxious face convinced me it couldn't be that.

"Okay," I said. "If you insist. What do I need to wear?"

Rose whittered on a bit about it being a really casual, low-key event, you know how people in the art world are, they turn up in paint-stained smocks to just about everything, so don't go to any trouble, Ellie, honestly. So I went and showered and spent half an hour straightening my hair and another forty-five minutes on my makeup, and put on a gorgeous navy blue silk DKNY dress that I'd found in the Black & White sale rail, and even painted my fingernails, because Rose is my sister and I've known her long enough to know when not to believe a word she's saying.

And I was right, of course. The function room at Quinn's was simply heaving with art types, and while I had no doubt that they were as paint-stained and scruffy as anything when they were working, they certainly scrubbed up well. Almost all the men were in dinner jackets, and if there hadn't been a slight tendency towards long, flowing hair, you'd never have known they weren't bankers or marketing execs or whatever; most of the women were in evening frocks, although quite a lot of them were vintage. I was glad I'd made an effort, partly because I was feeling really apprehensive about seeing Oliver again, for the first time since our disastrous evening together following the polo tournament.

When I heard his voice behind me saying, "Hello, Ellie," I felt the familiar lurch of excitement and apprehension in my stomach, and I turned around, fixing a careful smile on my face.

Honestly, it was as though the Oliver I had lusted after for all those months had been replaced by a not-very-convincing doppelganger. At least that's the only explanation I can think of for the fact that every last flicker of desire I'd felt for him had been extinguished. His hair was as silky as ever, but now when I watched him push his floppy fringe off his face I could imagine Claire saying, "Tory-boy hair." His voice was still deep and mellifluous, but now when he spoke to me I couldn't help remembering him whispering, "Gorgeous girl." Just, ick. His suit was another wonder of bespoke tailoring, but I looked at it and thought, "More money than sense." His hands were as long and slender as they'd always been, but now looking at them made me wonder what kind of vain tool he must be to spend his time sitting in a salon having manicures. I mean, really. That whole metrosexual thing is so noughties.

But I smiled sweetly and said, "Hello, Oliver, how lovely to see you," and accepted a glass of champagne from a passing tray, and chatted brightly away to him for a bit about the shortlisted artists and which one he thought was likely to win. He must have thought I'd been replaced by a doppelganger too, actually, because it was the first time I'd been able to sustain a conversation him without blushing and stumbling over my words and generally acting like a crush-struck schoolgirl.

"My money's on Jamie Cunningham," Oliver said. "Literally. Ten grand at six to one at Ladbroke's this morning. If he wins I'll make far more than that, of course, because I have three of his paintings and they'll all escalate hugely in value – by a factor of about ten, I'd imagine."

Then I'm afraid I did blush, because I was remembering the huge, blue nude in Oliver's bedroom, beneath which he and I had had our brief tussle on the sheepskin rug. Thankfully he didn't see, because he was looking across the room at Rose, who was standing talking to a tallish, gingerish man. I realised that as soon as we'd arrived, Rose had sort of melted away into the crowd and started networking away like mad, and I wondered with a shiver of concern whether the real reason she'd wanted me to come was so that she could avoid spending time alone with Oliver. "That's him," Oliver said. "Care to wander over and say hello?"

I said we might as well, because I didn't know anyone else there and didn't particularly want to be abandoned, and we pushed our way through the throng of people to Rose.

"Hello, darling," she said to Oliver, with a smile that was just a little too bright. "Hello, Ellie, are you having a nice time? This is Jamie, who's got a painting on the shortlist tonight, only he won't tell me any details about it. Come on, Jamie, it's going to be revealed soon so there's no point keeping us in suspense."

Jamie grinned and shook his head. "You'll have to wait and see," he said. He was looking at Rose the way most men did, as if unable to believe his good fortune at being in the same room, breathing the same air, as her, but he clearly wasn't going to let her get her own way on this one. I decided I rather liked him.

The lights in the room suddenly dimmed and a spotlight was trained on a raised dais, where a bearded man in evening dress stood at a microphone. "That's my boss, Edmund," Rose whispered to me.

He trotted out the usual platitudes about how glad he was that everyone could come, how the judges had had an enormously difficult task choosing between entries of such undoubted talent, how anyone who said that portraiture was a dying art would be proved wrong tonight, and so on and so on. After about ten minutes of it, people started to stir restively and cast longing looks at the waiters hovering by the door with their laden trays of canapés.

"And so it falls to me to reveal the results of hours of deliberation by our panel of judges," Edmund said. "Whilst selecting a long-list from the thousands of entries we received, and reducing that to a shortlist of ten, was challenging to say the least, I know our judges share my confidence that we have selected a worthy winner from this quite dazzling pool of talent. But although there can only be one winner, there is still acclaim – and large cheques, thanks to the generosity of our sponsors – due to the second and third placed entries. So please join me in congratulating Geraldine White, our second runner-up."

On the screen behind him flashed up a huge image of a teenage boy with bad skin, plugged into an iPod and glaring sullenly.

"The judges praised Geraldine's portrait of her son Glenn for its sensitive depiction of the tribulations of adolescence." A little ripple of laughter and applause spread round the room, and a large woman in brown shambled up to collect a white envelope that presumably contained the generous cheque. I glanced at Jamie to see if he looked nervous, eager or disappointed, but his face was unreadable.

"In second place, Marcus Brand, last year's winner."

I'd seen Marcus Brand's work before, of course, in brochures and things that Rose had left lying about the flat. His style was exactly what you'd expect from a wild child of Brit art: garish, brutal, undeniably brilliant, when he actually painted as opposed to just gluing discarded fried chicken wrappers to canvas. The subject of the painting was an elderly homeless woman, slumped against a wall in what looked like a Tube station, a toppled-over can of cider next to her and a scrawny looking dog lying sleeping with its head in her lap. Although the subject matter was shocking, I couldn't help admiring the obvious pain and empathy that had gone into producing the work, and wondered briefly whether the judges had simply felt it wouldn't be appropriate for the same person to win two years in a row, because it was hard to imagine that whoever got first prize could be any better. Marcus loped up to get his cheque, all flying hair and black leather, and made a little speech in which he said that Pam, the lady in the painting, was no longer on the streets, and while working on the picture he'd persuaded her to talk to various homelessness charities and addiction counsellors, and that she and her little dog were now living in Eltham and doing very well. I had to dig around in my bag for a tissue and dab at my eyes before my mascara started to run, he was so sweet and sincere.

"And I'm sure you will all share my and the judges' profound admiration for the time, dedication and passion that went into producing that work," Edmund said, and everyone applauded and several people blew their noses, "but there can only be one winner. So without further ado, let me present the Quinns/Bollinger Gainsborough Portrait of the Year, and award the fifty thousand pound first prize, to a painting which the artist tells me was completed after just one sitting."

The lights dimmed some more, and a new picture appeared on the screen. It was a woman, painted from the back. She was sitting on a bed, looking out of a window, her pale hair flowing over her slender shoulders, her face turned so that her profile was just illuminated. A strappy dress lay on the floor by the bed in a shimmering puddle, next to a pair of high-heeled shoes. The shades of blue that predominated reminded me unmistakably of the picture of Jamie Cunningham's I'd seen in Oliver's bedroom, although the treatment wasn't abstract at all – it was a tender, exquisite painting of a beautiful, naked woman. And it was immediately recognisable as Rose.

"I'm sorry I didn't tell you," Jamie said to Rose over the tide of applause. "It's the best thing I've ever painted; I had to enter it."

I just had time to register Oliver's enraged face when my phone started vibrating furiously in my bag, and I pushed my way out of the room to answer it.

An unfamiliar voice said, "Am I speaking to Ellie Mottram? I'm calling from Accident and Emergency at St George's Hospital. We have a gentleman who's here after a cycling accident, and you are listed on his mobile phone as his contact in case of emergency."

My hands were shaking so much I could hardly get my phone back into my bag. I pushed my way back into the room, looking for Rose, but she and Jamie were surrounded by a crowd of well-wishers and there was no way I'd be able to get to speak to her without hovering on the periphery for about twenty minutes. Then Oliver appeared next to me.

"You okay?" he said.

"No," I said. "Yes. But Ben's not. He's in A&E in South London and I have to get there now. Do you know where there's a cash machine near here? I can't get the Tube in these shoes, I'll need a taxi and I've no money on me." I could feel my lower lip trembling.

"Don't be silly," Oliver said. "I'll drive you. Or rather, Elliot will drive both of us. Come on. You text Rose while we're on our way. She'll be fine."

Through the clamour of my worry, I realised quite clearly that Oliver didn't want to be alone with Rose any more than she wanted to be alone with him. "Thanks," I said.

Oliver made a rapid-fire call and after a few minutes his car purred into view round the corner and Oliver told Elliot where we wanted to go, Elliot told the SatNav, and we were on our way.

Hospitals are strange places. There's this massive sense of urgency about everything, but also a huge amount of hanging around. We stood in a queue at the main reception before being directed to the A&E department, and then we waited for ages before any of the bustling nurses noticed us, and then they couldn't find Ben's name on the computer, and I was crying because I thought it must mean Ben had died, and Oliver came over all masterful and made them check again, and it turned out they had his name down as Benedict, not Ben, and he wasn't dead after all, but he'd been moved over to the Lanesborough wing, where the radiology department was, for a CT scan, and we'd have to wait.

I said, "That's a brain scan, isn't it?" and I must have gone a bit green and looked like I was about to faint and sustain a head injury of my own, because Oliver took my arm and steered me over to a hard plastic chair and made me sit down, and fetched me a cup of sweet tea. After a bit one of the nurses came over and told us Ben had had his scan and was waiting for the results, and his score on the Glasgow Coma Scale – at the word coma I felt a bit faint and queasy again – was up to fourteen, and we could go to the radiology place and see him, if we wanted. We trailed through a maze of corridors and after getting lost a few times we found the right place, and another nurse took us to a cubicle where

Ben was lying in a hospital bed. His eyes were closed and he looked so pale and vulnerable that I started to cry again, and when he heard me snivelling he opened his eyes.

"Hi, Ellie," he said.

I went over to the bed and sat down, and held his hand, and for a while I couldn't say anything. Then I said, stupidly, "Are you okay?"

"I'm going to have a hell of a headache," he said, "and my cycling helmet's seen better days. But I'll live."

"What happened?" I asked.

"I don't know," Ben said. "Can't remember a thing about it. But they tell me a lorry was trying to overtake me and got too close, and the wing mirror hit the back of my head and I went flying. If he'd been going a few miles an hour faster it would have been a different story, apparently." He managed a rather weak grin, and closed his eyes again, and I squeezed his hand as if I'd never let go.

I'd almost forgotten Oliver was there, when he said, "Would you like me to stay for a bit? I can wait outside and give you a lift home when you're ready?"

I was about to thank him and say that would be brilliant actually, if it wasn't any trouble, when we heard the sound of running feet on the floor outside, and Nina burst in, if you can be said to burst through curtains.

"Ben!" she wailed, "my..."

Then she saw Oliver, and stopped dead, and the two of them just looked at each other, and everything froze for what felt like a long, long time.

Then Oliver said, "Nina."

Nina said, "Oliver."

Oliver said, "Where is he?"

Nina said, "Who?"

Oliver said – actually, he kind of croaked out the words, his voice sounding all gravelly and harsh – "My son. Benedict. My boy."

Ben hoisted himself up on the pillows and I shifted over and held his hand a bit tighter, and we just sat and looked at two of them, like people watching a murder scene unfold in a horror movie – it's awful and you wish you could make it stop, but you're transfixed.

I'd never heard Nina sound uncertain or defensive before, but she did now. "With my mother," she said. It was also the first I'd heard of Nina having a mother – I suppose I'd imagined her springing fully formed into an unsuspecting world, like Athena from the head of Zeus.

"Why, Nina?" Oliver said. "Why didn't you tell me you were in London?" He was looking at her with the same sort of blind longing I'd seen on Ben's face when he'd first met her. Honestly, what was it about the woman?

Nina moved towards him and Oliver actually flinched away from her, the way you would from a wasp that looks like it's about to fly into your glass of Pimms. Then he seemed to accept his fate, and put his arms around her, and she buried her face in his shoulder, except it was more around the region of his breast pocket, Nina being so vertically challenged, as I think I've mentioned. I looked at Ben, dreading seeing devastation on his face at the prospect of losing her again, but he looked fascinated by what was unfolding. I could almost hear him thinking that a box of popcorn would go down well.

"I was so selfish," Nina whispered. "I didn't think you'd ever forgive me."

"You took my son away," Oliver said. "My son, who I loved and supported and lived with for two years, because you said you needed a clean break and seeing me would only confuse him."

"I'm sorry," Nina said. "I don't know what else to say. I'm sorry."

"What happened to New York?" said Oliver. I felt terrible for him, he looked so baffled and helpless and hurt, and furious too. "What happened to living the dream?"

"I was there for three years," Nina said defiantly. "I was working. I even auditioned for the New York Philharmonic. But I didn't get in." Her voice cracked. "I'm not good enough. So I came home."

For a moment I almost felt sorry for her, too. Then I said, "But why did you tell Ben..." and at the same moment Ben said, "But you let me think..."

Nina rounded on us and said furiously, "I told you nothing! You believed what you needed to believe! You contacted me on Facebook, you said you wanted to see me. What was I supposed to say? I needed a place to live."

"Why didn't you come to me?" Oliver asked.

"How could I?" said Nina. "After what I'd done?"

I remembered how longingly Oliver had talked about the child he'd lost, the love that had got away. But Ben was looking a bit knackered and grey-faced and it was all getting a bit too much like an episode of Jeremy Kyle, so I said rather primly, "Really, Nina, I wonder if this is the appropriate time and place..."

Oliver said, "Come, Nina. Take me to him."

He seemed to be over his wobble and was back in masterful mode, and Nina looked up at him admiringly and said, "Really?"

Oliver said, "Yes. Ellie, if you need anything, ring me. I'll be in touch with Rose."

And he took Nina's twig-like arm and the two of them swished back out through the curtains.

I was still holding Ben's hand, and I realised I was pressing it so hard it must have really hurt, but he didn't seem to mind. I guess they'd given him some good strong drugs, what with his bang on the head and everything. But I released my grip and was about to stand up, when he said, "Ellie?"

I said, "Yes?"

Ben said, "Come here."

I sort of leaned over him and squished up on the pillows, and he put his arms around me and squeezed me tight. He was wearing a hospital gown but he'd obviously been unceremoniously bundled into it, and I could see drifts of dried salt on his skin where he'd sweated on his long cycle ride, and smell the familiar smell of him. I could feel tears trickling down my face, and they tasted salty too.

"You want to be a bit more careful on that fucking bike of yours," I said.

"I know," Ben said. "I'm sorry. I will be in future, I promise."

"And what's more," I said, "You need to put sunblock on your hands, because you haven't been, just look at the tan you've got. And if you don't wear sunblock you might get skin cancer and die." My voice went all quavery on the last word, and it came out as a proper wail.

"I'm sorry, Ellie," Ben said again. "I'll wear sunblock next time. I'll wear it when I do the triathlon next week, if they don't make me pull out."

"If they don't... You're not still planning on doing it, are you?"

"Of course I am," Ben said. "Otherwise this would have been for nothing. And I've raised two grand for charity, and I'd have to give it back if I didn't finish."

"Which charity?" I asked, impressed.

"YEESH," Ben said. "I thought you'd be pleased."

There wasn't very much I could say after that. I half-sat, half-lay on the hospital bed, getting a horrible crick in my neck but not really minding. And after a bit one of the nurses came in with a sheaf of notes.

"Now," she said, "It appears you've been a very lucky man. The CT scan shows no damage to your skull or brain, although you'll probably have a sore head for a couple of days. We'll give you paracetamol for that." Which seemed a bit like trying to bring down a guided missile with a fly-swatter to me, but what do I know? "We'll keep you in overnight and reassess your Glasgow Coma Scale score again in the morning, and if it's up to fifteen you'll be free to leave."

"Great!" Ben said.

"However, with head injuries like yours, we're unable to release a patient unless there's a responsible carer to look after them at home. Do you live alone?"

I saw Ben realise that until about ten minutes ago, he'd lived with Nina, but now he definitely didn't.

"There's the cat," he said, doubtfully. "Which reminds me! Shit, Ellie, Winston will be needing his dinner. Do you think you could go back to mine and feed him, and get me some clean clothes to wear when I go home tomorrow?"

"As I said, Benedict," said the nurse rather sternly, "We're not able to discharge you unless there's a responsible person able to take care of you at home."

I stood up off the bed and picked up my handbag. "I guess that would be me then," I said. "Give me your keys, I'll go and feed the cat and come back with some clothes for you."

Chapter Twenty-Two

I was actually really looking forward to playing Florence Nightingale to Ben's wounded soldier, but I didn't get the chance. The next day he texted saying he'd had a panicky call from Lucille to say his presence was urgently required in her constituency because the Leader of the Opposition was paying a visit and Lucille, desperate to get back into his good books, needed to roll out the red carpet and make sure nothing went wrong. So Ben spent his convalescence writing sycophantic speeches for Lucille to make and scouring the constituency for signs with 'cock' on them, so he could make sure the dear leader wasn't photographed in front of any of them. He probably had a lucky escape, because I can kill a pot plant in five days flat.

So it wasn't until the weekend of the dreaded triathlon that he came home. We were sitting at his kitchen table eating pasta that Ben had cooked – and needless to say it was far superior to any effort I could have produced: lovely roast vegetables, wholemeal spaghetti and some sort of sauce that Ben said had sundried tomatoes in it. When I say we were sitting at the table, actually I was, and Winston the cat was too a lot of the time, because Ben kept getting up and going to check his kit, which was carefully packed into three separate different-coloured bags, and every time he did Winston jumped on to his chair and asked politely for tastes of grated Parmesan cheese.

"You need to eat something," I told Ben. "Come on, you're meant to be carb-loading, aren't you, not burning off more calories than you will the whole of tomorrow, pacing up and down."

Ben laughed. "Okay. Just let's run through this once more. You take my phone and read out the stuff on the list and I'll check that it's all there."

We'd been through this at least four times already: once when he got everything out of various wardrobes and drawers and carrier bags; once when he put it all into the bags; once when he took it all out because he found his energy gel things inside the pair of trainers he'd decided not to wear after all, and panicked that he'd got everything else wrong as well; and again for what he said was the absolute, final time to make sure. But I decided to humour him.

"Okay," I said. "Red bag: cycling shorts, cycling shoes, cycling helmet – and it had better bloody work – cycling gloves, socks. Towel, sunblock. Three energy gels, two bottles of energy drink, one bottle water, sunglasses, watch."

"All there."

"Blue bag: running shoes, running shorts, running socks, high-vis arm band, sunblock, baseball cap for sun protection, three energy gels, one bottle energy drink, two bananas."

"Okay."

"Special needs bag," I made the horrible politically incorrect face I made whenever I said 'special needs', and Ben looked disapproving. "Two Mars bars, one can Coke, one packet cheese and onion crisps, Marmite sandwiches. I'll make those before we go to bed. Christ, though, this is more like a bloody picnic than a triathlon. Are you sure you don't need to pack a corkscrew somewhere?"

"No corkscrew. No booze again, ever. Not until tomorrow night, anyway. Remind me again why I thought this was a good idea?"

"Because you're a man, and you do stupid, man things to prove your manliness," I said. "Speaking of which, tell me again what happened with Nina."

Ben abandoned his various bags and came and sat down again, scooping Winston on to his lap, and half-heartedly forking up some pasta.

"She sent me a friend request on Facebook," he said. "So I accepted it, because that's what you do. And I sent her a message, just to find out how she was, and then she suggested that we meet up. And when we did she told me she'd just got back from America and had nowhere to stay, and I was worried about her, because you know she's always been…"

"Barking mad?" I said.

"Emotionally fragile," Ben said. "I didn't know about her son then. But the next day she turned up at the flat with all her stuff, and him, and although she never said I was his father, she didn't say I wasn't, either. And the name… And she never mentioned that bloody Oliver. And he was okay, you know, the kid. I'd like to see him again."

I thought, over my cold, dead body. But I said, "Tell me again that you weren't sleeping with her."

Ben reached across the table and put his warm, dry hand over mine. There were calluses at the base of his fingers, from all the weight training and stuff he'd been doing in the gym – I could feel their roughness against my skin. "I didn't sleep with her," he said. "I got the sofa and she and Benedict got my bed, and Winston wasn't too pleased about it, were you?" He scratched Winston under the chin, and the cat began his thunderous purring, narrowing his eyes and looking adoringly at Ben. It's possible that I may have looked adoringly at him, too. "But what could I do? She needed me, she needed some sort of stability, and she told me she had nowhere to go. She certainly didn't say she had a Mum living in Croydon."

"Like I said, mad as a box of frogs."

"Emotionally fragile," Ben corrected me.

"But she's Oliver's problem now, I guess."

"Looks that way. They came round on Tuesday to collect Nina's stuff – not that she had very much. Oliver really seems to love her." Ben shook his head in bemusement.

"You loved her too, remember? I thought you still did."

Ben ate some more pasta. "I don't think it was ever love," he said. "I was infatuated with her, fascinated by her. And then I got sucked in by all her hysterics and drama, and once I got to the point of wishing I could end the relationship, she was threatening crazy things. I was devastated when she buggered off, because I felt so guilty about not having been able to make things right for her."

"You're too nice for your own good," I said.

"Unlike you," Ben teased. "Brazen hussy. Trying to shag your sister's boyfriend."

I cringed, feeling a blush creeping up my neck. "Don't," I said. "I feel so ashamed. I behaved horribly. But then so did Rose, of course."

"What happened with her and Oliver in the end?" Ben said.

"Well, he found out that Rose had slept with Jamie, the night before she sat for his portrait, which was Oliver's birthday, and afterwards too. And understandably he was absolutely livid, and dumped her. But Rose was like, 'You can't fire me, I quit!' because she'd realised that things between her and Oliver were never going to work. She was only really with him because she'd got it into her head that she needed to marry a rich bloke because she was in such a financial mess. And then Jamie gave her half the money he got for the Gainsborough Prize, and that little cat picture of his Rose bought is worth loads more now than she paid for it."

"Is that generous," Ben wondered, "or a bit creepy?"

"Oh, generous, I think," I said, "but generous with an ulterior motive. Jamie's absolutely smitten with Rose, you can tell."

"And Rose?"

"Smitten too, I think. Or at least ninety percent of the way there. Jamie's lovely, and he doesn't take crap from Rose."

"And now," Ben said, "why don't you tell me you never shagged Peter Barclay?"

I looked down at my bowl of pasta. There was still rather a lot left. "I can't," I said. "I can't even tell you it was rubbish, because it wasn't, really. But I can tell you it was never as good as with you. Nothing is."

"I was so fucking jealous of Oliver, you know," Ben said. "I let you think something was going on with Claire and me, just to try and give you a taste of how it felt. And then Claire told me about you and Peter, and I realised it had all backfired totally, and then Nina got in touch with me, and I thought, what the hell, I'd see if it was worth giving things another go with her. But I realised it couldn't work, and that I'd never really felt the same way about her as I did about you."

"And that is?"

"Ellie, don't be so needy. You know how I feel about you."

"I don't. You've never said."

"Come on, Ellie. I was completely batshit crazy about you from the first time you gave me an impromptu lager shower in the student union bar nearly eight years ago."

"Seven years, five months and sixteen days," I said. "But are you still? Even though I'm a brazen hussy, and stupid, and selfish?"

"You have been a bit stupid and selfish," Ben agreed, "but everyone is, at least some of the time. And you're those things much less often than lots of people, and you're funny, and brave, and brilliant and beautiful. And of course you're a brazen hussy, and that's really what I like best about you."

"Only 'like'?" I said.

"Blimey," Ben said, "It's like being under interrogation by the Gestapo. Okay, Ellie, I love you. I always have done. And unless something fairly drastic happens to change things, I suspect I always will. Now I have to be up at four in the morning to swim four kilometres, cycle a hundred and eighty, and then maybe knock off a quick forty-two K run, so we should probably get some sleep."

I looked at his gorgeous, familiar face, and felt a flood of happiness. Here I was with my favourite person in the world, we were friends again, and he loved me. Everything was going to be all right. And mixed with the relief, looking at his strong hands, the way his mouth moved when he talked and smiled, the lean muscles in his arms and the breadth of his shoulders, I felt the delicious glow of desire that I'd always felt for him, that had been there so constantly I suppose I'd stopped noticing it. It's a bit like when your favourite album is playing on your iPod, but you're doing something else, like the ironing or working out in the gym or you're looking out of the window of the bus or whatever, and it's just there in the background, until suddenly a familiar phrase brings you back to the music, and you start to sing along without really thinking about it.

"Not so fast, buster," I said. "I happened to be reading *Triathlete's World* the other day, and I happened to come across an article that said the theory that sexual intercourse before a sporting event impairs performance was long ago disproven."

"Is that so?" Ben said.

"Well, we don't have the opportunity to test the hypothesis properly, over a series of randomised trials with a control group," I said. "It comes down to one thing: do you trust *Triathlete's World* or don't you?"

"Implicitly," said Ben, and he stood up, tipping Winston on to the floor, and folded his arms round me and kissed me as if he'd never stop. Breathless with urgency, we pulled each other's clothes off and pressed our bodies together, rediscovering all the familiar things about each other and learning all the new ones (I felt rather smug about the fact that I was wearing really nice, lacy underwear that matched, and I'd had every bit of superfluous hair waxed off the day before, entirely co-incidentally), and it was as totally amazing at it had ever been. And afterwards, as we were lying sweaty and sated in each other's arms, with Winston in his proper place on my hip, purring away, I said to Ben, "I love you too, you know. Just saying."

If the love interest in your life ever asks you to come along and support him while he spends thirteen hours putting himself through mental and physical hell in the interests of raising money for charity, or just because he wants to see whether he can do it, my advice is, just say no. Step away from the lunatic fitness freak and go and find yourself some nice lardy bloke whose idea of vigorous exercise is walking to the fridge to get another tub of Ben and Jerry's. Seriously. Because if you do what I did, and loyally go along, this is what will happen.

Ben set the alarm on his phone for four o'clock in the morning – a time that as far as I'm concerned has no right to exist, except when you haven't been to bed yet. Then he made me set the alarm on my phone too, and found some online alarm clock and set that too. Then he was too nervous to get to sleep at all, and we lay next to each other and every now and then he'd say, "Why did I think this was a good idea, again?" Then Winston decided there was a mouse in the flat and spent about an hour thumping around, doing the special unnerving yowling he does when he's hunting. Eventually we did fall asleep, and it felt like about ten seconds later that all the alarms went off at once, and we sprang out of bed and launched ourselves into a frenzy of getting ready, with me checking off the to-do list Ben had made on his phone (and backed up on his laptop, and written down on paper just in case there was some sort of superbug that wiped out the world's electronic communications. Which I expect would have led to the wretched event being cancelled altogether, but I didn't tell Ben that, he was too stressed already, bless him). He was so anxious that he'd literally noted down every single thing he needed to do: "Get up. Shower. Drink coffee. Eat porridge." And so on.

Eventually everything on the to-do list was done, and we left the flat, laden with all Ben's bags, and got a train and then a bus to the start of the race, where he'd dropped his bicycle off the day before. It was heinously early and still actually rather cold, and neither of us said very much, because I was too sleepy and Ben was too nervous. But he held my hand in a kind of death grip until it was time for him to go off and squeeze himself into his wetsuit and prepare to dive into the murky waters of the Thames, which looked as cold and unpleasant as anything I've ever seen.

"I'll see you after the swim and at the halfway point on the run," Ben said. "And at the end. If I get there."

"Good luck," I said. "I love you."

Ben said, "Have you got my Marmite sandwiches?"

I said, "Durrr! Yes! Obviously," and off Ben went to get changed and start his swim. But of course I didn't have the shagging Marmite sandwiches, because, well, we'd been so busy shagging the night before that I'd forgotten to make them. His swim was only scheduled to take about an hour and a half, and I calculated that there was no way I'd have time to go back to his flat, make the stupid sandwiches, and get back in time to see him safely on to his bike. I was going to have to brazen it out. So I waited, watching all the totally identical swimmers ploughing through the cloudy water, until Ben emerged, changed again and set off on his bike, looking far less like the Creature from the Black Lagoon than anyone has any right to after swimming in the Thames. None of his fingers or toes had been eaten off by giant carp, or anything. As soon as he was gone, I retraced our steps – bus, train, Tube – back to Ben's flat, and spent fifteen minutes slicing bread and spreading butter and Marmite on it and cutting the sandwiches into triangles, and I'm ashamed to say I may have given each triangle a little kiss before I wrapped them up, and then I got the Tube and the train and the bus back to the race. I was there when Ben finished his cycle, smiling brightly and holding the special needs bag that contained the sandwiches (and making the not-very-appropriate face) and watched him get changed and set off to run a mere forty-two kilometres on the last stage of his journey to raise money for a cause I cared about. If I hadn't known before that I really did love him, I did then.

And when he eventually did cross the finishing line, he looked so amazing, shattered and sweaty but grinning like mad, and I felt so proud of him I just burst into tears. I thought how unbelievably lucky I was to have realised that this gorgeous, brave, kind, sexy man had been right there all along, under my nose, before it was too late. And I hugged him, and he wept a bit too, and I heard my voice, all muffled with crying, say, "Ben, will you marry me?"

And Ben, because he's not the kind of person to be constrained by the social and gender stereotypes that say it's the man who should propose marriage, and because he feels the same way about me, said, "Yes, please."

Or it may have been because he was puking and hallucinating with exhaustion, of course. I can't say for sure.

Chapter Twenty-Three

A funny thing happened at Ben's and my engagement party. Well, of course, any number of minor ones did, like Alex falling into the river when he tried to punt in a rowing boat, and Vanessa getting chased by an angry swan.

It was a totally perfect summer's day, and we were all sitting outside in the garden of Dad and Serena's house, and Rose did the catering and got predictably obsessive about it, except when she was being all neurotic and stressing about the strawberries needing to be chilled for the cocktails and there not being enough space in the fridge for them, Jamie took her face between his palms and looked into her eyes and said tenderly, "Rosamund, stop being fucking ridiculous."

And Rose looked back at him with a kind of searing passion that could take paint off a canvas, and the two of them disappeared upstairs to Serena's study for the best part of an hour, and Ben and I laughed and laughed about it, and said we expected that things would work out between the two of them.

Oliver wasn't there, and nor was Nina. I'd have been happy enough to invite them, but they'd flown off to Hong Kong a couple of weeks before, which Oliver was pleased about because it meant he'd make heaps more money and pay heaps less tax, and Nina was delighted about because it was the East and therefore somehow more spiritual than London, and Benedict would become fluent in Mandarin.

Ty turned up looking as heart-stoppingly gorgeous as ever, without Olya, and fizzing with excitement. He told Ben and me that finally, after playing gigs to almost empty pubs for years, he'd had a breakthrough: a song he'd written had been bought by an ad agency to be used in a fabric softener commercial. How I kept a straight face I will never know. But then he went on to tell us that he'd given Olya the push.

"I tell you what, mate, something like this makes you realise what's important," he said to Ben. "Look at you, you're settling down, like, stepping up to the plate, taking responsibility. I reckon it's about time I..."

Then he caught sight of Claire emerging from the house, where she'd been giving moral support to Serena while she fed William and Verity, who were only a month old. Claire walked out into the sunshine, her long legs tanned and perfect beneath the hem of her orange dress, with Pers toddling along behind her, and Claire looked around and said something to Pers and squatted down on the grass and lifted her daughter up and kissed her, and shook her glossy hair and laughed, and Ty said, "Excuse me a second," and raced off in her direction. I looked at Ben and Ben looked at me, and I knew he was thinking exactly the same thing I was.

We watched as Ty jogged up to Claire and took her hand and gazed into her eyes in just the same way he always used to. But Claire didn't gaze back. She listened to Ty for a while, quite gravely. Then she said something to him, laughed again and patted him on the cheek in a fond but totally unemotional sort of way. And Pers giggled and tried to stick her fingers up Ty's nose, and the moment was over.

Ty sat down on the grass with Pers while Claire wandered off to get a drink and talk to Dad about doing voice-overs on his new game.

Anyway, the funny thing happened right after Dad made his speech. I took a lovely gulp of champagne, and all of a sudden I was transported back to one hungover morning a few years ago when Ben and I had been to the Edinburgh Festival together, and I'd woken up on the floor of Rose's student flat and seen a can of Irn Bru on the floor next to me, and taken a huge thirsty swig of it, only to find that someone had used the can as an ashtray the night before. My champagne tasted just like that, and I promptly turned green and vommed into the nearest ice bucket. Ben ushered me inside and said, "Ellie, do you think..." and I nodded queasily, realising that all Rose's plans for our fabulous wedding would have to be put on hold, because there was no way she'd want to design things around a pregnant bride. Ruth and Duncan were there that day, and I'd been planning to ask them if they'd think about giving me my old job back, but Ben suggested I take a look at my contract at Black & White, and see what the maternity leave allowance is like, and I'm glad I did. I can't wait to see Barri's reaction when he finds out that I'm going to be starting a year off on full pay almost exactly twelve months after commencing my employment there, I really can't. I may have to remind him that there's no 'I' in 'Team'.

Acknowledgements

Although *It Would Be Wrong to Steal My Sister's Boyfriend (Wouldn't It?)* took less than three months to write, the journey to publication has been a long one and wouldn't have been completed without the help of many wonderful people.

Huge thanks to my agent, Peta Nightingale at LAW, for believing in me and supporting me, and for all her hard work and excellent advice. My sister Jassy Mackenzie and my friend Lucy Brett read the first draft and provided constructive criticism and some very welcome praise – thank you, you are both amazing. Thanks also to Tash Webber for the gorgeous cover design; to Rachel Alexander for her advice on the world of book publishing; to iron woman Fi Hourston for letting me pick her brains on triathlons; and to Sarah Harman and Jane Brooke for inspiring the Minge Bus.

And finally to Hopi, for being by my side every step of the way. You're the best and I love you.

About the Author

Sophie Ranald is the youngest of five sisters. She was born in Zimbabwe and lived in South Africa until an acute case of itchy feet brought her to London in her mid-20s.

As an editor for a customer publishing agency, Sophie developed her fiction-writing skills describing holidays to places she'd never visited. In 2011, she decided to disregard all the good advice given to aspiring novelists and attempt to write full-time. After one false start, *It Would Be Wrong to Steal My Sister's Boyfriend (Wouldn't It?)* seemed to write itself.

Sophie also writes for magazines and online about food, fashion and running. She lives in south-east London with her amazing partner Hopi and Purrs, their adorable little cat.

If you would like to get an email when Sophie's next book is released please sign up at sophieranald.com. Your email address will never be shared and you can unsubscribe at any time.

It would be great if you would consider leaving a review on Amazon to let others know what you think of *It Would Be Wrong to Steal My Sister's Boyfriend (Wouldn't it?)* It only needs to be short and it would be much appreciated.

Discover more sparkling romantic comedies
by Sophie Ranald

If you enjoyed *It Would be Wrong to Steal My Sister's Boyfriend (Wouldn't It?)* why not read *Who Wants to Marry a Millionaire*? for FREE?

Sign up to Sophie's newsletter at sophieranald.com to claim your copy and receive updates and news of future giveaways!

Contact Details:
Website: www.sophieranald.com
Twitter: @SophieRanald
Facebook: SophieRanald

Made in the USA
Monee, IL
04 December 2020